Assassin's BANE

MARINA FINLAYSON

FINESSE SOLUTIONS

Cover design by Karri Klawiter
Editing by Larks & Katydids

Published by Finesse Solutions Pty Ltd
2021/08
ISBN: 9781925607079

Author's note: This book was written and produced in Australia and uses British/Australian spelling conventions, such as "colour" instead of "color", and "-ise" endings instead of "-ize" on words like "realise".

A catalogue record for this book is available from the National Library of Australia

1

———

The freezing wind caressed my neck and wriggled icy fingers through every vulnerable gap in my layers of clothing. Sure, the Realm of Winter was pretty—all fantastical swirls of snow and icicles festooning every tree. Hell, if I stood still long enough, I'd probably be covered in icicles myself. But I was a Spring girl through and through, and cold feet just made me cranky.

We'd been trudging through the snow for most of the morning. The Hawk's magical sword could open a gate to anywhere within the fae Realms—but, of course, there was a catch: he had to have been there before. And naturally he hadn't been anywhere near this remote part of the mountains of Winter.

Looking around at the icicle-laden pines and sharp rocks that poked up through the snow like black fangs, I couldn't say I blamed him.

Our party consisted of the Hawk and another of the king's Chosen knights, the Lion, each leading a dozen of the king's strongest guards, plus Ash and me. Between the lot of us, we probably had enough magic to level the average city.

Would it be enough to destroy the Nest of the Vipers, the notorious fae assassins that Ash and I had so recently been part of? Time would tell—as long as I found the damn secret entrance before we all froze to death.

Only a Winter fae could enjoy weather like this. Fae could regulate their own body temperature with magic, but there were limits—at least, there were for this half-fae.

I cast a sidelong glance at Ash, my favourite Winter fae. He'd donned a thin coat that clung to the strong muscles of his back and shoulders, but that was his only concession to the weather.

He moved like a predator, wary and ready for action. Watchful grey eyes roved ceaselessly across the landscape, alert for threats. When he felt the weight of my attention, he smiled at me. It was just a small curve of those full lips, accompanied by a warming of his gaze, but a flush of pleasure made me forget the cold for a moment. Those smiles of his were all too rare. I treasured every one.

That smile might have warmed my heart, but the rest of me was another matter. I focused on the magic coursing through my body and directed it towards defrosting my toes, which had left *freezing* behind hours ago and had moved on to *despairing of ever being warm again*. Even after all these weeks, I sometimes had to remind myself of the power I now possessed. Having grown up with very little magic, thanks to my scumbag of a father, I'd always had to conserve what little magical strength I had. Using magic didn't come as instinctively to me as it did to the fae all around me.

Finally I spotted a rock formation that matched my memory. My breath fogged the air in a great white cloud as I sighed in relief. *Soon*, I promised my toes. *Soon we'll be out of this icy hell.*

"This is it." I stopped in front of the mouth of a small cave, and the group of knights and guards gathered around me.

Snow was piled up, almost obscuring the cave's entrance. Even if that hadn't been the case, a subtle Aversion had been cast on the opening, which encouraged anyone fool enough to be roaming these mountains to look away, to pass by without their gaze ever stopping on this nondescript cave.

It was like so many others in this region, except for one small detail: *this* opening could lead into a cramped and uninviting cave, as inhospitable as the rest of this benighted Realm—or it could take the right person through a sneaky little back door to the Nest of the Night Vipers.

And for "the right person", read: "the leader of the Night Vipers", since up until now, the Serpent of the Vipers was the only person who had known it existed. But two days ago, *I* had been the Serpent of the Vipers and, even though I'd given up that position and all its tainted power, I still remembered the location of the hidden entry.

The only question was: could we still use it?

The Hawk gave soft orders to the group of fighters, though there was no one else to hear him but the wind and the snow that fell lightly, dusting our shoulders like icing sugar. Freezing bloody cold icing sugar.

"Are you ready?" he asked. Though he spoke to me, his golden gaze drifted to the man on my right. Those eyes of his were mesmerising, like the eyes of the bird that was his namesake. They'd certainly ensnared my friend Allegra, who was head over heels in love with the stern knight.

For myself, I found I preferred grey eyes. I turned to Ash, too. His cool gaze already rested on me. His black clothes stood out starkly against the snow—and against the coloured livery of the guards and the knights. The Hawk wore gold, and the Lion at his shoulder was all in Autumnal russet. Though their clothes were practical, suited to a sudden raid on enemy territory, still they managed to look like what they were: Knights of the Realms.

But Ash in his practical blacks looked like the assassin he had so recently been. He was a shadow to their light, the danger lurking in the darkness. I made a mental note to take him shopping when this was all over. There was no sense in reminding people of his past. They were already wary enough of him.

I raised an eyebrow, and he nodded. "Ready."

The Vipers made their Nest in a sith, a small piece of the Realms which had been broken off by magic and sealed into its own little bubble, a world within a world. Siths could range in size from a small room to a large estate, and the Vipers' Nest was the largest I had ever heard of. Within its bounds were acres of forest and a large lake, in addition to a generous sprawl of buildings. The gates of these siths could be anchored like balloons on a string to any part of the mortal or fae worlds. They were just as movable as any balloon, too, making them the perfect refuge or hideout for those lucky enough to possess one.

It would be up to Ash to open the gate to the sith, if he could. I was no longer a Viper, so the gate wouldn't respond to me. Neither was Ash, of course, but, in my time as the Serpent, I'd built a specific exemption for him into the wards that guarded the Nest. I was counting on the fact that my father, the new Serpent, wouldn't have noticed that yet. The hidden gate was only known to the Serpent, but it would open for any Viper, so it should also open for Ash.

I had every frozen finger crossed that it would, because otherwise we were up shit creek without a paddle, and our grand plan to destroy the Vipers was dead in the water before we'd even begun. There *was* no Plan B. Our scouts had already confirmed that the only other entry to the Nest had been moved, and there was no way for us to find it. It could be anywhere in the human world. If this gate didn't open to Ash, we were screwed.

The Hawk and the Lion pressed in close at my back as I stepped up beside Ash. The Hawk had his sword out already, its silvery length shimmering in the dull Winter light. The Lion winked at me, and my nerves settled as I smiled back. Behind them, the guards waited in two lines, ready to leap forward the minute the gate opened.

If the gate opened.

The weak Winter sun shone directly overhead, doing

absolutely stuff-all to warm the frigid air. Since the Night Vipers, like other fae, lived a nocturnal life, the middle of the day was the best time to mount a surprise attack on their stronghold. Thank the Lady it hadn't taken me any longer to find the damned gate.

Ash stepped up to the cave mouth and swept the snow away with a gentle swirl of his Winter magic, revealing a tumble of small bones scattered across the floor of a shallow and uninviting cave. Then he focused his magic on the threshold and an unnatural mist rose up from the ground, boiling around the entrance to the cave and obscuring its shallow interior once more.

"That's a good sign," the Lion breathed behind me.

Optimist. A gate had formed—that didn't prove that it led us to the right place. My stomach tightened with anticipation as Ash stepped into the mist and disappeared. A long moment passed, but he didn't reappear looking disappointed. Thank the Lady. He was in.

"After you, my lady," the Lion said.

I nodded, gathering my Spring magic tight around me until my veins thrummed with power. I had no sword like the two knights, though a pair of throwing knives was nestled under my vest. This would be more a battle of magic than a battle of weapons. Every man and woman behind me had been chosen for the strength of their magic and their skill in wielding it offensively. I took one last look back at them. Two dozen barely seemed enough for an attack on the Vipers, whose numbers were at least three times that many, even without counting support staff. But numbers didn't always mean that much in fae battles. It always came down to who had the most power, and these were some of the strongest mages in the Realms.

Besides, marching a whole army into the Nest would hardly go unnoticed, even in the middle of the day. We were hoping to avoid any battles at all, magical or otherwise, and rely on stealth. Which would be a pretty poetic end for a bunch of assassins whose work had always involved sneaking around.

I took a deep breath and followed Ash through the gate. Threshold magic shivered over me, like the touch of invisible hands or tiny insects marching over my skin. When I emerged from the mist, I found myself by a lake that glittered in the midday sun—a considerably warmer sun. I shrugged off my heavy coat, revelling in the feel of air that didn't bite my throat all the way down to my lungs.

The forest that took up most of this sith stretched off to one side. Behind me, a small pavilion by the lake shore concealed the Serpent's gate, which was still open and admitting the rest of my companions as I watched. We'd decided to leave it open until we left—just in case.

Across the lake, the towers and turrets of the main building stabbed into the blue sky. It looked like the country mansion of an English billionaire, though it had a foreboding look that even the bright sunshine couldn't completely erase. It reminded me a little of Hogwarts, though it was a much darker place than the fictional wizarding school. Evil Hogwarts, then.

I studied the windows as I waited. There was no apparent sign of life, but that didn't mean no one would be watching. Everyone *should* be asleep at this time of day, but what plan ever went so smoothly as that? Maybe my experiences had made me jaded, but I was fully expecting the alarm to be raised at any moment.

Not for the first time, I wished that I still had the power of light-weaving. When I'd had all the powers of the Serpent at my disposal, I'd been able to make myself—and Ash—invisible with that nifty little bit of Day magic. Standing here on the lake shore in broad daylight, I felt horribly exposed.

If anyone else felt the same, they didn't show it. We had all cast an Aversion on ourselves, of course, but an Aversion was a poor substitute for the invisibility of light-weaving. Still, there was no use wishing for what we couldn't have—and that power had come with such terrible strings attached that, all in all, I was glad to be rid of it. Just because I had the occasional hankering for the almost limitless power of Ni'ishasana, the Serpent's unholy dagger, it didn't mean I wanted to go back to being possessed and shoved around like a puppet by the trapped souls that powered it.

I fell back and let the Hawk take the lead, with Ash at his side. They had been over and over our plan in the hours before we had left the palace, and everyone knew what they were supposed to do, but there was still no substitute for Ash's intimate knowledge of the Nest. All the hand-drawn maps in the world couldn't replace it.

My shoulders were tight with tension, but no alarm was raised as we approached the main building. The Lion led two-thirds of our group around the side towards the training grounds and the individual houses beyond. Ash, the Hawk, and I, with a handful of others, entered the building in search of my father.

Honestly, I wasn't expecting him to be here. He'd given me such a strange look when I'd accused him of tricking me out of the dagger in order to become the leader of the Vipers, as if the Vipers had never entered into his plans. It was the dagger itself, and the power it conveyed, that interested him. It wouldn't have surprised me if he hadn't shown his face here at all and perhaps didn't intend to, despite the bonds that would have formed between him and the Vipers the minute he took up the dagger.

"Fallon must be stopped," the king had said, his mouth set in a grim line, those famous Brenfell blue eyes showing the strain of the bad news I'd dumped on him.

We'd been planning this raid in a small parlour at Whitehaven—well, as small as anything got at the palace. The room was probably as big as most people's houses and lavishly furnished.

The Hawk nodded. I did, too. My father had been a feared necromancer even before the power of Ni'ishasana had been added to the mix. Now he was the kind of bad news that no king wanted running around, free to wreak havoc.

"Of course, sire," the Lion said, the same way most people said *sure, honey, I can stop at the store on my way home*. As if "stopping" Fallon were no harder than grabbing milk from the supermarket.

I knew that the king and his knights phrased it that way because no one wanted to come right out in front of me and say that our mission was to kill him.

I'd bitten my lip and said nothing. I'd lived with that power in my veins—I *knew* what we were up against. There was no simple way of "stopping" a man like Fallon. They were either alive and kicking your arse, or they were dead.

So here we were, ready to become assassins ourselves and drown the Vipers' organisation in a wave of blood. As for my father ...

How were we meant to kill someone with so much power? If we got lucky, and he was asleep, and we managed to sneak in without waking him, and no one raised the alarm, and ... and ... and. We would almost certainly *not* get that lucky.

But he had to be "stopped"; we were all agreed on that. There was no other way to defuse the enormous threat he posed. We had fae from every Realm but Fire here, hoping to counter his enormous power, and we still might not be able to do it.

But I would have to be grateful if we could—grateful to see my own father die.

I mean, it wasn't as though I *loved* him anymore. He hadn't been a real father to me in years. Yet, through all the discussions about stopping him, memories from happier times kept intruding. I'd recall the smile on his face the day he'd given me my first horse, or I'd remember how my heart had leapt every time he walked into Lord Thistle's Court after one of his many absences.

Talk about mixed emotions. Hopefully, he wouldn't be here and the terrible task would fall to someone else—

some time when I wasn't there to witness it. If that made me a coward, too bad.

My heart thundered a nervous tattoo as Ash led the way inside and we crept down the familiar carpeted hallways. The Serpent and his zombie servants were the only ones who lived in this vast building, though at night it came alive with Vipers and support staff. In the middle of the day, there should be no one around.

A floorboard creaked under the Hawk's foot, and everyone froze instinctively—everyone but Ash, of course, who threw an impatient glance over his shoulder at the rest of us and moved on, taking the stairs up to the next level. We followed silently all the way up to the floor where the Serpent's quarters were. A strange sense of déjà vu crept over me as we approached the familiar door. This had been my own apartment so recently.

My nerves were wound tight as Ash eased the door open. I wanted to shout, to run, to hit something— anything to release the tension building inside me. All this sneaking about was killing me.

Please, I begged the Lady silently, though I wasn't sure exactly what I was praying for.

We burst into the room, but there was no one there.

As we turned to leave, a servant entered. One of the guards gasped, but the woman took no notice of him, or any of us. She didn't even blink. As if she were completely alone in the room, she knelt before the fire in the main sitting area and poked it back to life, adding two more logs.

"She only has enough will to obey orders," Ash said.

His voice was so unexpected in the quiet room that I jumped. "She will take no notice of us."

The Hawk's gaze was glued to her in disbelief. "Will she betray our presence?"

"If she is asked what she saw in this room, she will tell," Ash said, "but not otherwise."

"Then we should kill her."

"She's a victim of the dagger," I said with some heat. This was a subject close to my heart.

"She has no will of her own?" The Hawk studied Ash rather than me. The knight had been reluctant to allow Ash to join this mission. Only Ash's superior knowledge of the Nest and its inhabitants had swayed him in the end. It was clear he didn't believe that Ash had truly turned against the people he'd lived and worked with for so long.

"She's a slave to the dagger," Ash replied. Sadness flickered in his eyes, though the Hawk wouldn't have known it for what it was. He didn't know him as I did.

"Then it would be a mercy to release her from servitude," the Hawk said, stepping toward the woman who still knelt at the fireplace, tending the fire.

I cried out, but it was too late. He pulled a knife from a hidden sheath and slashed her throat, then lowered her dying body gently to the floor. He cleaned the blade on the carpet and resheathed it before taking up his sword again.

"Why did you do that?" I snarled at him. "She was no threat to us!"

His expression could have been carved from ice. "If she were ordered to fight us, she would, wouldn't she?"

"Yes, but—"

"There is no *but*," he said. "We would be fools to leave a threat behind us."

He led the way from the room. I lagged behind, bringing up the rear, my worldview shaken. I had been used to thinking of the king's Chosen as noble men, loyal and brave. And so they were—well, except for the Dragon, who had disappeared when it became apparent that he wasn't the upright knight everyone thought he was.

The part that hadn't registered with me, though, was that they were also killers who would stop at nothing to ensure the security of the kingdom. What had I expected? That we would break into the Nest and arrest its inhabitants, then take them to court, the way they did with criminals in the mortal world? I was half fae, and I'd lived with the fae all my life. I should have known better. The fae were ruthless, and they didn't bother with lawyers and arguing the criminal's case. Justice was swift, deadly, and entirely arbitrary.

I comforted myself with the reflection that that poor woman's soul had fled long ago. When the dagger reanimated a dead person and bound them into slavery, they weren't really that person at all anymore, but only a shell. Perhaps the Hawk was right and it would be a mercy to kill all the servants, but my heart balked at such a slaughter.

We descended the stairs, retracing our steps. I breathed a little easier now that I knew my father wasn't here. He would hardly be out on the training grounds when everyone else was asleep. In the hallway, our group fanned out, checking each room.

I took the handle of the nearest door, only to have it

jerked from my grasp. I stumbled, half-dragged into the room. Using my momentum, I dived forward into a roll, which took the man behind the door by surprise. His knife darted out, but instead of ending buried in my gut, it slashed a line of bright fire across my shoulder.

The room was dim, the curtains drawn. I had a brief impression of bookshelves and heavily upholstered chairs as I rolled and bounced back to my feet. The man himself was a black-clad figure in the shadows.

It was a small room, one of several used as offices and retreats by the more senior Vipers. There wasn't a lot of space to manoeuvre. A blast of Summer heat came at me and I dived behind a chair, making myself small. Even so, the smell of burnt hair filled the room and my face smarted as though I'd just stuck my head in an oven.

Out in the hallway, I heard shouts and running feet, but I didn't have time to wait for rescue. This guy would barbecue me in the time it took for the cavalry to arrive.

I surged to my feet and heaved the chair at him. Terror and half-fae strength managed to heft it straight at his face. He leapt aside and blasted it out of the air, leaving it smouldering on its side up against a bookcase, but it had served its purpose.

It had moved him closer to the windows and distracted him at the same time. Before he could turn his magic on me again, I *pulled* with all my might, dragging the green, growing energies of Spring into the room.

Glass shattered as a massive oak branch lanced straight through the window. The man dodged—right into the path of a second branch. Its tip, moulded into a sharp point, speared straight through his back and burst out of his chest. He dangled there, his body jerking, his mouth forming a silent scream. The slow drip of blood onto the carpet below was the last sound he heard as the light left his eyes.

I let out a shaky breath as Ash burst into the room, the Hawk hard on his heels.

"Are you hurt?" Ash looked as though he wanted to pat me down, just to be sure.

"Fine." I was *so* not fine. I swallowed hard. *Don't throw up. Don't throw up.* I recognised the man—he was one of the younger Vipers.

Magic was all fun and games until you used it to skewer someone like a kebab. In that moment it was clear to me that I would never be a true fae. When they were handing out ruthlessness, I must have been behind the door. I could kill people if I had to—but just because magic made it simple didn't mean it was *easy*.

The fact that I knew this guy seemed to make his grisly death worse. The contrast between the living man I remembered and the sagging corpse in front of me was too cruel. I folded my arms, tucking my hands into my armpits to hide their shaking from the Hawk. He would never understand regret over the death of an enemy.

Ash's hand rested briefly on my shoulder, where my half-fae healing had already begun to close the knife's slash. I leaned into his touch. "One less Viper," he reminded me gently.

The Hawk nodded. "Only seventy more to go."

2

———

sh took the lead again when we left the building. The bright sunshine seemed such an odd contrast to the dark scene we'd left behind, as if the world could no longer be the same after what I'd just done. My hands were still shaking, but birds sang in the trees regardless.

It was him or me, I reminded myself. And it was why we'd come. Killing Vipers was the whole point—so why did I feel so sickened? The image of that tree branch bursting out of his chest would be with me whenever I closed my eyes, for a long time.

We passed Ash's old house, tucked away among the pine trees. It should be empty now, but, just in case someone else had taken up residence there, Ash and the Hawk headed inside. The Hawk didn't seem to want to let Ash out of his sight.

In a moment they reappeared, a quick shake of the Hawk's head assuring us there was no one there. We headed off again, moving without a sound.

It was eerily quiet as we approached another cottage. This one was larger than Ash's tiny home, with neat gardens flanking the path that led to the front door. A bright blue ball lay in the grass, nestled up against the rocks edging a garden bed, as if a small child had dropped it there when they'd been called inside to dinner.

A family lived in this cottage. I dimly recalled a small blond girl and a couple of older boys, quiet and serious. My memories of my time as Serpent were hazy, and children hadn't been important to the dagger, so I'd barely noticed them.

At the Hawk's signal, our party split into two. Half of the guards circled around the cottage, ready to rush the back door while the rest of us took the front.

Suddenly afraid, I caught at the Hawk's arm. "What about the children? We'll leave them alive, won't we?"

Those golden eyes surveyed me dispassionately. "We have orders to eradicate the Nest, Sage. What did you think they meant?"

"But the children are innocent. It's not their fault that their parents chose this life."

Ash reached out and took my hand. "The older ones have already begun combat training."

"So?" I jerked my hand from his grasp. "So have most fae by the time they're teenagers, and nobody's running around trying to kill *them*." I turned my attention back to the Hawk, desperate now. The king was coming to inspect the Nest and its secrets once the Hawk gave the all-clear.

"At least wait until the king gets here. Don't kill any of the kids before then. Let him decide."

The Hawk gave me a weary look. "Who do you think gave the orders?"

The first guard laid his hand on the door, and I swallowed my outrage. Arguing would make no difference.

When had I become so human? I'd grown up in the Realm of Spring, watching Willow's father, Lord Thistle, deliver summary justice whenever necessary, and I hadn't blinked an eyelid. Probably because no one else did. It was just the way the world was.

But then that same "justice" had been turned on me, and Lord Thistle had exiled me for my father's actions, which had nothing to do with me and over which I'd had no control. It hadn't mattered to him that I'd saved his daughter from death at Fallon's hands. It only mattered that I shared his tainted blood, so I'd been exiled to the mortal world for someone else's crime.

I guess that was the moment that I began to question the fae way. Then my time in the mortal world had shown me it didn't have to be like that. Justice wasn't always achieved by the humans either, but human law seemed a damned sight fairer than the fae method, where some Lord or king had the power to order anything at all and it would be done, and might was always right.

Children being punished for their parents' bad decisions was a sore point with me, and I wasn't going to stand by silently while the king's forces slaughtered innocent children.

I surged forward and entered the house hard on the

heels of the first guard. The layout was similar to Ash's cottage and most of the homes in the sith—a central hallway with rooms opening off either side. A small ornamental table stood against the right-hand wall of the narrow hall, holding a spindly vase that looked suspiciously like a child's first efforts at pottery. A few branches of a flowering shrub were tucked into it.

I drifted to the side, letting my hip nudge the table as I passed, hard enough to bruise—and hard enough to topple the vase. It smashed to the hardwood floor in a rain of greenery, water, and pottery shards.

As if the sound had been a starter's gun, the guards leapt into action, throwing doors open and barging into rooms, weapons drawn. I bolted for the door at the end of the corridor. If this house followed the same pattern as Ash's, this would be the second bedroom.

A roar of wind filled the hallway as I opened the door. Behind me, a man was shouting and all the mess on the floor had whirled into the air. I flinched and ducked inside as the table was swept up and slammed into a guard's back.

A boy who couldn't have been more than eight years old stared back at me with frightened eyes from his place at the window. His dark hair was rumpled from sleep, and he was staggering under the weight of the little girl in his arms. He had her half-balanced on the window sill, and his arms were shaking with effort. She wasn't that much smaller than he was.

I plastered my back against the door, holding it against any guards who might try to enter, and we stared at each other for an endless, frozen second. Then larger hands reached in through the window and dragged the girl out in a flurry of blond hair and kicking feet. I caught a glimpse of an older boy's anguished face before they both disappeared, leaving me and the eight-year-old staring at each other.

"Go on, then," I said as the sounds of battle in the hallway died down. "Get out of here."

As if my words had brought him to life, he scrambled out the window without a sound. I opened the door, coming face to face with the Hawk.

"No one here," I said, feeling like a child caught with her hand in the cookie jar and trying not to show it.

His gaze took in the two rumpled beds, the open window, and the curtains still swinging from the boy's abrupt exit. Then it turned on me, and there was fury in his eyes. "Whose side are you on, Sage?"

He knew what I'd done. He knew my banging into the hall table was no accident, that I'd done it to give the children a chance to escape.

"The one that doesn't murder kids in their beds."

He looked monumentally unimpressed, but a shout split the silence outside, and we turned as one to bolt out of the house. Beyond the hedge at the back of the house, swords clashed against each other. A powerful burst of Air magic buffeted me, ripping green leaves from the trees and hurling them in my face as I forced my way through the hedge in the Hawk's wake.

A sudden rush of power filled me, but it wasn't my Spring magic, which already swelled within me, begging for release. It was something stronger, deeper. Older? I didn't know why it felt that way to me—power had no age, for God's sake. I'd last experienced this feeling when Atinna died, and I'd been kind of hoping I'd never feel it again. It had rushed into me the night my father stole the dagger from me, and I wanted nothing to do with anything that came from him.

Back then, I'd actually thought I must have imagined the whole thing, but there was no mistaking it this time. My body tingled with power as I raced through the trees after the Hawk.

We burst into a cleared area where three houses huddled close together, as if telling secrets to each other under cover of the forest boughs that shaded them. An Air mage who looked about seventeen or eighteen was holding off five of the king's men. It was the boy I'd glimpsed through the window, who'd snatched the little girl—probably his sister—to safety. There was no sign of her blond head, or of the boy I'd urged out the window to join them.

The clash of swords in the forest behind him suggested he was covering the retreat of others, who had run into more of the king's forces among the trees. Were those little kids in there? A desperate glance over his shoulder confirmed his fear for the unseen fighters, but he returned to his task with renewed determination, hurling two of his assailants from their feet with a wind that felt like a hurricane.

One of the guards who was still standing returned fire with a bolt of Summer heat that should have cooked the boy on the spot, but his Air magic was so strong that he managed to turn it aside so that it hit a house instead. The wood of the house creaked and groaned in protest under the onslaught, the boards warping in the heat. Every plant in the garden turned up its toes and expired on the spot, but the boy paid no attention.

Then he saw us emerging from the trees and a look of sheer desperation appeared on his face. He retreated towards the forest, and one of the men he'd knocked from his feet with the hurricane gestured. Trees bent toward the boy, bent on capturing him with their twiggy fingers, but he saw the danger at the last minute and ducked aside.

But now he was trapped. He couldn't retreat into the forest, for fear of the Spring mage turning it against him, but he could no longer stand against such overwhelming numbers.

Except, of course, he was an Air mage. Magnificent white wings appeared, and he leapt into the air, soaring out of reach of the trees' grasping fingers. The Summer mage hurled another wave of heat after him, but the boy was so fast he must have been beyond its range, because he didn't flinch or falter.

The Hawk leapt after him with a muffled curse, his great eagle-like wings snapping into being on his back as he took to the skies. They were deep brown and tipped with gold, bigger even than Raven's wings.

Not that this was the time to be comparing wing sizes or thinking about the mercurial Night lordling at all. Always charming, never serious, he had midnight eyes that could make any girl long to uncover the real man beneath that mocking smile. But we'd parted on bad terms when

I'd brought the news of his father's death to him. If he thought of me at all, it wouldn't be with any fondness.

The Hawk quickly gained height, closing the distance between himself and the boy. I guess size really did matter. The boy's white wings, though beautiful, were nowhere near big enough to allow him to outrun the knight. The Hawk was also far more experienced than the teenager and buffeted him with such strong winds that he could no longer control his flight and came tumbling back to earth.

My heart was in my mouth as he fell, tumbling over and over, the white wings outstretched but unable to regain control. Just before he smashed into the ground, he managed to arrest the headlong fall, but he still landed heavily, staggering like a drunkard.

The Hawk landed gracefully beside him and grabbed his arms. Then he hauled him over to our little group and shoved him to the ground at my feet.

"Don't move," he warned the boy. He wasn't even breathing hard—unlike the boy, whose chest heaved as he tried to regain his breath.

"Do as he says, Igan," Ash said.

"Are you with them?" Igan spat on Ash's boots. "Traitor."

Ash regarded him evenly. "Call me whatever you like, but don't move or you're dead."

Igan glanced around the circle of impassive faces until his gaze lit on my face. His eyes widened. "Serpent? I thought you were dead. What is happening?"

"The king is bringing his law to the Vipers," the Hawk said before I could speak. "That's what's happening."

"Kyrrim," I said. It was probably breaking protocol to address the Hawk by his given name instead of his title, but his pride was the least of my concerns right now. Keeping this kid alive was all I could think of. "Don't …"

He stared at me for a long moment, his expression unreadable. Then he sighed and cocked an eyebrow at Ash. "I assume there is somewhere here we can confine prisoners until the king arrives?"

My whole body slumped in relief, but the boy's eyes widened and he leapt up, producing a knife from its hiding place in his boot. As he came at me, I found myself thinking that he must have had some warning of the attack, even beyond my "clumsiness" with the table—had he heard some noise from the Lion's group? Because no one wore boots with knives in them to bed.

Maybe that was a strange thing to be thinking at such a time, but, as often happened when I was attacked, time seemed to stretch and slow, so that I had plenty of time to indulge in odd thoughts, even as my body was reacting in a more appropriate manner. I had side-stepped neatly and was drawing my own knife when Ash slid smoothly between us.

His knife was out and there was death in his eyes as he buried the blade in Igan's chest with cool expertise. With his other hand he disarmed the boy, flicking his blade harmlessly aside.

Igan coughed, his hands going to the hilt that stood out from his body, his eyes staring at it in disbelief. He dropped heavily to his knees, sagging forward.

"No!" I cried, falling to my knees beside him. He

stared at me as if he couldn't understand what was happening. I prayed that his little brother and sister weren't watching from the forest. "We were supposed to take him prisoner."

Ash stared down at me, unbending. "He attacked you."

"But I could have stopped him. You didn't have to kill him!"

Igan toppled onto his side, one hand reaching out, though I wasn't sure he could see whatever he was reaching for. His eyes had an empty, wounded look, and his breath was coming in short gasps.

I took his bloody hand in mine. There was nothing else I could do for him but sit with him while he died, so that he wouldn't be alone. I leaned forward and whispered in his ear. "You did a brave job, Igan. You would have made a fine Viper."

I don't know if he heard me, because a wave of dizziness hit me. I felt him go, felt the snuffing of the spark of his life like a twisting sensation within my own breast. I didn't need to see his eyes glaze over or feel his grip on my hand loosen to know that he was dead.

I rubbed a hand against that spot in the centre of my chest where I'd felt his life end and looked up. A new figure had joined our group, and I stumbled to my feet with a shout.

Instantly Ash was at my side, supporting me, gazing around wildly. "What is it? What's wrong?"

"Igan ..." I said, staring at him.

"He's dead," Ash said, calming as he decided there was no threat.

"No. Not him," I said, and pointed at the newcomer. "*Him.*"

It was Igan himself, standing by his dead body. A pale blue light clung to him. "I feel strange," he said to me, and I heard him as clearly as I'd heard Ash a moment before. He looked down with a puzzled frown. "Who is *that*?"

"That's you." My voice shook.

"Who are you talking to?" Ash asked sharply.

"To Igan," I said. Why was this happening? I was as confused as Igan himself, who continued to hover above the body he'd so recently inhabited. I realised I could see the trees through him, and a cold shiver ran all the way down my spine. "Apparently I can see ghosts now."

3

———

I might as well have said I was made of glass. Ash stuck to me like glue for the rest of the raid. There were no more pockets of resistance, but he shadowed me everywhere as we searched the houses and grounds of the Nest, never more than a short step away.

Eventually our search took us to the gardens I used to look out on from my window when I was the Serpent—the same gardens where I had fought Atinna, a longstanding pain in my backside and the woman who had assassinated Raven's father. She might have killed me, too, if Ash hadn't turned up in time to save the day.

Today, all was calm, with no enemies lurking in the shrubbery to disturb the gardens' peace. Blowsy roses drooped over the fountain in the next walled courtyard, visible through a wide archway. The weight of their heavy heads pulled them down as if they wanted to kiss the water, their perfume scenting the air.

I should have been thrilled that we'd taken the Nest so

easily, but we hadn't found a single Viper among the dead or the prisoners, apart from the one I'd killed in the main building. The only people the knights had in custody were non-combatants—children too young to fight, like Igan's little brother and sister, or other family members of the Vipers.

So where were all the Vipers? What the hell was my father up to that he needed all seventy-odd assassins? I knew I should be worried, but for the moment, alone in the peaceful rose garden with Ash, I tackled the more immediate problem.

"I saw him standing right there next to his body, as plain as you or me," I said, making no effort to conceal the irritation in my voice. "You don't need to dog my steps. I'm not having a mental breakdown."

"You were hallucinating," Ash said.

I wasn't buying that theory. It had felt way too real to be a hallucination. But Ash was frowning at me like a mechanic examining a broken engine, his grey eyes narrowed as if he could find the problem by sheer willpower. I stared right back, fuming. It was funny how I could still want to kiss him even when I also felt like punching him.

I sighed. I seemed to have a type. Raven had often had a similar effect on me.

I stuffed down the habitual sadness I felt now whenever I thought of Raven, down into the dark where I didn't have to look at it. Our friendship was in tatters, but there'd been no time to fix it.

No time even to explore what was happening between

me and Ash. I stared into those infuriating grey eyes and remembered a completely different look in them—a smoking hot look that had nothing to do with trying to analyse me. My insides quivered at the memory of the hunger in their depths, of his deep voice saying *I think you know what I want.*

And I'd wanted it, too. Everything had been crystal clear in that moment. I could have stayed forever in the strong circle of his arms.

But stupid reality had an annoying habit of intruding. My father, the dagger, and now this—whatever it was. Ghosts? *Really?* As if I needed anything more on my plate.

No, now was most definitely not the time for thoughts of love or the future, not when the damn present was screaming for attention like an overtired two-year-old. But as soon as this mission was over, we were going to have a talk. I needed at least *some* certainty in my life.

"Ash," I said, trying for calm, "that was no hallucination."

Long and lean, he stalked to the archway and swept his gaze over the fountain and the gardens beyond it. He moved like a panther, all coiled energy, ready to strike at a moment's notice as he checked for threats. He'd spent so many years checking for threats that it was as natural as breathing to him now. It made me a little sad. No one should have to live like that.

When he was sure that our immediate environs were safe, he turned back to me. "What, then?"

I took a deep breath, refusing to let his obvious disbelief rile me. The Hawk had looked just the same. When I'd started speaking to Igan's ghost, the Hawk had stared as if I'd suddenly become a liability, and wasted no time in bundling me off to search the stables, where he clearly thought I could do no damage to his precious mission. But Ash—I'd expected more understanding from him.

"He appeared within moments of death—which, by the way, I felt happen—and spoke to me just as you're speaking to me now." Only not so *annoyingly*. "But as soon as I told him he was dead, he just disappeared."

Laying out the facts made me feel better. I knew what I'd seen, and I wasn't crazy.

"Disappeared," he repeated.

"Yes. One minute he was there, kind of blue and see-through. Then I told him he was dead. He looked so surprised." I couldn't get that look of disbelief and horror out of my mind. His form had simply faded into the air. "And then he just dissolved into sparkles of light."

"Sparkles."

"Yes, sparkles. Stop repeating everything I say."

"And you insist that this wasn't a hallucination." He leaned against the stone of the archway, hands in his pockets, a sceptical look on his handsome face.

"It wasn't." I was absolutely sure of that.

"But you've been under so much stress lately. You're still not recovered from Ni'ishasana's possession. Couldn't this be a symptom of that?"

I considered it for a moment—an extremely fleeting moment—then shook my head decisively. "Nope."

"But you saw things that weren't there all the time

when you were the Serpent—these shadow people you told me about."

Many of the previous owners of the dagger had appeared to me as people made of shadows. Some of the more recent ones, like Umarenthe and Celebrach, had even spoken to me. In fact, Umarenthe had been downright hard to shut up.

"They were there, all right. It was just that no one but me could see them."

He kicked at a white pebble that had strayed from its place among a sea of other pebbles onto the path. "And isn't this exactly the same? You're seeing things that no one else can see."

"My point exactly! He was *there* and I could *see* him, but no one else could."

"Because he was a hallucination."

"If you say hallucination one more time, I'm going to strangle you. No, not because he was a bloody hallucination. Because there's something that makes me different to everyone else. Again."

"As I said, the dagger—"

"This is *not* some holdover from the dagger! Do you think I wouldn't *know* if it still had some kind of hold on me?" No, Ni'ishasana had wasted no time dumping me as soon as a better prospect had appeared. "This is something new. Something changed the night my father did that ritual and took the dagger. I feel ... different."

He straightened, and the scepticism fled, leaving concern—no, alarm—in its place. "He did something to you?"

"Maybe? But not on purpose." I thought back to that night. We'd been in the middle of a ritual to raise my mother from her grave—or so I'd thought. It had all been bullshit, of course. Fallon had raised lying to an art form. But he'd managed to persuade me that I needed to transfer ownership of Ni'ishasana to him for the ritual to work. He'd had some help there from the dagger, which, for reasons of its own, wanted him as its wielder instead of me, so it had been applying some pretty heavy-handed mind control.

"Why is this the first I've heard of it?" Ash demanded, trying to disguise worry as anger.

"I thought it was nothing."

"*Nothing*? Sage, you just saw a ghost."

"Well, I didn't know *that* was going to happen. That night my father tricked me out of the dagger—we were in the middle of the transfer, and I finally realised what was happening and started fighting back." Ni'ishasana's power had slipped through my fingers like sand. "It was too late to hold on to any of the dagger's magic, but all my pulling on the end of the bond between me and my father managed to tug *something* free. Some kind of power flowed into me at the end."

And my father hadn't looked too happy about it—which meant it had to be a good thing, right? Whatever annoyed Fallon had to be a win for me. But it wasn't Spring power—I already knew how that felt, and I didn't recognise the "flavour" of this magic. And I didn't know of any magic that allowed someone to see ghosts.

Except one.

"I don't like the sound of that." He looked kind of green, to be honest.

I sighed heavily. "Me neither."

I didn't know much about necromancy, and information on it was hard to find. Most fae spoke of it in whispers, if they discussed it at all, but I knew it was something you had to learn, not a power you were born with, like the powers of the Realms. It involved rituals and sacrifices. It was the sacrifices that had given it its dark reputation.

Well, the sacrifices and the whole zombie thing. People didn't take too kindly to having their dead relatives reanimated to become the slaves of some necromancer. Fortunately, necromancers were few and far between. Not a popular career choice at all, for some reason. In fact, Fallon was the only one I knew of, though I supposed someone must have taught him. Or was necromancy something you could learn from a book? It would have to be one hell of a twisted book.

"Do you think it's—"

I cut him off. "Can't be."

I stepped through the archway, as if I could leave the conversation and the awful speculation behind me. I'd been standing right by that fountain when Atinna attacked me. Not a happy memory, but it was still a beautiful garden. All the greenery and flowers appealed to my Spring nature, and I felt my tension ease.

Ash followed a moment later. The rich perfume of roses filled the air. Small trees lined the stone walls, forming a soft green backdrop for the flowering shrubs that marched down the four paths towards the central fountain. Three stone dolphins leapt from a wide circular basin there, thin streams of water flowing from their open mouths into the pool below.

The pattering of the water hitting the basin made me think of Spring. There were always water noises in a Spring fae's home, from a fountain or a little brook or creek. Something. Spring was the Realm of new life, and water was essential to that. I'd grown up going to sleep to the sound of the gentle pattering of water into a small pool outside my bedroom.

I relaxed as the sound of water worked its magic on me. Sometimes, the simple everyday magics of scent and sound were the best.

"Fallon's a necromancer," Ash said, sitting down on the stone edging of the fountain and pursuing the topic with dogged determination. "Do you think *he* can see ghosts?"

I shrugged. "I guess so. But I'm not a necromancer, so why can I?"

Maybe this seeing ghosts thing was only temporary, some kind of weird side effect of the tussle with my father. Perhaps Ash was right after all and this strange new feeling of power was somehow caused by the dagger—its parting gift to me. Nothing to do with Fallon.

I sighed and ran my fingers lightly through the water. If only I could believe that.

I watched the water dripping from my fingers, something nagging at me. A tickling between my shoulder blades. The roses still filled my nostrils with their luscious scent, but the pattering of the fountain had lost its soothing power. A feeling that I was being watched grew to a certainty.

Something moved in my peripheral vision, and I whirled. My heartbeat quickened. *Not again.*

A figure stood by the trees to my right, and the damned trees were clearly visible through the figure's body. I could sense a presence like a chill breeze through my soul. Why was this happening to me?

I took a step closer. Ash, ever alert, rose to see what I was looking at, but I could tell from the way his gaze continued to search that he couldn't see what I saw. It was a woman, outlined in soft blue light. She wore black, as she had in life, but her skin was a silvery blue. Her blond hair had lost its golden shine. Her eyes stood out in her pale face like black pits.

She stopped moving when I noticed her, and hovered there, her feet almost on the ground but not quite. Her face was twisted into the same expression of rage and hate that she'd worn when I'd last seen her, right here in this garden. Back then, she'd been trying to choke the life out of me.

"Hello, Atinna," I said. If I had to see ghosts, why couldn't they be the friendly kind, like Casper? I thought I'd seen the last of Atinna, and finding out I was wrong wasn't improving my mood any. "What are you hanging around here for? Shouldn't you be in hell by now?"

"Atinna is here?" Ash asked in an urgent undertone, his hand going to the hidden sheath inside his shirt.

That wouldn't do him any good against a ghost. There

was a tree branch sticking right through her shoulder, which obviously wasn't concerning her in the slightest.

"Hell is a human construct," she said, and I heard her as clearly as I'd heard Ash. "But I would happily send you there."

She rushed at me, and I flinched back, instinctively calling on my Spring magic. Normally I'm pretty steady in a fight, but I'd never fought a ghost before, and the whole thing was weirding me out. The trees stretched their branches after her, and the plants bordering the path whipped at her, roses grasping at her with their thorny branches, but they found nothing but empty air.

And then she was on me, hands curled into claws. I felt a chill that raised gooseflesh all over me as she passed right through my body and out the other side. I spun to face her as she checked her headlong rush.

"Eww," I said. "That was gross. Stay out of my body, you dead freak."

She snarled in frustration and drew a knife from its sheath on her belt. It was as ghostly and see-through as she was, so I wasn't worried, though I still flinched when she hurled it at me. It passed through me, just as she had done, and I didn't feel more than the smallest shiver in my chest.

"Nice throw. That might have killed me if you weren't a useless dead monster."

She screamed right in my face, and another shiver ran through me.

"We should leave," Ash said. His dagger was in his

hand, his gaze uselessly roaming, trying to find the threat he couldn't see.

"She's no problem," I said. "And I kind of like winding her up. How does it feel to be so sad and pathetic?" I asked her. She'd caused me so much grief when she was alive. It was time for some payback.

Her eyes narrowed, and the temperature dropped noticeably. Like, really, *really* dropped. The sound of water pattering into the fountain's base abruptly ceased.

The fountain had frozen over. The streams from the dolphins' mouths were solid ice, and you could have skated on the surface of the pool below them.

"Did you do that?" I asked Ash, suddenly wary.

"No." He caught my hand and tried to tug me back through the arch, but I resisted his pull.

The dark pits of Atinna's eyes lit with a bright blue glow. That couldn't be good. One of the frozen streams broke with a loud snap, and the pieces clattered onto the ice below. The biggest was the length of my arm, with jagged points at each end. Atinna reached out as if she meant to pick it up, but instead she stood there, arm outstretched, and stared at it. One end shuddered, forming scratches in the surface of the frozen pool.

What was she doing? Trying to pick it up with magic? She'd discovered that ghost weapons couldn't harm me, so now she was trying to affect the physical world. But surely ghosts couldn't still access their magic? She'd frozen the pool, and she'd been a Winter fae—but I'd heard of cold spots associated with a haunting before.

Admittedly *cold* was a little different than *frozen abso-*

lutely bloody solid. My heart beat faster as I stared at that jagged spear of ice. There was too much I didn't know.

But if ghosts could use magic—that was pretty big news. Magic elevated haunting to a whole new—probably fatal—level. I was certain I would have heard about it. Ghost stories would be a whole 'nother ball game with magic in the mix.

It had to be something to do with the damn dagger— one more sin to lay at its door. She must still have some kind of connection to it that gave her abilities that the average ghost didn't possess.

"It's not safe here," Ash said, pulling on my hand with more force. "Let's go."

And leave her here like this? The spear of ice shuddered again and lifted a handspan from the surface before falling. Soon she would figure it out, and then we'd have a magical poltergeist on our hands. Bad news all round. I had no idea if she could leave this garden, the place of her death, but if she could, all the king's guards were in danger from a threat they couldn't see or defend against.

The ice spear lifted into the air, and a grin of triumph split Atinna's face. It wavered, but didn't fall, as she turned it so that it pointed directly at me.

Ash stepped between us, forming an ice shield as he moved, a wall as thick as my hand that separated us from Atinna. "We have to leave."

His face was pale, his brow creased by a worried frown. It seemed that I wasn't the only one unnerved by facing off against a ghost. And he couldn't even see her. He tried to herd me back down the path toward the archway.

Behind him, Atinna simply stepped through his ice wall. Somehow, she brought the ice spear with her—and now it was pointed at Ash's unsuspecting back, barely a foot away.

"No!"

The spear drove forward at lightning speed. It was too close. There was no time to duck, no time to do anything. I threw my hands up in desperation to ward it off.

Power surged within me and blasted free. Ash was hurled sideways into the rose bushes. Atinna flew backwards, as if picked up by an invisible wind, and a mist boiled up out of nowhere, swallowing both her and the spear with such uncanny speed that I blinked in surprise. The mist sparkled with silver and flashes of blue. I froze in place, uncertain what was going on.

Ash untangled himself from the broken rose bushes. "What's happening? Where is she?"

"I'm not sure. I can't see through the mist."

"What mist?"

That sent a chill through me. The mist was *right there*, impossible to miss. Why couldn't he see it?

I couldn't sense Atinna's presence, or see anything beyond the billowing mist. My skin prickled as all the little hairs on the back of my neck and up and down my arms stood to attention. The garden was silent but for the movement of leaves stirred by the breeze. I held my breath.

Gradually I became aware of another sound, almost on the edge of hearing. It sounded like a fae flute, and the mist sparked and swirled in response to the yearning melody it played. It grew louder, as if the flautist approached, and the melody curled around me, calling to me. Every fibre of my being wanted to find that flautist, to see who could play a tune that spoke so directly to my heart. I took a single step forward, and felt the first pricklings of threshold magic.

But this was nothing like the usual sensation. This wasn't tiny insect feet tickling on my skin. It was needles piercing me; a thousand—no, a *million* fiery stabs that burned every surface of my body. Yet I still wanted to push forward against the pain, the melody of the flute calling to me, as if calling me home. I knew that if I persevered in spite of the pain, I would be happier than I'd ever been before. Everything I wanted was waiting right there, on the other side of the thick, silvery mist.

I trembled, leaning forward, and took a step. Somewhere in the distance, hounds bayed, and I sensed figures moving in the mist all around me, their movement setting the mist swirling in silvery patterns. Another step. Another. The pain was almost gone.

"Sage!" Ash's voice behind me sounded very far away. I couldn't see him, but the panic in his voice made me pause. In everything that we'd faced together, he'd been a rock; a steady, reliable presence. Nothing ever disturbed his equilibrium. The only time I'd heard such terror in his voice before was when he'd thought I was dying, poisoned by the deadly venom of a night viper. "Where are you?"

I looked back. I couldn't see him through the mist that boiled around me. It was so beautiful with its flashes of blue and sparkling silver. The music of the flute called me, and I was turning back to it when Ash called my name again.

Reluctantly, I turned toward the sound of his voice and took a single step. The bite of the needles faded and the garden appeared, shadowy and somehow distant, as if I gazed at it through a veil. Ash was there, his arms outstretched, spinning in place as he called my name with ever more urgency.

I took another step, and reality jarred into focus. Ash's face lit up and he swept me into his arms.

"Where did you go?" he asked, almost squeezing the breath out of me, as if he feared I would disappear again if he let me go. "One minute you were there, the next you were gone."

My face was pressed against his chest, his heart racing beneath my ear. A familiar ironbark scent clung to him, and I took a deep breath of it before turning my head against his shirt and looking over my shoulder. There was no sign of the mist, and the ice of the fountain had melted. Once again water flowed from the dolphins' mouths, pitter-pattering into the pool below. The only hints that anything had happened were a couple of mangled rose-bushes, a few snapped branches, and a shower of leaves and rose petals strewn across the path.

There was also no sign of Atinna. I pulled away from Ash and inspected every corner of the garden, but I couldn't see her anywhere. That sense I'd had of her presence, that chill that had gripped my soul, was gone.

Ash caught at my hand. "What did she do to you? Let's get out of here before she does it again."

"She didn't do it." I allowed him to pull me along as I studied the now-empty garden, but it held no clues for me. No mist. No achingly sweet melody played on a fae flute. No sense of other people moving just ahead of me—waiting for me? "It was all me."

That strange power felt almost familiar now. It had surged up in the face of danger and blasted Atinna right out of existence. I was sure of that. There'd been something niggling at my senses when we'd first entered the garden, even before Atinna's ghost had shown itself. Some sense of a presence, though I couldn't say now how I had known. But I could certainly tell that it wasn't here anymore.

"I think I banished her."

4
——————

*a*sh peppered me with questions as we went to find the knights, but I cut him off. I wasn't ready to answer his questions when I had so many of my own. He still held my hand, and I was glad of his touch. His warm skin against mine seemed to ground me. Otherwise I might have floated off into the sky, or the earth could have opened up and swallowed me whole. I was reeling with the implications of what had just happened. I could tell from the way that Ash sneaked sidelong glances at me that he might be silent now but he was making the same horrifying deductions that I was.

It didn't make any sense. Necromancy was a thing of rituals, of black candles and chanting and blood sacrifice. A thing to be learned in the dark places of the world. My father had journeyed far and studied for years to become what he was.

And though I'd pulled some kind of power out of him in that last desperate struggle over the dagger and its powers, it couldn't have been the power of necromancy—except I was becoming ever more certain that it actually *was*.

How else could I explain the things that were happening? I'd seen two ghosts in the space of an hour. When that poor boy had died, I'd felt as if something in my own chest had snapped. In fact, now that I thought about it, I'd felt that same sense of something being severed when Ash had killed Atinna, though at the time I'd put it down to some lingering effect of the bond I'd had with all the Vipers when I was the Serpent.

And now it appeared I had destroyed Atinna's ghost by somehow hurling her into the sparkling silver mist. That mist had felt like a threshold, but different to any threshold I'd experienced in the past. I'd been at once attracted and repelled by it, longing to follow the siren song of the fae flute even as the threshold magic had been biting into me.

That must have been the threshold between the worlds of the living and the dead. What else could it have been? I'd hurled Atinna's ghost through, and she hadn't reappeared. Perhaps the painful threshold magic had been a warning to my living body not to cross, despite the yearning I'd felt to join those mysterious figures waiting on the other side.

I shivered. I didn't want to be a necromancer. I'd never heard a single good thing about them. They were universally reviled and feared among the fae, probably because death was such a taboo subject and necromancers were all about death. Their presence was a constant reminder that even the seemingly eternal summer of life that the fae enjoyed would one day turn to winter. It was funny, really, considering they were such a long-lived race. Why should they fear death when it might be centuries before it came for them?

Maybe that was the very reason. Humans saw death all around them, experiencing an aging process that made the approach of death real and inescapable. But to the fae, death was rare and aging something that only drained their strength in their last handful of years. They had so much more to lose than mortals. Death was a thief that stole an eternal youth that they considered their right. And with their birth rate so low, every death was a terrible loss. No wonder they hated and feared it so much.

Even the Vipers, those dealers of death, rarely spoke of it. They talked of hits and targets and contracts, making it all sound safely dry and professional, leaching the fear out of it.

"Where do you think the rest of the Vipers are?" I asked, breaking the silence as we emerged from the gardens onto the lake shore again, near the pavilion that housed the hidden gate. The Lion was there, his thick russet hair shining in the sun. I couldn't see the Hawk. The rest of the king's people stood guard over a small number of prisoners, mostly children, though there were a handful of adults among them. They were seated on the ground, heads bowed in a sullen silence, even the smallest toddler.

"I don't know," Ash replied, his eyes roving over the crowd, as if counting their number and coming up woefully short. I knew there had been many more support staff and families of Vipers living here. The rest must be dead. "You know your father better than me. Where is he likely to go? What are his goals?"

I shook my head. I'd thought Fallon's goal was to bring my mother back to life, but I'd been proven wrong. "I have no idea. But I suspect we won't like whatever he's doing."

"That seems certain," Ash said, a grim set to his mouth. But he squeezed my hand encouragingly. He knew how guilty I felt about this whole thing. I should never have let my father get his hands on Ni'ishasana.

But if I hadn't, *I* would still be trapped in service to the dagger, and I wasn't particularly keen on that outcome either. There seemed no way to win here. Both alternatives were appalling. I had settled for the slightly less appalling one, and there was no way to undo my choice, even if I had wanted to.

"How are you feeling now?" the Lion asked as we reached his side.

"Fine," I said, the word clipped short just this side of rudeness. There was nothing wrong with me. I wasn't hallucinating; I was suffering the effects of necromantic power, apparently. But that wasn't a fact I wanted to disclose to him or anyone until I had more of a handle on it myself.

Two figures appeared in the swirling mist between the columns of the pavilion. I shivered at the reminder of the sparkling silvery mist, but this was an ordinary threshold. The Hawk strode down the steps, sword in hand, followed at a more leisurely pace by the king.

Rothbold wore a simple golden circlet, not his heavy

crown of state, but he looked every inch the king in a dark blue velvet robe that swirled around his feet as he moved. Golden embroidered vines looped down his sleeves from shoulder to wrist, glinting in the sunlight. He didn't look at all tired, despite being still awake in the middle of the day, his eyes, as blue as the sky above, taking in every detail as he approached the seated prisoners.

He nodded a greeting to us, and I stepped forward. "Sire, what are you going to do with the prisoners?"

"Question them, of course." He frowned at me as if that should have been obvious. "We need to find out where the missing Vipers are."

"I mean after you've questioned them."

Rothbold raised one eyebrow. "Do you wish to dispatch them yourself?"

"No!" I stared at him aghast. "Of course not. I don't want them *dispatched* at all."

What a strange way to put it. It made them sound like letters to be sent through the post. But they were people, and we were talking about their lives. How could he discuss them so clinically?

"Really? I seem to remember you begging me to make an end of the Vipers not so long ago. Have you forgotten our purpose? We're here to wipe out this Nest and remove the threat of the Vipers from the Realms forever."

"The threat of the Vipers, sure. But these people aren't Vipers. Most of them are *children*, for the Lady's sake. Would you execute children for the crimes of their parents?"

"Small hatchlings grow to become dangerous snakes."

The king surveyed the prisoners without a trace of emotion before turning those cool blue eyes on me. "Do you think they will love us for sparing their lives? No. They will hate us for killing their parents and destroying the only home they have ever known. And then they will seek vengeance."

"There is no enemy more dangerous than a child seeking revenge on its parent's killer," the Hawk said gravely. He had put his sword away, but his hand still rested on its hilt, as if he was ready to draw it at the king's signal and personally *dispatch* every prisoner there.

"Of course there is!" I said heatedly. "How about an enemy in possession of the Thief of Souls and commanding the Vipers? Why are we focusing on innocent children when Fallon is running around out there somewhere?"

"You have a tender heart, Sage, but kings can't afford to follow the dictates of their hearts. Things are seldom as black and white as you would imagine—even such apparent truths as the innocence of children." Rothbold's voice was weary, as if years of difficult decisions weighed on him. "Most of these will have begun their training already, and they will certainly have been indoctrinated into the Viper way of thinking. They would kill us without hesitating if we gave them the opportunity."

"But they didn't choose this life," I argued, "and indoctrination can be undone."

"By whom? Who would care to take on such a risk with such little hope of reward? Only a fool." He lowered his voice, speaking calmly but very firmly. "And I am not a fool."

Great. Now the king was convinced I was insulting him.

"They won't expect mercy," Ash said, as if that might help me feel better.

"Then why should we expect them to tell us what we want to know? If they know they're going to die anyway, why would they co-operate? But if you give them a reward, a reason to help us, it will be a different story."

"There are ways to find out what we need to know without their co-operation," the Hawk said, a flinty expression on his face.

"I'm sure Ash knows all about them," Rothbold added. His eyes held a challenge.

Ash met the king's gaze without expression. "I do."

"Good. Find out where the Vipers are and what Fallon Domani is up to."

Ash bowed in acknowledgement, but I stared at the king in horror. "You want him to torture children?"

"Of course not. The children won't know anything."

"So just the people he's lived and worked with for years, then." Rage quivered within me and I could hardly contain it. I wanted to slap the king silly, until he came to his senses. Why was he being such a hard-ass? He wasn't usually like this. Was this some kind of test of Ash's loyalty? Did he think Ash's defection from the Vipers was fake and this was all part of some elaborate plan against the throne?

"He is more likely to be able to tell truth from lies than

anyone else," the king said, "since he knows more about the Vipers and their operations than any of us."

"But that's ..." Brutal. Heartless. Utterly fae.

I took a deep breath, trying to calm myself enough to argue logically rather than just screaming in inchoate rage.

"It's all right, Sage," Ash said, stopping me with a hand on my arm. "I'll do it. If it means the end of the Vipers, I'll do it."

But he shouldn't have to. It was too much to ask of anyone. Even though Ash hadn't joined the Vipers willingly and he'd hated his time there, he wasn't made of stone. He'd had *some* personal connections with the other members of the Nest. To force him to torture these people now was barbaric. That Rothbold expected it took my breath away. I had always thought him a benevolent ruler.

"At least offer him a reward for doing this," I said.

"What kind of reward?"

"Allow these people to live." Ash hadn't said anything, but I knew he wanted that. Probably he'd kept quiet because he knew how bad it would look to have him, an ex-Viper, pleading for his former associates' lives. Clearly he'd been conscious all along that he was in some kind of probationary period himself, as far as the king was concerned, though I'd been oblivious. Ash was far better at this Court intrigue crap than I was.

A rather cool silence fell on our little group and I forced myself to stand strong and not fidget under the weight of the king's stare.

"I make no promises," he said finally. "Each of them

must be judged on his or her deeds. But they will not be executed until they have had a chance to plead their case."

Some concession. Still, if that was all Rothbold was willing to give, I'd take it.

"Should we move the prisoners now, sire?" the Hawk asked.

"Yes. Clear this place out. I have work to do."

"What work is that?" I asked, still seething, as the Hawk nodded to a pair of guards, who began herding the prisoners through the gate. Once they were outside the Nest's wards, the Hawk could use his sword to open a direct gate to the palace's dungeons.

"I intend to make an end to this sith." The king smiled wolfishly. "The missing Vipers will get an unhappy surprise when they try to return home and discover that their Nest no longer exists."

"You can destroy siths?" That was news to me.

"Of course. They have been detached from the Realms in the first place. For the right person, reattaching them is easy."

I glanced at Ash. He looked equally surprised. Did "the right person" mean someone of the king's level of power? I certainly couldn't imagine attempting it. It had been taxing enough to move the Nest, big as it was, and back then I'd had all the dagger's powers at my command.

Still, it was often easier to destroy than to create. I looked around at the lake and the forest, at the massive building on the far shore with its turrets and towers. "Reattaching", huh? This should be interesting.

"Should we leave, sire?" the Lion asked.

He was the last of the king's forces here, as the others had gone through the gate with the prisoners. But at least one of the Chosen always stayed close to the king when he was out of the palace. Rothbold was an insanely powerful Earthcrafter, as I had already discovered during my recent abortive raid on the palace. As king, he also had a certain magic that came from the Realms themselves, which allowed him to perform other feats beyond Earthcrafting. But he didn't have eyes in the back of his head, so his Chosen guarded him carefully.

Because holy hell did that man have enemies.

"No," Rothbold said. "I need to be inside the sith to do this. As long as you stay close to me, I can keep you safe."

I took a big step closer to the king. I didn't want to be accidentally destroyed along with the sith.

Rothbold laughed. "Not that close, Sage. I only meant that you shouldn't stray."

I stepped back, doing my best to ignore the Lion's grin. What did he have to laugh about? He wasn't exactly giving the king a wide berth either.

Ash hadn't moved. He was staring across the water at the huge building that had been the centre of his life for so long. He might have felt grim satisfaction that it was about to be destroyed, or sorrow at seeing it go—it was impossible to tell from his carefully expressionless face. Ash had had too much practice at hiding his feelings. But I was betting on the grim satisfaction. He had no reason to feel nostalgic about his time here. He'd been as much his father's prisoner as if Celebrach had bound him in chains.

The king raised his arms and closed his eyes, and a

rumbling started under our feet. Was this Earthcrafting or his royal magic? If I'd still had the power of the dagger, I would probably have been able to tell. It was pretty disconcerting, either way. I liked my solid ground to stay *solid*, not quiver like a jelly.

Would my necromantic power be activated by the death of the sith? I shuddered a little. I'd managed to go a whole quarter hour without thinking about necromancy while I argued with the king and his knights about the prisoners. Now it was back in the forefront of my mind.

I gritted my teeth as the rumbling became a shaking and the air shimmered, like a heat haze on a summer's afternoon. The sith was so big that I couldn't see its edges from where we stood, except for the part near the front gate, where the enormous wall marked the boundary. Something strange was going on over there.

The ground writhed, reminding me uncomfortably of the ritual where my mother's dead body had climbed out of her grave. The great wall teetered, swaying like a sapling in a high wind, then crumbled, its blocks crashing to the ground. A great cloud of dust and soil fountained into the air.

A roaring like a jet engine drew my attention back to the main building. Spires tumbled. Turrets exploded. At any minute I expected some giant creature to climb out of the earth, shrugging the house off its shoulders with a shake of its pelt.

The noise was incredible. I covered my ears, watching blocks of stone crash against each other, cracking and grinding. The whole house collapsed in on itself. Eagerly the ground swallowed it up, writhing and shivering as it ingested its meal. Yet the lake in front of us remained serene, not a ripple on its smooth surface.

"What of the night vipers, sire?" Ash asked.

"They will never find this place again," the king replied, surveying his handiwork with satisfaction. The great building lay in ruins. Most of it was gone, swallowed by the earth as if it had never existed, but a few stones lay tumbled. The grass lapped against them as we watched, and moss and vines crept over the top of them. In less than two minutes, the headquarters of the Night Vipers had gone from a looming mansion to something that looked like an ancient ruin.

"Not the assassins," Ash said. "The actual snakes. There are hundreds of them here in a special facility in the woods."

I shuddered. Evandir had thrown one of the green- and yellow-striped snakes straight at my face there once. Only Ash's quick intervention had saved me from a deadly bite. And then Atinna had tried to kill me in my sleep by sneaking a few into my room and using magic to make them bite me. I had no love for the night vipers.

"They keep them in pits," I said.

The king's eyes gleamed. "Take me there."

Ash led the way, followed by the king, with the Lion hard on his heels. I brought up the rear, marvelling at what Rothbold had done. The effects of his magic were everywhere. Not a building was left standing. Some of them, the earth had swallowed whole, and there was only grass where houses had been. The cluster of pines that had stood guard over Ash's little cottage guarded only empty space now. Ash didn't even turn his head to look.

The training grounds were the same as ever. They'd only been well-trampled dirt. But the large building next to them that had housed the storerooms and changing facilities was gone without trace. I wouldn't have known where we were, except for the familiar trees and gardens. Those, the king had left.

I felt a prickling on my skin as we entered the forest, similar to threshold magic, though not as strong. The path we followed was still the same, so at first I dismissed it as my imagination. But the prickling persisted, and the hairs on the back of my neck rose.

The trees seemed to cluster together more closely than I remembered. The undergrowth was thicker, and the further we went into the forest, the more it impinged on the path. Before we reached the clearing where the snakes were kept, Ash was forcing his way through bushes that I could have sworn weren't there before. The trees reached down to brush against the king as he passed, like fans longing to touch their idol.

Finally, we broke through into the clearing. The king's magic had been at work here, too. The building that had housed the equipment for collecting the snakes' venom was gone. Only a vine-covered tumble of bricks marked where it had stood. The low brick walls that had lined the edges of the three pits where the vipers lived were gone, too, though the pits themselves were still there.

We gathered at the edge of the first pit. A few bricks lay at the bottom, and a couple of snakes lay unmoving, killed by falling bricks. The others were restless. In the middle of the day, they usually lay unmoving, basking in the warmth of the sun, but now they coiled and hissed, their scaled bodies twining over and under each other. The tumbling bricks had disturbed them, and they were looking for something to take out their annoyance on.

"So many," Rothbold said in tones of wonder. "I thought that these were extinct."

"You cannot let them live, sire," the Lion said. "They will breed unchecked in the Realms."

"Will you plead for *their* lives, too, Sage?" Rothbold asked. "After all, they are only dumb creatures who have no inclination to interfere in the affairs of the world." I shook my head, and he glanced at Ash. "What do you say?"

"Bury them deep," Ash said with ferocity, "where their venom can never take another life."

"Then we agree," the king said. "Step back, everyone."

As we moved, the ground around the pits began to crumble. Soil pattered down onto the snakes in a gentle rain at first, then the surrounding earth heaved and rumbled. I was close enough to see into the nearest pit, and the bottom simply fell away, taking the snakes tumbling into an abyss. The mouth of the pit contracted, and all at once there was smooth grass where once there had been a massive hole.

Even the clearing had shrunk. As I watched, new growth sprang from the earth. Flowers clustered around the king's feet. Seedlings turned into saplings in the space of a breath, and a moment later into trees. I raised my eyebrows, impressed. I had thought only Spring mages could do that. The king was an Earthcrafter. It must be his deep connection to the Realms that allowed him to coax plants into life.

But still that uneasy feeling persisted. "Does anyone else feel that tickling sensation?" I asked. "What *is* that?"

The king smiled and waved his hand. The bushes had closed completely over the path back through the forest, but they bent aside at the king's command, opening a way for us.

"That is the Wilds you feel," he said, leading the way.

I hurried to catch up, leaving Ash and the Lion to bring up the rear this time. The feeling was growing, and hearing it was caused by the Wilds, that dangerous place between the worlds, didn't make me feel any better.

"The Wilds?" I didn't understand what they had to do with anything.

"I have brought this sith back into the Realms, but not any part where the assassins will be able to find it. I've hidden it deep in the Wilds." Trees bent to caress him with their leaves, and flowers sprang up from nowhere, blooming as his robe brushed the ground.

I remembered the Wilds behaving in a similar fashion for his sister Yriell once. She'd told us then that they were the remnants of the old Realm of Earth. It had once been a mighty Realm, but centuries ago it had been split in two. Its Lord at the time had banished its darker aspects to please a wife who shrank from them, and the reduced Realm had been renamed Flowers. It hadn't lasted long after that. In a matter of decades, which was practically the blink of an eye as the fae measured time, Flowers had become part of Spring.

The Wilds had grown stronger and darker in exile between the worlds, until their magic had twisted that place. I'd heard that long ago it had been a simple matter to move between the Realms and the human world, but now it took magic and a strong will to find your destination. Many had been lost on its ever-changing paths, and as for those who left the path—well, let's just say that leaving the path wasn't a great idea.

But the Wilds remembered their old masters, and still loved them in spite of the rejection. Any of that long-ago Lord's descendants were still treated to a warm welcome, and paths miraculously opened for them.

When the Wilds eventually ushered us back to the lake, everything had changed. The shimmering in the air that had concealed what lay beyond the sith's walls was gone—as were the walls. Now the trees encroached over the tumbled blocks of stones almost to the lake shore and extended in the other direction as far as the eye could see. Trees grew where the huge main building had stood, and its ruins were almost lost among the bushes that had sprung up there. The Wilds had swallowed the sith whole.

The Nest of the Vipers was no more.

5

Three days later, Lord Nox's funeral took place.

I hadn't wanted to go, convinced that Raven's family would all blame me for his death, but Willow had made delicate enquiries—which surprised me, because Willow was rarely delicate about anything—and she had received a message back that all of the Spring ruling family would be welcome.

So apparently I was now considered Lord Thistle and Lady Feronique's honorary daughter. I bet that was news to them.

It was all politics, of course. Night was the king's oldest and proudest ally, and they knew I had his favour, so they wouldn't turn me away. It was the same reason Lady Feronique had made overtures of friendship to me at Allegra's ascension. I was Someone, now, and people were prepared to overlook the taint of my father's blood in a way they had never overlooked the human stain of my mother's when I was growing up.

Although, to be fair to Lady Feronique, she had helped me out that terrible night when I'd crashed the ball Spring was throwing to welcome Lord Nox. I'd been sent to kill him, but fortunately, I'd managed to slip him something that only made him *appear* to be dead, and appearances were enough to satisfy the watching Vipers, at least for a time. Then it had all gone to shit, and I'd ended up possessed by the damned dagger and leading those same Vipers.

Fun times.

Poor Lord Nox had been assassinated a few weeks later anyway, despite my efforts that night. Strictly speaking, his death had been nothing to do with me, but I felt responsible because I knew Atinna had only killed him to piss me off.

And clearly Raven considered me responsible, whatever diplomatic noises the rest of his family made. He hadn't looked at me once all through the long ceremony, staring straight ahead while fae flutes wailed and the pungent scent of the herbs burned to guide Lord Nox's soul on its way to the Realm of Death wafted through the air.

Bobbing faelights lent a soft glow to the scene. We stood in a meadow where tiny sweet-scented yellow flowers nodded on long stems, and fireflies flitted through the tall grasses like miniature faelights themselves. We all stood together in a loose circle, Lords and Ladies rubbing shoulders with the members of the Lord of Night's household in the perfumed night air. A cook with flour on one cheek sobbed quietly next to the Lord of Winter, wiping her tears on her apron. She must have come straight from preparing food for the wake.

Others had had time to put on their best to honour their fallen Lord. Judging by the size of the crowd, Lord Nox had been a popular man. Swathed in silks in the blue and black colours of his House, his body lay on the grass in the centre of the gathering. Many had come to lay flowers at his feet. Even the fireflies danced around his body as if they'd come to pay their respects.

Raven's oldest brother, Quinn, spoke movingly of his father's life. He was pale and grave, as if the burden of stepping into his father's shoes as Lord of Night rested heavily on his shoulders. The mourners listened in respectful silence, heads bowed. All the Lords and Ladies of the Realms were in attendance, and many of their families and closest retainers, so it was quite a crowd.

Well, *almost* all the Lords and Ladies of the Realms. Lord Orobos of Fire hadn't been seen outside his Realm in years, so his absence was hardly a surprise. But Willow's parents, Lord Thistle and Lady Feronique, were also missing, though they had been expected. Willow was here to represent the ruling family of Spring, but it was strange that they hadn't turned up—particularly as Lord Thistle had so recently been negotiating with Lord Nox for a marriage between their Houses, a little tidbit that I hadn't yet had the guts to share with Willow. It seemed doubly odd to shun the funeral of a man when you were trying to foster closer relations with his family.

Allegra, the new Lady of Illusion, was here, surrounded by her people, who had all brought their rainbow drakes. The drakes were like miniature dragons, only with less fire and a lot more cuteness. Squeak, Allegra's drake, rode on her shoulder, half hidden in her hair. Moonlight glinted silver on his scales when he moved. I was looking forward to catching up with Allegra and hoped that Squeak might let me pat him.

Night itself was a surprise. I'd expected something dark and sombre, given its name, but what I found was a city as light and bright as Whitehaven itself, if a little less formal. The Lord's estate was less of a palace and more an enormous sprawling manor house. But unlike any human idea of a lord's manor, this one had flat roofs that were all accessible from within or reached by stairs from the many open courtyards scattered within the building. The Night fae spent nearly as much time relaxing on these roofs, which were used as informal gathering spaces, as they did inside the buildings. Each roof had a lavish garden, many containing quite large trees and fountains.

The meadow where we stood was only a short walk from the sprawling house, and a trail of faelights lit the way back to it. The house bulked black against the night sky, all its windows dark, as if it, too, mourned the passing of its Lord.

When Quinn finished, an Earthcrafter stepped forward. Only the poorest fae dug graves. The rest employed the services of an Earthcrafter to bury the body without fuss. But the king stopped her with a hand on her arm.

"Allow me the privilege of laying my dear friend to rest," he said.

Lady Fiana, Lord Nox's widow, bowed her head in acknowledgement of the honour, and Rothbold bowed back. Queen Ceinwen didn't stir or even seem to notice that her husband had moved. As usual, she looked pale and bloodless, as though she'd been carved from a block of ice. In contrast, beside her, Princess Lily, who'd been let off her leash for the occasion, glowed with health. Her time in the sunlight of the human world with Willow had transformed her from a pale copy of her mother to something a lot warmer. I wasn't ready to admit that it might have improved her character as well, but she certainly *looked* better.

Besides, I had bigger things on my mind than Lily. Raven stood with his family, almost directly opposite me in the circle of mourners, but he steadfastly refused to meet my gaze. He was on one side of his mother, and Quinn was on the other, and they each took one of Lady Fiana's hands as Rothbold stirred the earth with his magic and Lord Nox's silk-wrapped body slowly sank into the ground. My own eyes welled with tears, but they remained dry-eyed, Lady Fiana even retaining control of herself enough to thank the king in a steady voice as the grass reformed and a mass of the tiny yellow flowers bloomed on her husband's grave, their sweet scent intoxicating.

Later, in the largest of the roof gardens, the family stood in a receiving line to welcome their guests and accept their condolences. Fireworks in silver and blue burst soundlessly overhead as I waited my turn to speak to them. They weren't like human fireworks; these were fae ones, which weren't restricted to sparkling flower shapes in the sky. These were fuelled by magic, not explosives, and they showed scenes from Lord Nox's life. A wild hunt where he skewered a boar the size of a small four-wheel drive. A massive state occasion, which looked like his wedding to Lady Fiana. Small moments where he chased a trio of dark-haired boys through a garden or rode a magnificent horse through a wood of tall, pale trees. Each scene would burn bright for a moment or two, hanging suspended in the night sky, before fizzling away as fireworks did and being replaced by another bright burst. I was getting a crick in my neck from craning skyward, but I couldn't look away.

We were almost at the head of the receiving line. Spring was one of the last contingents to be received. The others had dispersed around the garden, watching the sky show as they nibbled on delicate cakes and drank sweet fae wine. A subdued murmur of conversation hummed in the background, voices mingling with the sound of a fae flute playing a melancholy air and the soft trickle of water in the central fountain.

Finally, it was our turn. Willow moved from Quinn and Paxyl, the second brother, on to Lady Fiana and Raven, last in the line. I was next. I nodded to Quinn and Paxyl, but didn't stop until I reached Lady Fiana.

"I'm so sorry for your loss," I said. "Lord Nox was a wonderful man."

I hadn't known him that well, but he'd been kind to me at the fateful ball at Spring, and it spoke to the kind of man he was. Fae Lords weren't often kind.

"Thank you," Lady Fiana said.

"I did my best to keep him alive," I said, driven by an urge to have it all out in the open. "I was supposed to kill him for the Vipers at that ball in Spring, but I gave him starbright instead. It's a weed that grows in Spring," I added at her look of incomprehension. "It can put you into a sleep that mimics death."

"Why are you telling me this?" she asked.

"Because he wasn't supposed to die! When he collapsed, the Vipers were satisfied, and that should have been the end of it. I became their leader after that. No one else should have touched him, because it was my kill to make, and I never had any intention of killing him."

Lady Fiana looked pained, and it occurred to me belatedly that describing the details of the Vipers' procedures may not have been the right thing to say at her husband's funeral. But I wanted her to understand how sorry I was. I'd really thought he was safe.

"But they did, didn't they?" Raven said, his tone icy. His eyes were hard, too, and I looked back at his mother, my face flushing at the rebuke in his voice.

"The king has explained the circumstances," Lady Fiana said stiffly, giving her son a warning look. "We bear no ill will towards you."

"Speak for yourself, Mama," Raven said. He turned on me, those coal-black eyes alight with fury. "You should have issued an explicit order, not just left it hanging as if it was of no consequence. It wasn't some trivial matter. My father's *life* was on the line."

"I'm sorry," I repeated helplessly. What else could I do

but apologise? "But I never thought any of the Vipers would do such a thing without an express order."

"You never *thought*." His mimicry held a vicious undertone that made me flinch. Several nearby guests were looking our way, their curiosity stirred by Raven's raised voice. "And your thoughtlessness stole my father from me." His glance raked his family almost contemptuously. "*They* may forgive you, but *I* never will."

6

———

"Why did I come?" I asked bitterly. "I shouldn't have done it. I knew how he felt."

"He'll get over it," Allegra said with an assurance I was far from feeling. She'd found me in a quiet corner of the garden, cradling a drink and wondering if getting drunk would make things better or worse. I'd never missed Ash's calm presence more, but he was still at Whitehaven. "Raven can be a bit unpredictable, I grant you. But I've never known him to be unreasonable. That was his grief talking. When the loss isn't so fresh, he'll come around."

And when would that be? "Fresh" could last a long time, considering how long the fae lived. With my human blood, I might be an old woman before Raven got over his father's death sufficiently to consider forgiving me for my part in it.

"Or he might just hate me more and more as the years go by," I said gloomily, looking out into the night. The fireworks had finished, and now only the stars shone down on the rooftop gardens of Night. All the houses had them, not just the Lord's residence. A sea of small trees and fountains covered every roof, and many had people on them. The folk of Night were mourning their Lord's death just as we were.

Squeak winged in for a landing on the low wall that encircled the rooftop garden. At least, I assumed it was Squeak. I wasn't familiar enough with him to pick him out from the crowd of similar-looking drakes wheeling above in the dark sky. But Allegra's warm smile of greeting made his identity clear.

He sidestepped along the wall like a parrot on a perch until he was close enough to nuzzle into her side. She scratched under his neck and his eyes closed in draconic bliss.

"Don't be so pessimistic," she said, still scratching. It seemed to give her almost as much pleasure as it did him, judging by the fond smile on her face.

"Easy for you to say. He's still talking to you."

For someone who'd been a changeling not so long ago, her life had turned out pretty sweet. Lady of Illusion, with a tiny dragon that doted on her and an attentive boyfriend, she had nothing to complain about anymore. Not that I begrudged her her happiness. It just made my own messed-up life look even worse by comparison.

Raven hated me, my father was up to something that would no doubt turn out to be an absolute shit-show, and half the people at this gathering were giving me the side-eye for what he'd already done. Not to mention the mess of my own making I'd only just managed to extricate myself from.

Or perhaps not *quite* managed—there was still the matter of my peculiar new powers. And how the hell I was going to sort that out, I had no idea. The best thing would be to get rid of them. I had absolutely no desire to be a necromancer. But I had a sinking feeling that it wouldn't be quite so easy to get rid of them as it had been to acquire them—at least not in any way that left me still alive and kicking.

Basically the only good thing in my life was Ash.

"You're smiling again," Allegra said. "What are you thinking about?"

"Nothing."

True, Ash made me smile. He even made my heart beat a little faster every time I saw him—and there was no doubt of his feelings for me. But we'd only known each other a short time. Could I be sure that these feelings for him were real and not just some kind of misplaced gratitude for making it through all the crap we'd been through together?

And did I really want to spend the rest of my life with an ex-assassin?

However good he'd been to me, there was no denying that Ash had killed a lot of people. Granted, he hadn't wanted to, but the fact remained that he'd done it. He wasn't exactly the kind of guy you could bring home to your mother. Assuming you had a mother, of course.

I stirred restlessly, and Squeak chirped in disapproval as Allegra stopped scratching under his chin.

"I think I'll go for a walk," I said. "One more conversation about how wonderful Lord Nox was is going to kill me. I feel so bad."

She gave me a direct look. "You shouldn't. It's not your fault, Sage."

"Tell that to Raven."

"Have another drink and you'll feel better."

"Maybe I'll do that, too. Catch you later."

I left her there with Squeak and headed for the nearest staircase. There were gardens down below, too, and I'd spotted an empty courtyard with plenty of tall trees, where no one would notice me. I could hide there until Willow was ready to leave.

But the inside of the building was surprisingly labyrinthine, and I got turned around and came out instead into a small space that was barely big enough to be called a courtyard. A single jacaranda in the middle spread its leafy boughs across a small fishpond and the bench beside it, and that was all.

Someone else stepped into the space at the same time, from a corridor opposite. It was a tall man, and his footsteps made no sound as he glided toward the stone bench and sat down. Then he looked up at me and smiled. I gasped.

It was Lord Nox.

I froze on the spot. Did Lord Nox have a twin that no one had told me about? Biting my lip, I moved closer and realised that I could just make out the textured trunk of the jacaranda through him, and the faintest shimmer of blue surrounded his form. Dammit. Another ghost.

"Lord Nox," I said, giving him a bow of respect. "I didn't expect to see you here."

Understatement of the century. I hadn't expected to see any ghosts, *ever*, and now they were popping up all over the place. For good or ill, it seemed I was a necromancer now.

"You're Fallon's daughter," he said, and I tensed up. Was he going to launch into a rant about my father and the taint of his blood? I had expected better from him, but perhaps being assassinated had put him in a bad mood. I could see how that could piss a person off.

"Yes. My name is Sage."

"I remember you," he said. "I met you once when you were a child at Thistle's Court. I see you don't recall the occasion."

"We met again more recently," I said.

"Yes, but I didn't recognise you then. You were trying to save me, weren't you?"

I nodded, surprised. But he'd always had a reputation as an astute man, so perhaps I shouldn't have been. He'd probably done a lot of thinking in the aftermath of that debacle.

"I did my best," I said. "I'm sorry my best wasn't good enough."

He waved that aside. His ghost still wore the massive ring of the Lord of Night on one long, elegant finger. He was dressed in black velvet embroidered with silver stars, and it occurred to me that I'd never heard any details of his death. Was this what he'd been wearing when Atinna struck? I didn't even know how the deed had been done. I hoped it had been an easy death, but that didn't seem like something I could ask Lord Nox's ghost.

"Don't blame yourself, child. When the Lady decides to cut your thread, it is not for men to argue." He patted the bench beside him. "Come and tell me why you can see me. I've been wandering the halls and rooftops all week, but no one else knew I was here."

I sat down gingerly, keeping as much space between us as possible on the small bench. The air was noticeably colder this close to him, and I wasn't exactly dressed for fraternising with the dead. Some people said a ghost's touch could kill. My experience with Atinna's ghost proved that wasn't true, but I still preferred to keep my distance.

Fae believed in ghosts, but I'd never expected to see one myself. Meeting ghosts was something that happened to the heroes of stories that people liked to tell late at night. They were usually vengeful and pretty much insane, not urbane figures who invited you to join them for a cosy chat.

How much should I tell Lord Nox? It wasn't as though he could betray any of my secrets, but I barely understood what was going on myself.

As I considered my answer to his question, footsteps approached and I looked up. It was Raven, and he recoiled when he saw me.

"What are *you* doing here?"

"This is one of his favourite spots to be alone," Lord Nox said. His gaze was fond as it rested on his youngest son. "As a boy, whenever he was in trouble, I knew I could find him here."

"I'm not doing anything," I said to Raven. "Just sitting here." *Talking to your father.*

He turned to leave, and I leapt up. "Raven, wait. Let me explain—"

"I've heard your explanations before." He spun around, his eyes hot with anger, the words almost spat at me. "Explanations don't bring my father back, do they?" He grabbed my wrist and hauled me with him back down the corridor. "Come with me."

"Where are we going?" I tugged, but he refused to let go. And since I wanted to know what he was up to, I let myself be pulled along.

He didn't answer, just kept towing me along, marching with furious strides past rooms full of beautiful furniture and priceless works of art. It was all I could do to keep up. He came to a silver staircase that glittered in the moonlight shining through a skylight high above and took the stairs two at a time. Wherever he was going, he sure was in a hurry to get there. We didn't pass a single soul; they must all have been on the roof still.

Striding down a new corridor, we passed under the watchful gaze of dozens of portraits done in the fae style. The magic of the artists made their subjects appear three-dimensional, as if you were gazing through a window into an actual room or scene, and not looking at a flat canvas. The people looked as alive as Raven or me, and most bore an obvious resemblance to Raven, making it clear that these were family portraits.

Towards the end of the hall, the portraits reached the current era. One painting showed three dark-haired, dark-eyed boys together, their mischievous grins captured for all eternity. Another showed Lord Nox and Lady Fiana, perhaps on their wedding day. She had flowers in her hair, and he looked down at her with a smile that warmed his whole face. I bit my lip, reminded again of Lady Fiana's loss.

Not that I could forget it, with her son dragging me off in such obvious fury. He threw open the door of a room near the end of the long hall, a black door with a swirling silver design on it that reminded me of comets blazing across the night sky.

Inside lay a bedroom. The emblem of Night adorned the wall above the bed, which was draped in a dark blue velvet coverlet. A black cat snoozed in the middle of it. He lifted his head and regarded us blearily, then lowered his head again and closed his eyes, evidently deciding that we weren't worth waking up for.

The size of the room and the grandness of the furnishings suggested that this was the Lord of Night's own bedroom. Raven dragged me to a stop in the middle of the vast blue carpet and pointed dramatically at the floor.

"This is the place where your murderer killed my father. Gutted him and left him to bleed out like a bull for slaughter. Tell me again how *sorry* you are, and how you didn't *mean* it." His black eyes challenged me, and the room crackled with power, as if he were only just maintaining control of his magic.

"They did well to get that stain out of the carpet," Lord Nox's voice observed. His ghost appeared, standing close enough to touch Raven and gazing thoughtfully down at the floor. Surely Raven could feel the chill in the air?

But perhaps his rage kept him warm enough. Unable to help myself, I glanced down at the carpet. Lord Nox was right. You could never have guessed that someone had died messily here. How could he speak so nonchalantly about his own death? Did ghosts somehow lose touch with their emotions, the way they lost touch with their bodies?

The cat meowed, wide awake now and staring with rounded eyes at the former Lord of Night's transparent form. It leapt down from the bed and prowled closer, never taking its eyes from Lord Nox.

"Poor Midnight," Lord Nox said as the cat tried to rub itself against Lord Nox's non-existent legs and almost fell over. "He can't understand what's happened to me."

"He can see you?" I asked.

"What's wrong with you?" Raven asked roughly. "Who are you talking to?"

I weighed my options and decided that honesty was the best policy, even if he thought I was crazy. "Your father."

If I'd thought he looked angry before, that was nothing to the rage that twisted his face now. "You dare mock my grief?"

I gave him a level look. "I'm not mocking anything. Your father is here. Standing right next to you, actually. Can't you feel the chill?"

The ghost's presence was raising goosebumps on my own arms. Poor Midnight stalked in high dudgeon towards the door and showed himself out, trying to pretend that had been his intention all along. Evidently he didn't approve of ghostly owners who couldn't even offer a cat the attention that was his due.

"You think you can distract me with this rubbish?" Raven demanded, though a little uncertainty had crept into his voice. Maybe he did feel the chill in the room.

"Tell him that only a fool acts in anger," Lord Nox said.

"Your father says only a fool acts in anger," I repeated dutifully.

His eyes widened in shock, then narrowed again. "Who told you to say that?"

"Your father," I said wearily.

"I used to tell him that all the time when he was a child," Lord Nox said, "because it applied to him so often. Youngest children can be so difficult."

"You're lying." Raven's voice was flat.

Now my anger stirred. I was well aware of my own flaws—stubbornness and a tendency to leap before I looked being the main ones—but dishonesty wasn't one of them, and I disliked being called a liar.

"Right. Because obviously I would have researched your childhood interactions with your father before I came here, so when you dragged me off to his bedroom I'd be able to quote some obscure maxim he used to say to you. Sorry to break it to you, but being able to see the future isn't one of my strengths."

He cleared his throat and stared at the floor for a moment. I'd rarely seen him in anything but black and tonight was no exception, but his clothes were particularly fine for this occasion. His shirt was the finest silk and the sleeves were thick with delicate silver embroidery. There was more embroidery on his vest and even on his shoes.

He raised his head and pinned me with an intense glance from under arched black eyebrows. "If he is truly here, tell me something that only he would know."

I looked at Lord Nox and waited.

"He once told me he'd rather kiss an angry boar than a girl." Lord Nox chuckled at the expression on my face. "In his defence, he was only twelve at the time."

I duly repeated the information and Raven stared at me for a long moment. Hope and fear of disappointment warred in his coal-black eyes. I knew that feeling all too well. I'd felt the same not so long ago, when Fallon had been promising to resurrect my dead mother.

Sadly, there was no hope of resurrection here. As Fallon had so comprehensively proven, there was no way to bring back the dead, even for a necromancer. Not if you wanted more than a zombie.

"He's really here?" Raven bit his lip, his eyes shining with unshed tears. "Papa, can you hear me?"

"He's nodding," I said, and Raven stopped searching the room for something he could never see and looked at me again.

"Can you let me hear him speak?"

I sighed. "I don't know how."

Fallon had brought my mother's spirit into a revenant's body so I could hear her speak to me. Not only did I not know how to do that, but I didn't *want* to do it. Zombies creeped me out, and I was having nothing to do with them —and as little to do with these necromantic powers as I possibly could. I couldn't help seeing ghosts, apparently, but I was damned if I was actively exercising this dark magic. I hated it. Necromancy was not for me.

"Then how is it that *you* can hear him? How are you doing this?"

Lord Nox watched me with just as much interest as his son. Both of them stood with their heads tipped slightly to the right, like the bird that Raven was named for. The family resemblance between them was unmistakeable.

I was sorry to disappoint the dead Lord. "I don't know for sure, but I suspect I managed to steal some of my father's necromantic powers."

Briefly I explained the circumstances of that eventful meeting, and how, when Ni'ishasana had stopped controlling my thoughts, I'd come to my senses and tried to claw some power back from my father. By then he'd taken all the dagger's powers for himself, but I had managed to pull some unfamiliar strength into myself at the last minute.

I wouldn't have fought for it so hard if I'd realised what it was.

Raven stared at me, frankly disbelieving. "But necromancy isn't magic that simply dwells within someone. It's a dark power that comes from rituals and sacrifices."

I shrugged. "That's what I thought, too. But I can't see any other explanation for why I can suddenly see ghosts." And even banish them to the Realm of Death.

Lord Nox shook his insubstantial head. "So I thought, also, when I was your age. But a Lord must deal with many problems in his lifetime, including necromancers." He smiled. "Fortunately, I only ever met one. But I learned that necromancy is a power that comes from the Realm of Death. It is no different to the magic of any other Realm."

"How can that be?" I asked him. "No one is born with the magic of the Realm of Death already inside them."

"Of course not. Otherwise they would be dead."

"What is he saying?" Raven asked.

"That necromancy is the innate power of the Realm of Death," I said. He raised his eyebrows, clearly as surprised as I was.

"It is true that the power of the Realm of Death is difficult to acquire," Lord Nox said. "The would-be necromancer must kill some unfortunate person and ride their soul into the Realm of Death. Then, he or she must survive the journey back to their own body with the power. It is hard for an unbodied soul to resist the pull of the Realm of Death. It takes great focus and strength, especially the first time, to escape the Realm with the power intact. But once they have returned to the world of the living, that power lives within them in the same way that the magic of their birth does. So it is entirely possible that you could have stolen some from your father during the transfer of power between you."

I stared at him. Everything he'd just said raised more questions than it answered. If the pull of the Realm of Death was so strong, how did so many people who were killed manage to resist it and remain in the world of the living as ghosts? And how could anyone travel outside their own body, following a dying person's soul into death?

"But ... Then why do necromancers use their rituals, if necromancy is a magic that simply lives within them, the same as Spring magic, or Ocean magic? Shouldn't they just be able to use it naturally, without black candles and blood sacrifices?"

"The rituals are simply a focusing tool," Lord Nox said, "because the magic of the dead is hard to control for a living person. It helps them resist the call of the world beyond."

"I reckon I could resist it just fine," I said, shuddering at the thought of following Atinna through that shimmering silver mist and never seeing the sun again. Never seeing any of the people I loved again either—at least not until they also died. And since most of them were fae, that could be a hell of a long time.

Maybe my words fooled him, but I wasn't fooling myself. Despite the pain I'd felt when I'd hovered on that threshold, I'd wanted to walk through that gate. Something that lay beyond called to me, and I had nearly given in to the temptation. Only Ash's voice had pulled me back to the world of the living before it was too late.

Raven grasped my arm in frustration. "Sage, what is he *saying*?"

Quickly, I repeated the gist of our conversation.

"Always so impatient," Lord Nox observed, smiling at his son.

"The magic of the dead is hard to control?" Raven asked. "Perhaps that's why there are so few necromancers."

"Or perhaps it's because becoming a necromancer requires you to *kill* someone," I said pointedly. And probably in some horrible way, considering the terrible reputation of necromancy in general.

But I could easily believe it was hard to control. I certainly had no say in whether I saw ghosts or not. I wondered if there were some way to block them out. It would be horribly unsettling to go the rest of my life seeing random dead people pop up all over the place.

"I suspect you would not find it as easy as you think to resist the pull of Death," Lord Nox said, "in spite of your obvious reluctance to claim its power."

"I don't want it," I told him. "I didn't mean to take it."

"That will help. Many necromancers can't resist going just a little further, clutching at a little more power, when they travel into the Realm. And then they die for real."

That wasn't going to happen to me. I was never heading into that silver mist. "When you say travel, do you mean astral travel?"

"Sometimes. But apparently it is possible for a necromancer to travel bodily into the Realm. It is riskier, but the rewards are greater, so some of them attempt it."

Raven shifted restlessly beside me. "Sage. Let me talk to my father."

"Of course." I'd been hogging Lord Nox, discussing my own problems, while Raven waited. "Go ahead. I'll tell you what he says."

"Papa—why haven't you gone on into the Realm of Death? Are you staying with us permanently?"

He looked like a small child begging for a treat, and my vision misted with tears. Lord Nox's end had come so suddenly and unexpectedly that his son hadn't been able to say goodbye.

"I must stay until my death is avenged," Lord Nox replied.

"He says he can't go on until his death has been avenged," I said. "But Ash killed Atinna, my lord."

"That is excellent news," he said, "But nothing less than the destruction of the whole Viper organisation will satisfy me."

Well, that aligned nicely with my own current goals. I outlined the results of the mission against the Vipers for them both, lingering on the destruction of the Nest.

"I wish I could see you," Raven said, a wistful note in his voice.

Lord Nox reached out and cupped his son's cheek in his hand. "I wish you could, too."

"Is he close?" Raven asked me. "It seems colder than it was."

"He just touched you." My heart was breaking for them both. "On your right cheek."

Raven's hand drifted to his cheek, a lost expression on his face. "I love you, Papa. I miss you more than you can possibly imagine."

"I think he can imagine," I said quietly, observing the pain in the ghost's dark eyes. It seemed that ghosts didn't lose *all* their emotions. What must it be like to not even be able to touch the people you loved? To see them walking past you every day, oblivious to your presence?

No wonder ghosts became bitter. All those tales I'd listened to wide-eyed as a child, about vicious ghosts who hurled things and haunted places, driving people from their homes, made a lot more sense now.

"I miss you, too, son."

He gave Raven messages to deliver to his mother and brothers.

"Have you no message for me?" Raven asked when his father fell silent at last.

"Do you remember the time you broke my favourite sword?"

A small smile blossomed on Raven's face as I translated. "I tried to use it to cleave a boulder in two. You were so angry with me."

"Yes. But I forgave you. My message to you is to be liberal with your forgiveness. Forgiveness is a gift that benefits the giver even more than the receiver." He paused to let me repeat his words. "You are angry that I was taken from you, and that is understandable. But a lot of your anger is because you feel guilty that you weren't here to save me—even though that would likely have been impossible. And so you focus your anger on this young lady here, which is not right. It's not how I would have a son of mine behave."

I quailed under Raven's gaze as I spoke his father's words. But there was no heat in it anymore—heat had been replaced by a bone-deep sorrow.

He sighed wearily when I was finished. "As always, you are wise, Papa." He slanted a glance at me. "Thank you for being my father's voice."

I nodded. Lord Nox's form shimmered, becoming more silvery-blue and less substantial. I could clearly see the bedroom furnishings through his body now. Did ghosts get tired?

"Papa—" Raven began.

"He's gone," I said.

Raven's shoulders slumped. "Well," he said, rubbing at the cheek his father had touched as if it was still cold, "that was unexpected. It seems that necromancy has some positive uses after all." He drew himself up, straightening his shoulders. "And now I have some messages to deliver. Thank you, Sage."

He hooked one hand around my neck, pulling me to him, and brushed my forehead with his lips. I looked up at him. We were standing very close in the dim room. His lips were only a heartbeat away.

And yet I felt nothing.

I still cared for him—very much—but there was no spark of excitement anymore at his nearness. Those coal-black eyes studied me for a long moment.

"I don't know if you can understand ... I take my father's words about forgiveness to heart. But I still ..."

I waited, but no more words were forthcoming. "You still blame me for his death?"

"*Blame* is a strong word." There was a glint of the old, mischievous Raven in his eye. "I don't blame you, but I don't ..." He sighed. "I don't know. You seem very close with that assassin. Have you really left the Vipers behind?"

"We both have. How can you doubt it? You know how I feel about the Vipers."

"I thought I did." His hand dropped and he took a step back. "But the Sage I knew wouldn't be friendly with a Viper—even an ex-Viper. And it seems to me that you are more than friends."

Was he jealous? Surely not. Raven's conquests were legendary, and he hadn't been serious about a single one of them. I was convinced that our relationship had been no different.

"We are," I said steadily, holding his gaze. I refused to apologise for Ash, or to feel ashamed of him because of his past.

"I see. A dangerous choice. Some might even say a foolish one. I hope you don't come to regret it." His mouth quirked in a wry smile. "Still, where's the fun in life if we can't make stupid mistakes for love? As long as he is good to you. He *is* good to you, isn't he?"

I nodded. Somewhere along the way, my heart had been given to a stern-faced assassin with haunted grey eyes who always seemed to know exactly what I needed. Raven would always be dear to me, but as a friend, nothing more.

"Good. He'd better be. I'll be watching." Then the smile faded and he sighed. "Life has become very complicated and serious all of a sudden."

"You're grieving. I understand."

"It's not just that." He ran a hand through his midnight hair, leaving it standing up in crazy peaks. "My family has dropped a bombshell on me. Papa was arranging a marriage for Paxyl, but now, Paxyl is Quinn's heir until Quinn marries and produces a child. He's suddenly a whole lot more important. And the alliance that was arranged isn't suitable for an heir."

I struggled to follow. "I'd heard your father was trying to arrange a marriage with Willow."

"Exactly." He looked relieved; it was probably something he wasn't allowed to tell me. "But you can see that's now impossible."

I shook my head. "Your faith in my perceptiveness is flattering, but I have no idea what you're talking about. Why is it impossible?"

"Because if something happened to Quinn, and Paxyl became the Lord of Night, Night and Spring would eventually become one combined Realm, since Willow is the heir of Spring. And nobody wants that."

"So the marriage is off?" Willow would be glad to hear that—if, in fact, she'd ever been told of her father's plans. And if she hadn't, I certainly wouldn't be the one to enlighten her. Willow knew that, as the heir, she would one day have to do her duty and enter into a political marriage, but as far as she was concerned, that was something for the dim, distant future. Not right now. She'd be furious that her father had been trying to marry her off so soon.

"Not exactly. The wedding's still on, but the identity of the groom has changed."

I stared at him, open-mouthed. Was he saying ...?

"I'm the expendable brother now. *I* will have to marry Willow."

7

—————

was still reeling from Raven's bombshell as we headed back to the rooftop to rejoin the others. He didn't speak again, and I was glad of the silence. Willow and Raven! What would her reaction be to the news? Thank the Lady that I wouldn't be the one to tell her. There would be fireworks, for sure.

The rooftop was eerily quiet. Coming up the stairs, I wondered if everyone had gone home already. I mean, it *was* a wake—people hadn't exactly been partying—but there'd been a steady buzz of conversation and the clinking of glassware when we'd left, and now silence reigned.

Everyone was staring at a small group gathered around the king and Lady Fiana. Raven pushed his way through the silent crowd, and I followed, wondering what was going on.

A woman stood before the king and the rest of Raven's family, who were gathered in a rough half-circle about her.

She had her back to me, and her body was wreathed in shadows—but that voice!

Dread gripped me as I circled around to get a look at her face.

"I claim the privileges of any ambassador," she was saying. "An ambassador shouldn't be wrapped in spellcraft and treated like a prisoner."

Her whole body was covered by the writhing shadows. Only her face was clear, and I recognised her immediately. Nuah hadn't changed a bit. She faced the king with the same sneer that I'd seen all too often when I'd been a lowly Viper apprentice.

She had balls coming here, that was for sure, to a place where the Vipers had so recently struck. Not that assassins were ever welcome. Quinn's face was dark with fury, and his fists were clenched at his side. His mother's features were calmer, but her steely composure suggested that she was every bit as angry as her son.

"Who is this?" Raven demanded, striding into the middle of the confrontation. He glanced at Quinn. "Why is she wrapped in your shadows?"

"She's a Viper," his brother replied through gritted teeth. "Turned up at the gates a few moments ago, demanding entry."

Raven's scowl darkened. "Why didn't you strike her down on the spot?"

"Don't doubt your brother's thirst for vengeance," Rothbold said. "I stopped him."

"I'm an ambassador of Lord Fallon," Nuah said. "Release me at once."

Lady save me. What was my appalling father up to now?

"The shadows are as much for your protection as ours," Rothbold said drily.

Evidently, they held her immobile, because she moved her eyes rather than her head as the speakers changed.

"How do we know she's a Viper?" Raven asked.

I stepped forward. "She is. Her name is Nuah, and she's one of the Serpent's Adepts. She's very highly placed among the Vipers." She'd been right behind Ash in the Viper hierarchy. Now he was gone, she must be top dog.

"I'd say it was good to see you again, Sage," she said, "but I'd be lying."

"And she's also a bitch," I added, though if they'd had more than thirty seconds alone with her, they'd probably figured that out for themselves. At least she wasn't here to kill anyone, if she'd turned up at the gates rather than sneaking in. Unless that was a plan to lull her victim into a false sense of security. "Don't trust her."

"There is no fear of anyone here doing that," Lady Fiana said crisply.

I glanced across at Meritt, the current Lord of Summer. He stood to one side with his aunt, the queen. They shared the same white-blond hair that was common among the ruling family of Summer. The previous Lord of Summer must have trusted the Vipers at least a little, as he'd charged them with invading the chambers of the king's daughter in a pretend attack.

But Meritt was studying Nuah with an expression on his face that said butter wouldn't melt in his mouth.

"Who is this Lord Fallon you speak of?" Quinn demanded. His voice was steady, even if his eyes were hot with anger. If Lord Nox was watching, he would be proud of his heir. "Fallon Domani the necromancer is no Lord."

"He is Lord of Ruin now," Raven said. "His Nest has been destroyed."

If that was news to Nuah, she didn't show it. She slanted a sly smile at Willow, who stood with Princess Lily. "He is Lord of Spring."

"What rubbish," Willow said. "If you're going to lie, at least make it believable. You're wasting our time."

"I don't care if you believe me or not. You're no one now, girl." She focused her gaze on the king once more. "My Lord sends me with greetings. I am to tell you that you may consider the Realm of Spring no longer part of your domain, as Lord Fallon declares it a sovereign Realm. He does not recognise your claim."

Willow strode forward, the faelights highlighting flushed cheeks and an angry spark in her eyes. Only someone who knew her as well as I did could see a hint of panic in the way she clenched the folds of her diaphanous gown in her fists, and the faint sheen of perspiration on her brow. "This is ridiculous, sire. Why do you listen to this liar? My father will have something to say about this. Fallon is no one."

Ouch. Well, he was my father, but not even I had much time for him anymore, so I wasn't sure why that stabbed at me. Maybe it wasn't the comment so much as the way people's gazes were sliding over to me, then slipping away when they realised I saw them.

Once again, they were judging me for something that had nothing to do with me—if my father had indeed done anything. The absence of the Lord and Lady of Spring from this gathering was concerning, though, and Willow wasn't the only one whose pulse raced in alarm.

"Speak plainly, Nuah," I said. I needed to know. It was better to hear the bad news at once than have it doled out in dribs and drabs. Might as well rip off the Band-Aid and be done with it. "What has Fallon done?"

I purposely didn't call him my father, but everyone knew it. Lord Merritt shot me a look of pure venom before turning back to Nuah. He was the last person who should be condemning anyone for the actions of their father. Talk about the pot calling the kettle black.

"Lord Fallon has taken over Spring," she said, "and now proclaims himself its Lord."

"Impossible," Willow said at once, but there was a sick look in her eyes.

"This is outrageous," Lord Voltirren said. The Lord of Air's wings had popped into view in surprise, and he didn't seem to have realised it yet, though he'd nearly knocked the diadem from his Lady's head. "Fallon has no claim to Spring."

Nuah eyed him with a smug smile. "Lord Thistle has forfeited his claim to rule by dint of his actions."

"What actions would those be?" the king demanded coolly.

"My family has ruled Spring since time began," Willow said. The fabric of her poor dress was taking a real mauling as she ground it in her clenched fists. She looked as though she wished it was Nuah's neck in her hands instead. "Fallon has no right to it."

"Right of conquest," Nuah said succinctly, and the shadows closed over her face, obscuring her for a moment.

"Lord Quinn," the king murmured.

"Sorry, sire," Quinn said, and the shadows receded again.

Nuah didn't look quite so cocky once she reappeared. I wondered if the shadows had cut off her air when they closed in.

"Where are my parents?" Willow demanded, and now the panic was apparent to everyone.

Nuah glanced at Quinn before she answered, as if afraid of his reaction to the news, and my heart skipped a beat. I had no great love for Lord Thistle and Lady Feronique, but Willow did, and I would hate it if anything had happened to them.

Particularly if my own arsehole of a father had been the cause.

"They are in Spring," Nuah said. "They are both alive and well. For the moment."

Willow took a deep breath at this news, though she still looked tense. Like me, she was probably waiting for the other shoe to drop.

"My lord has a particular message for you," Nuah continued. "He says that if you wish them to remain that way, you should present yourself at his Court to acknowledge his rule immediately. You have forty-eight hours."

"Don't do it," I urged immediately. "It's a trap."

A hubbub of voices broke out as all the gathered Lords

and Ladies added their own opinions. The king held up a hand, and silence descended once more.

"Is that all you came to say?" he asked.

"It is." Nuah managed to sound bored with the whole thing.

"Then you may leave us." Rothbold gestured to the Hawk, who came forward, drawing his sword.

That rattled Nuah's calm. Her eyes widened and she opened her mouth to protest, but the knight wasn't there to kill her. He slashed his sword through the air, and its peculiar magic opened a gate. Mist and a flowery perfume billowed through it. Faintly through the mist I made out a grove of pale trees heavy with delicate pink blossoms.

It looked—and smelled—like somewhere in Spring, though I didn't recognise it. But the billowing mist reminded me uncomfortably of the dense silver mist that shrouded the gate to the Realm of Death, and I suppressed a shudder.

"Tell your master there will be a reckoning for his actions," the king said.

He nodded to the Hawk, who gave Nuah a firm shove. As she stumbled through the gate, the Night shadows that had wrapped her fell away, but before she could do anything with her newfound freedom, the gate snapped shut on her heels.

A handful of pink cherry blossoms wafted to the ground at the Hawk's feet as I stared at Willow with a growing feeling of dread. I knew that look on her face.

We were in trouble.

8

"I know it's probably a trap," Willow snapped as we turned into the street where the entrance to her sith was hidden. "I'm not stupid."

The human world was still mostly asleep at this early hour, but already the sun had a bite to it, promising a hot day to come. There was no dew left on the grass on either side of the concrete strip of footpath.

"There's no *probably* about it. And the king specifically forbade you from going to Spring."

It was a wonder he'd even let her leave in the state she was in. But Lily and I knew he expected us to keep her from doing anything stupid. And in case we needed help with that, two of the royal guard followed at a discreet distance, ready to take on assassins or zombies or whatever my father decided to throw at us.

I doubted Fallon would do anything of the sort. He'd delivered his ultimatum, and now he'd sit back and wait for us to come to him. The king must have thought so, too, otherwise he wouldn't have let his only daughter wander around with only two guards for protection when such a threat to the kingdom existed.

"Can't you see it doesn't matter? I still have to go. They're my parents." For a long moment, the click of her heels striking the pavement was the only sound other than a passing truck making an early morning delivery. "But I suppose you don't understand that, considering who *your* father is."

I stiffened at that. The fact that my father was a homicidal nutjob didn't make me any less aware that other people enjoyed good relations with their parents. Quite the opposite, actually. And I didn't care for her tone. Willow had always been on my side, even to the point of going into exile with me when her father cast me out of the Realms. She'd never even breathed a word of reproach when my father had tried to kill *her*.

But now that he threatened her *parents*, there was that same judgemental tone that I'd heard so often from other fae, tarring me with the same brush as Fallon, just because he'd fathered me.

And I didn't see why that tied me to his fortunes forever. There was no reason I should thank him for being a sperm donor. He certainly hadn't created a child from any altruistic motives. I'd be willing to bet good money that at the moment of conception he'd been thinking of something else entirely.

"You don't have to go anywhere," Lily said firmly. "My father will take care of it. Without risking you."

The king had promised to descend with force on

Fallon, well within the forty-eight hour time limit. It would take him a little time to organise a raid of that magnitude, but I had faith that he would manage it.

"But what if Fallon kills them as soon as the king attacks? As soon as he realises I'm not coming?"

I sighed. We'd been over this several times already. The king was convinced Fallon wouldn't kill such valuable hostages as the Lord and Lady of Spring out of hand. He had nothing to gain from such an act other than the king's eternal enmity.

"Your parents are worth more alive than dead. He will want to use them as bargaining chips with my father."

"But you can't be sure of that, can you?" Willow insisted. "Why would he ask for me if all he wants is to negotiate with the king?"

"Three hostages are better than two," Lily pointed out with weary patience.

In the end, the king had had to order Willow back to her sith, since she wouldn't stop arguing with him and trying to plan his assault. I got it—she was scared for her parents. Anyone would be, in her position. But it seemed to me that the purpose of sending Nuah to Lord Nox's funeral with her declaration was to challenge the king's authority. Otherwise why do it so publicly? The ultimatum was meant to force *him* into action, not Willow.

The prickle of early morning sun on my bare neck was suddenly chased away by a chill that brought the tiny hairs there to attention. I stopped abruptly, only a few steps from Willow's gate.

Her small brick house slumped on its neglected block, the paint on the windowsills peeling, and the mesh of the flyscreen door sagging down from the top corner. Paspalum stalks stood tall all over the lawn, which had bare patches the size of a small car. The unappealing exterior hid a sith of uncommon beauty, full of birdsong and the trickle of many fountains, and smelling like the inside of a florist's shop.

But the chill in the air had nothing to do with the ugly little house. Willow looked back impatiently at me standing on the boundary between her property and the neighbour's.

"What's the matter?"

"Don't you feel it?" I asked. "Like someone just opened a freezer door right behind you?"

My eyes were roving as I spoke, seeking out the source.

Lily rubbed her arms. The princess wore a Glamour of a long-sleeved shirt and jeans to disguise the jewel-encrusted dress she'd worn to the funeral, but underneath the Glamour her arms were bare.

"I thought I was imagining it," she said. "It's as if a cloud suddenly crossed the sun."

She and Willow both looked up instinctively, but the sun still rode low in the sky, and there wasn't a cloud to be seen.

"That's a ghost," I said.

The sensation of cold I was experiencing couldn't possibly be mistaken for the sun going behind a cloud, but maybe my new powers made me more sensitive to the telltale signs of a spirit's presence than most people. I looked around and found a translucent figure, outlined in a faint blue glow, lurking behind the camellia bushes in the neighbour's front yard.

In an instant, I was transported back to the night the Vipers attacked Willow's sith. I'd found Nevith's body right there. He'd been killed by the assassins once they'd forced him to let them into the sith.

"Nevith?"

The ghost drifted closer, his form pale and hard to see once he left the shade of the bushes for the sunlit footpath.

"What are you doing?" Lily asked impatiently.

I hadn't told her, of course, about my newfound abilities. The princess and I weren't the best of friends, and only tolerated each other for Willow's sake.

But I'd told Willow, and she strode over, a strange look on her face, part curiosity and part dismay. "Is he here?" she whispered.

"Standing right there."

I gestured toward the glossy green leaves of the camellia. Nevith's ghost appeared in the same clothes he'd died in, complete with large and horrifying blood stains all down his shirt. Funny. Lord Nox had appeared in full Court attire with not a mark on him, though I'd heard he'd been killed during the day, when he'd presumably been wearing his pyjamas. Or whatever he wore to bed. Lord Nox's nightwear wasn't something I'd ever given much thought to.

Did ghosts choose the look they presented to the world? Or was their appearance something to do with their power? I had no idea. The more I learned, the more I realised how ignorant I was about anything to do with necromancy. It was starting to be seriously annoying.

"Can you hear me?" I asked the ghost.

So far, he'd done nothing but stand there. I wasn't even sure he knew we were present—he seemed to be looking at something in the distance. I restrained an urge to look over my shoulder, my skin crawling. Who knew what ghostly eyes could see?

"So cold," he whispered.

My heart clenched at the forlorn expression on his face. He'd been such a cheerful kind of guy in real life, always laughing. Always trying to persuade me to have one more drink, one more round of darts, one more slice of cake. It was as if he'd somehow known how short his life would be and had been trying to cram as much living into his years as he possibly could.

"Nevith," I said, more firmly. "It's me, Sage. Talk to me."

Go, me. Look how far I'd come in a few short days. I'd started off horrified that I could see ghosts, and now I was demanding that they talk to me.

It seemed as though he wouldn't answer, and then his head slowly turned. "Sage?"

His voice was no more than a whisper on the wind, and it raised the hairs on the back of my neck. Willow rubbed her arms unconsciously as she drifted closer.

"I can't see him."

"What are you both talking about?" Lily demanded. "Who's Nevith?"

Willow ignored her, which warmed the cockles of my

vindictive little heart. *It's not about you, princess.* Surely she'd heard us talk about Nevith before? Had she forgotten so quickly? The guards had moved closer to her, spooked by the way Willow and I were behaving.

"Yes," I said to Nevith. "It's me. Why are you still here?"

"It hurts, Sage," he breathed, his eyes empty pools of darkness.

My gaze was drawn to his horrific wound. His throat had been slashed open and I could see far more of his ghostly innards than I was comfortable with.

"Your ... your neck?"

"It hurts," he said again, as if he hadn't heard my question. "I can't bear it. Why did I let them in? My Lady Willow. Zinnia. You. All dead because of me."

Oh. Understanding dawned. He didn't mean a physical pain. He was tormented by the thought that his actions had led to our deaths at the hands of the assassins.

"I tried to be strong," he said, and ghostly tears slid down his cheeks, like glimmers of blue light leaving tracks on his transparent face. "But they hurt me. They hurt me so much."

"But we're not dead," I said gently. "Look at us. Here's Willow, right next to me. And Zinnia and Yarys are fine, too."

His eyes narrowed as he peered at me, as if he was trying to see something way off in the distance. Did the sunlight hurt his eyes? Or was he lost somewhere in between the worlds of the living and the dead, unable to clearly perceive our world anymore?

"Lady Willow," he breathed, and a look of relief washed over his face.

He drifted closer to her, his outstretched hand reaching for her. She shivered at his touch and glanced at me, though she didn't move.

"What's going on?"

"He just touched your hand. He's standing right in front of you now. He was afraid that he'd caused our deaths by opening the gate for the assassins."

She looked straight ahead. "Nevith, you are in no way to blame for opening that gate. We know you had no choice. And none of us were hurt."

He nodded, ghostly eyes fixed on her face. "Yes, Lady Willow." A smile touched his lips, and he looked up into the light of the early morning sun. "No one was hurt."

"We killed those bastards for you," I told him. I hated to think of him trapped here in the place where he'd died, tormented by the idea that he'd been the cause of all our deaths. He should have been enjoying the peace of the afterlife. "And now we've destroyed the Nest they came from. The Vipers are on the run now, and we'll have them all soon. You can rest now. You'll be avenged, I promise you."

He smiled, his pale form floating back towards the bushes where his body had been found, mist licking at his feet.

Wait. Where had that mist come from?

"Do you see mist?" I asked Willow in an urgent undertone.

Something tugged at my centre, as if a rope stretched from my belly button into the gathering mist. It was harder to make out Nevith's form against it.

"Where?" she asked, which pretty much answered the question.

The tugging grew stronger, and I shivered. Damn. Not an ordinary threshold, then. But I hadn't hurled Nevith away as I had with Atinna. Back then, I'd been in a fight for survival. My new magic had responded to the danger by opening a gate to the Realm of Death and shoving her through. But Nevith was no threat. I hadn't consciously tried to open that final gate—I had no idea how to. Apparently simply wishing for Nevith to be at peace was enough to open it again.

His substance was shredding, little bits of him drifting away at the edges, swirling towards the mist. Becoming one with it. "Do you hear me, Nevith? I promise you that."

Almost nothing was left. He was the faintest of outlines, disappearing like smoke. Next time I blinked, he'd be gone.

No one was hurt drifted back to me, more of an echo than a sound.

"Hold my hand," I said to Willow, fighting back the urge to follow him. "Don't let me move from this spot."

She grabbed me, the feel of her warm hand against mine a welcome anchor. I shut my eyes, focusing on that grip. It had been shockingly easy to open this gate. That scared me. I needed to figure out how to close it as easily.

"Tell him we're sorry for what he suffered," Willow said, and her voice seemed to break a spell.

The insistent pull vanished, and I opened my eyes. The bushes were just ordinary bushes. There was no sign now of any otherworldly mist, and I breathed a sigh of relief.

Willow let go my hand, looking at me curiously. "You okay?"

"Yep," I said, and we stared at each other for a long moment until she seemed satisfied with what she saw. "He's gone."

"Your lost servant's ghost was here?" Lily asked.

I cleared my throat, swallowing a lump, and nodded. I was glad I'd seen him again. Maybe Raven was right, and there were some good uses for necromancy after all.

"Let's go inside," Willow said. "Unless you think he'll be back?"

She sounded hopeful, but I knew deep in my bones that Nevith was gone for good. The dead didn't return through that gate.

"He's moved on," I said. "I think it was only his guilt that was holding him here. And once we reassured him that there was no harm done, he was free to go."

Finally, all my striving to find justice for Nevith had borne fruit. Being able to assure his ghost that his killers were dead and the rest of their organisation was in the firing line was an indescribable blessing. Knowing that his spirit was finally at peace left my own soul feeling soothed.

Willow led the way into the sith. The threshold magic shivered over my skin and the traffic sounds of the human world abruptly cut off, replaced by birdsong and the faint trickle of distant fountains. Before us lay a flowery meadow where bees buzzed and magpies warbled in the trees beyond. Deeper in the sith, the peaks of white pavilions reared above the greenery, and Willow set off down the path that led under the trees towards them. The grasses brushed lovingly against her legs as she walked, and I felt the energy of the green life that powered them as I followed. Lily and the guards brought up the rear.

Coming here was a very different experience now that I was flush with Spring power. The trees leaned down to welcome me just as they did to Willow. When I ran my hands over leaves and branches, I could feel the sap rising within. I could even sense the potential of seeds sleeping in the dark earth, and the promise of buds still tightly furled. Everywhere I turned, I sensed the life of the green, growing things, and my magic rose like a tide inside me in response.

"I wonder why some souls linger and others don't," Willow said as we entered the largest pavilion. Its cool shade housed the main living areas, and we settled in the dining room.

One side of the room was completely open to the gardens, and the two guards took up station there, looking out as if they expected more assassins to leap from among the flowering rhododendrons. I wondered where Christian was.

Lily and Willow sat down at the table that ran nearly the length of the room. It could have seated twenty but was only set for four at the moment. Zinnia was expecting us for dinner, and I could smell the tantalising aroma of baked potatoes drifting from the kitchen pavilion already.

But I wasn't hungry. I stood looking out into the

garden, too, though I wasn't searching for any threats. Rather, I was hoping to see a certain grey-eyed assassin—but all I got was a cat. Kel sauntered out from underneath the bushes and wandered in, brushing past my ankles on the way but pretending that the touch was accidental and not actually an indication that he might kinda sorta like me.

"Some stay because they have a strong attachment to a place or a person," Lily said, eyeing me warily from where she sat. "Maybe they have left something important unfinished. Most of the documented cases I've seen were murder victims, who couldn't seem to come to grips with their untimely ends or harboured a vain hope of gaining justice. But that's not really the important point to note, here, is it?"

"It isn't?" Willow asked lazily, moving her legs out of Kel's way in case he got any ideas of rubbing up against her. She hadn't stopped complaining about the cat since Ash and I had arrived back here with him. To be fair, Kel seemed to delight in leaving half-dead lizards and mice in her bedroom, so her dislike of him wasn't exactly without provocation.

Lily sighed huffily and glared directly at me. "Since when have you been able to see ghosts?"

"Ghosts, plural? How do you know it wasn't just this one?" Willow said. "Nevith was a good friend of hers, after all."

The princess shot her an impatient glance. "He was a good friend of yours, too, but *you* couldn't see him. It's something to do with that father of yours, isn't it?"

I rolled my eyes. I was sick to death of hearing about *that father of mine.* "It's all right, Willow. It's not as though I'm going to be able to keep this a secret. Yes, it's been happening since my confrontation with Fallon."

Lily's eyebrows shot up. "And you wanted to keep it a secret? Does my father know?"

"Of course he does. Along with half his knights and most of the palace guard." And all Raven's family by now, too.

That didn't appear to mollify her. If anything, she seemed more annoyed, but that probably had more to do with the fact that it was simply more proof that she wasn't back in her father's good books yet than anything to do with me.

"But what happened? How is it possible?"

I shrugged. I was getting sick of telling this story already, and I had a feeling there were plenty more retellings still in my future. "Apparently a lot of things are possible for a necromancer."

"Including taking my parents hostage," Willow said. "But I still don't understand that. There are probably only three people in all the Realms who are more powerful than my father. In his own Court, with all his people around him, how could anyone harm him?"

"Ni'ishasana is ridiculously powerful."

"None of the previous wielders could have managed it," she insisted.

I shrugged. None of the previous wielders had been a necromancer, either, but I was sick of talking about my father.

"Well, it doesn't matter," she said. "I'll sort the bastard out when I get there."

Lily drew herself up and looked down her long Brenfell nose at Willow. "You're not going anywhere. I'll chain you up myself if I have to."

9

———

I had never expected to agree with Lily about anything, but I guess there was a first time for everything.

Of course, I didn't agree with her handling of the situation, but that was to be expected. I knew Willow too well to try issuing ultimatums. I could have predicted the argument would end in the shit-show it did. Willow shouted at Lily; Lily shouted at Willow. Zinnia tried to distract everyone by serving dinner, but that only gave Willow literal ammunition.

"I can't believe you ever got mad at me for simply threatening to dump eggs on Lily's head," I muttered as a plate of vegetables went flying past, flung in a fit of rage by Willow and dodged with surprising deftness by the Crown Princess. Green beans and yellow squash pelted down like rain as I raised an eyebrow at one of the guards. "Shouldn't you be pulling them off each other or something?"

The man didn't respond, though his partner shifted

nervously, his eyes following every plate's flight path. He must be new. The other guy had the right idea: do your job and ignore the goings-on of the nobility. It wasn't his fight.

It wasn't mine, either, though as dinner entertainment went, it wasn't half bad. I had no more intention of letting Willow endanger herself like that than Lily did, but I wasn't stupid enough to order her around. Instead, I ate another mouthful of Zinnia's very fine fish pie, appreciating the delicate flavours of the filling and the delightfully flaky pastry. If only Ash were here to join me in the meal it would be just about perfect. I was pretty sure that the antics of Willow and her house guest wouldn't bother him at all—he'd dined with Vipers, after all.

"This pie is divine," I told Zinnia, who was still hovering uncomfortably by the table, scrunching her apron in her hands as if she wished she could stop the two combatants but was afraid to try.

"I'm glad you like it," she said automatically. "Sage, can't you stop them? Someone's going to get hurt."

"Rubbish," I said. I, too, had dined with Vipers. This little spat was nothing. "It will do Willow good to blow off some steam. She might be able to think better, once she's done that."

Zinnia sank into the chair next to me, which showed how flustered she was. Under normal circumstances, she would have seen this as "taking liberties", even though we all sat together around the kitchen table happily enough. But apparently the dining table was sacrosanct and only for Willow and her guests.

She was a gentle soul, with neatly braided hair as fine

and pale as cornsilk and brown eyes that usually held a smile for everyone. They weren't smiling now.

"Is it true that Spring has been invaded? What has happened to everyone?"

Zinnia, like us, knew everyone at Lord Thistle's estate, and she had many friends there.

"I don't know," I said, suddenly losing interest in the pie. "I hope that Fallon would know better than to harm them. Surely he doesn't want to draw the wrath of the king down on his head."

"But what *does* he want, then? Why would he do such a thing?"

I suppressed a twinge of annoyance. Zinnia was only wondering aloud, not asking me to be my father's spokeswoman. "Lady only knows."

I wouldn't be surprised if this move was why he'd wanted the dagger—but I had no idea what the thinking behind it could be. Surely he had no real ambition to be the Lord of Spring? I mean, Nuah had come to proclaim him Lord, but it seemed absurd, a gimmick designed to catch the king's attention. Fallon already had more power than anyone before him had ever held. Why would he want to add the responsibility of governing a Realm onto that?

Particularly considering that responsibility really wasn't his jam. He hadn't been bothered to look after one small girl. A whole Realm would be completely beyond him.

Besides, he had to know that Rothbold would never let his rule stand. Someone with that much power was a threat to the king himself. If he allowed Fallon to take Spring, how long would it be before the zombie armies were marching on Whitehaven itself? No, there had to be more to it.

"Nobody tells me what to do in my own house!" Willow shouted, striding around the table on Lily's heels. "I don't care who your father is."

"Oh, dear," Zinnia said, biting her lip as she watched Lily square up to her, hands on hips. "But Lady Willow is the heir. She can't endanger herself by giving in to your father's demands." She turned those big brown eyes on me. "Who would take the Lord's seat if ... if ..."

She couldn't bring herself to finish the sentence, but she was right. Willow was the last of her line, the final Andrakis. There weren't even any distant cousins. If Willow and her father both died, the rulership of Spring would go to some other family. And that was why the king had forbidden her from getting involved.

There might even be a war over who got to warm Lord Thistle's empty seat, if he and Willow both died, though hopefully King Rothbold wouldn't let it get that far. My mind recoiled from thinking any further about a Spring without Willow, and I tuned back in to the argument.

"You have a duty to protect yourself," Lily was saying. "As the heir—"

"Trust me, I know all about my *duty* as the heir," Willow spat. "I'm an only child—it's been drummed into me since birth." I was hoping she'd got over the urge to throw things. There was a plate of blueberry tarts on the sideboard that was too near her hand for comfort. Blueberry tarts were one of Zinnia's specialties and a particular favourite of mine. "Marry for political advantage. Produce an heir—and a spare as well, if possible."

"And protect the heir when the head of the House is in danger," Lily said quietly. "I'm an only child too. I know how it works."

There was a pregnant pause. We were probably all thinking the same thing. Willow's father could live another two or three centuries—if Fallon let him. If he wasn't dead already.

"I don't feel hungry," Willow said, the fight going out of her all of a sudden. "Tell Christian to wake me when he gets home. I'm going to bed."

She stalked out, head held high, but I would have bet money that she wouldn't sleep. Who could, with a threat like this hanging over their family and their Realm?

I didn't think I would, either, so I wandered out into the garden, Kel slinking along after me, carefully pretending it was only by sheer accident that we happened to be going in the same direction. The little furball must have missed me.

Or perhaps he missed Ash. My serious assassin had a soft spot a mile wide for this particular bundle of fluff.

I missed Ash with a soul-deep ache. It was scary how fast he'd become essential to my existence, like the air in my lungs. All I wanted was to spirit him away somewhere and show him that the world wasn't as dark a place as he'd always thought, to coax one of those rare smiles of his to his lips.

His lips. Mmm. Okay, so maybe that wasn't *all* I wanted.

It was still cool under the trees, and the light lay in stripes across a small clearing as it slanted between the tree trunks. I often came to this spot in the garden. There was no fountain, no artfully planted bed of flowers, but a small creek wandered through the trees, and the wild grasses of the clearing sloped down to meet it.

The creek reminded me of a similar spot on Lord Thistle's estate, where I'd spent a lot of time lying on my belly watching some fish dreaming in the moonlight, or listening to the calls of a hunting owl. There wasn't enough water in the creek to make a noise, but its shallows were as clear as glass, showing an array of smooth pebbles in grey and brown, and the roots of the reeds that clung to the edge of the bank.

I sat down with my back against my favourite tree trunk and closed my eyes. Orange spots danced behind my eyelids. It would be hot later, but it was always cool here, at any time of day.

I hoped Ash would be back soon. I had an urgent need to get to know him much, *much* better. I wanted to explore every inch of his lean frame. Personally acquaint myself with the smooth interplay of muscles across his shoulders. Run my hands across his broad chest and watch those cool grey eyes burn with need. I lost myself in a daydream of bare skin warm beneath my questing fingers, and a hard mouth hot and insistent on mine.

I'd never been in love before, not like this. Sure, I'd thought I was—I'd even thought I might be in love with Raven at one time, but my eyes had been opened. Love wasn't the big, romantic gesture that Hollywood kept pushing. It wasn't flowers and charm and dinner dates. It wasn't even being so obsessed that you couldn't think about anything else.

Admittedly, I *was* having trouble not thinking about Ash. But this wasn't about romance. I doubted Ash had a romantic bone in his body. But that was okay. Romance was just the fluffy layer of icing on top. Real love was the whole cake. Real love was holding each other up when we stumbled, and always being there for each other.

Real love was the constant feeling that something was missing when he was away, and saving up things to tell him because no one had ever listened to me with such focus as he did. Real love was seeing the constant tension in his face soften when he caught his first sight of me after we'd been apart. Real love was being prepared to kill to defend him.

That last one probably wouldn't be going on any motivational posters any time soon, but it was absolutely true. There was nothing I wouldn't do for Ash, and I knew he felt the same way about me.

I sighed. And now I'd made myself feel even lonelier without him. Resolutely, I turned my mind to other things. The Lady knew, I had plenty of other things clamouring for my attention.

Willow, for one. The king's order would only hold her for so long, I was sure. She was beside herself with worry for her parents, and I could absolutely understand that. They could be dead already, or they could be fine, or anything in between.

Perhaps Fallon had no intention of harming them. At

one time, Lord Thistle had been one of his dearest friends. This could all be part of some ruse that only he understood. But we had no way of knowing, and the uncertainty made the fear unbearable.

I'd lost my own mother so suddenly that there'd been no time for fear. One minute she'd been there, the next gone. The same with Lord Nox—gone in an instant, leaving his family in shock. Even for fae, life could be uncertain.

I sighed. Losing a loved one was always hard. Speaking with my mother's spirit recently had been the first contact I'd had with her since I was seven years old, and I longed to hear her voice again.

But I wasn't prepared to raise a zombie to house her spirit as my father had done to get what I wanted. I indulged in a daydream for a while where Mama hadn't died, and the three of us—no, four of us, I guess, because the baby probably would have lived, too—lived together in Spring.

The daydream got rocky, though, when I tried to imagine my father as part of that happy scenario. Damn him. And now I had his stupid necromantic powers. What use were they?

Lord Nox had told me that necromancers could visit the Realm of Death. Perhaps that was a way to see my mother again. My heart lifted as I considered it, until I recalled that he'd also said it was dangerous. And I'd felt the pull of that dark Realm twice already. I had no faith that I'd be able to return once I succumbed to that pull.

A sudden sense that I wasn't alone made me open my

eyes, expecting to see the cat again, but he was sitting in the only patch of sun in the little clearing, staring fixedly at something in front of me.

For one heart-stopping moment I thought it was an assassin and adrenaline flooded my body. I leapt up, heart pounding.

In a way, I was right. It was an ex-assassin, another ghost—because of course it was. I couldn't move lately without tripping over the damn things. And that chill in the air was more than the cool of the shady spot I'd found.

It was the ghost of one of the Vipers who'd invaded the sith the night Nevith had died. Not one of my kills, although I recognised him. Willow had put him in the ground, but here he was again, popping up like some undead jack-in-the-box.

I held my breath, but the ghost did nothing except stand there. I backed up, keeping a wary eye on him. Kel flicked a glance at me, then returned his attention to our visitor, his tail idly flicking from side to side. He seemed relaxed. Maybe I should be, too.

Now you're looking to a cat for guidance? You're an idiot.

I groped inside myself for that deep strength I'd stolen from my father. Considering it had turned out to be necromancy, it was kind of odd that I experienced it as a strength. You'd think something so dark would feel wrong or evil somehow, but this didn't. I hadn't thought about that before.

Now wasn't the time to consider it, either. Not with the ghost of a Viper standing in front of me.

"If you're hanging around here looking for vengeance,

you're wasting your time," I told him. No way was any dead Viper spirit getting the jump on me.

He simply stared at me, and I stared back. I'd seen so many ghosts lately that I was almost used to them. They didn't lift the hairs on the back of my neck anymore, though the chill of their presence raised goosebumps on my bare arms.

He could have plenty of friends floating around these gardens. That wasn't a happy thought. There would be more ghosts than people in the sith, if every one of the assassins we'd killed that night still lingered here in spirit form.

I folded my arms across my chest. "You're the strong, silent type, are you?"

He'd been an Air mage, like the Hawk, blindingly fast with a blade as well as with his magic. He had large eyes, and he didn't blink at all, which became unnerving as soon as I noticed it. It was like being stared down by a cat.

I glanced at Kel, who was also doing the unblinking thing, and remembered how fascinated he'd been by Umarenthe, the shadow woman whose soul inhabited Ni'ishasana. He'd given her that same unblinking stare. Lord Nox had said that cats could see the dead. Was that why they sometimes stared at nothing—or what seemed like nothing, at least, to a person who couldn't see them?

I sighed. Life had been simpler when I'd been one of those people.

"Do you want me to send you on to the Realm of Death?" I asked. I might do that regardless of his wishes— my favourite part of the gardens would be off-limits if I knew some dead Viper was going to come stare at me every time I went there from now on.

Had he been doing this before, and I just hadn't known? That felt a little creepy. Maybe it was better to be able to see who was watching after all.

Finally, the spirit spoke. "No. I must kill her first."

"Who?"

"The one who killed me."

He meant Willow. The Hawk had taken out a couple that night, and so had I, but Willow had done the lion's share of the work, fighting to defend her home.

"Right. And how do you propose to do that?" Atinna had found a way to access her magic from the grave, and I had the sinking feeling it was something to do with the dagger. Otherwise, there'd be a lot of ghost stories that ended differently. Did that mean that this guy could do it, too?

A second later I had my answer. Something slammed into me from behind, sending me shuddering to my knees. A burst of Air, like a mini tornado. Branches whacked into me, lifted by the gale, even whole plants. All I could do was urge the trees to shelter me. How did you fight back against a ghost?

"I'm growing stronger every day," he said, smiling in satisfaction as the wind blasted me. "I can be patient—I have all of eternity. One day I will be strong enough to kill her."

I squinted against the gale. A faint line of blue light trailed off into the distance behind the ghostly form—connecting him to something?

I lunged up from the ground, slicing my hand through the blue line. "Not if I have anything to do with it."

The ghost cried out as the Air magic stopped abruptly. He glared at me with confusion in his face—and a little fear.

Good. He *should* fear me. Cutting that line of light had cut off his magic. I had no doubt that that line had connected his soul somehow to the dagger—and now that he was no longer connected: hey, presto! No more magic.

This time, instead of hurling him away as I had with Atinna, I reached for him. My hand passed through his insubstantial body, but I felt a definite resistance, as if I'd pushed my hand through water. The ghost retreated, a pained look on his face.

So I lunged after him, following the broken line that trailed behind him, and my hand closed on something within him. It didn't look any different to the rest of him, nor did it feel any more substantial. But it thrummed in my hand, and the Viper cried out in shock.

I squinted, focusing hard on that spot. Was it a deeper blue? Something shimmered, and the harder I concentrated, the clearer it became—a blue flame, burning cold.

When I looked away, it disappeared, and it took a real effort of will before it became visible again. Was this necromancy or imagination? But I wasn't imagining the look of fear on the ghost's face, or the fact that he stayed still as the grave, my hand buried in his chest. Was that because he *couldn't* move away?

I concentrated again, and this time the blue flame

came easier, responding to my magic. What had I caught there?

Was I holding the dead Viper's *soul* in my hand?

I nearly puked at the idea. That was so many kinds of wrong. Necromancy was vile, and I wanted no part of it. And yet ... here was a ghost determined to harm my friend, and here was I, apparently with the means to stop him.

"Does it hurt you when I do this?" I squeezed my fingers tighter.

The ghost's moan answered me. Yep, that hurt. The soul, or whatever it was, fluttered like a trapped bird in my hand. It was all I could do not to release it, but I thought of Willow and hardened my heart. The Viper had already tried to kill her once. There would be no second chance.

"Tell me about the Realm of Death," I demanded.

"I know ... no more of it than ... you do. I haven't been there."

He had a point there. I chewed my lip, thinking. "What if I send you there now, then call you to ask again?" Not that I would, of course. I was still firmly in the *no zombies, no way* camp.

He smiled past his obvious pain. "Then I can tell you whatever you want to hear."

That was interesting. It hinted that spirits in the Realm of Death could lie to their summoners. And perhaps that now, with his soul in my grasp, he couldn't.

Shame I couldn't think of anything useful to ask him. His information on the Vipers was more outdated than my own—and my hand around his soul was starting to ache from cold.

I summoned the gate with a thought—it was getting easier every time—and hurled him through it. This time, when I closed my frozen fist again, the gate slammed shut, its siren song cut off before it could get a grip on my mind.

But it still took a long time before I stopped shaking.

10

*A*s night fell, I woke to the certainty that there was someone in my room. The fountain still played in the garden outside, but the frogs and chirping cicadas had fallen silent, as if someone had passed that way a moment before.

I stiffened, readying myself for sudden, violent action, but before I could unleash a wave of deadly Spring magic, I felt a weight on the bed and a familiar ironbark smell drifted on the air.

"Ash!" I opened my eyes and flung my arms around him, almost taking out his eye in the process.

He gathered me to him and took a deep breath, his face buried in my hair. Maybe he liked the way I smelled, too. He was warm and solid, and we stayed that way for a long moment, my whole body relaxing into his. It felt glorious just to hold him. I knew I'd missed him, but I hadn't realised just how much until he was here again, stronger and more beautiful even than I'd remembered.

"I'm sorry to wake you," he said, drawing back to look at me. His eyes roved over my face, as if committing every detail to memory.

"Don't worry about it." I glanced outside. It was nearly full dark—time to wake up anyway. "I'm so glad to see you."

"Are you?"

Could he really be so uncertain of his welcome here? "What's wrong?"

He looked tired and there was something about his eyes that I didn't like. It reminded me of the old Ash, the one I'd first met, who was as cold and unyielding as a block of ice.

But that coldness had come from a place of fear. He'd been hurt so badly once that he'd shut himself off from the world, presenting a façade to keep himself safe. It was a necessary façade in the impossible position his father had forced him into. Beneath it he was a gentle soul who could not have become the ruthless killer he needed to be in order to survive.

"What's wrong?" I asked again, lifting my hand to his cheek. "You look ..."

He turned my hand so that he could plant a kiss in my palm. "Old? Tired of living in a world where people live only to hurt each other?"

I leaned forward, resting my forehead against his. "Was it very bad?"

The king had commanded Ash to interrogate people he had lived among for years. I had been trying not to think about it the whole time he'd been gone, though my imagination had supplied some pretty gruesome scenarios. Rothbold could be ruthless when he needed to be, just as any fae could, but in his case it was worse. When a whole kingdom was at stake, sometimes there was no place for kindness. I just hoped someone had broken early, so that Ash didn't have to repeat the process with too many of his former colleagues.

"It was necessary," Ash said, his voice bleak. "Anyone would have done the same in Rothbold's position."

Well, maybe not *anyone*. Plenty of humans wouldn't, but we weren't talking about humans. Fae lived by different standards. And to make Ash do it was a typically fae twist.

"I hope he's now satisfied of your loyalty, at least." Because of course that was why Rothbold hadn't ordered one of his knights to carry out the unpleasant duty. He wanted to make sure that Ash really was an *ex*-Viper.

Perhaps the king didn't understand how cold the Vipers were. They had no loyalty to anyone but the Serpent. All of them could have done what Ash did. None of them would have suffered for it the way Ash was suffering now.

I pulled him down on top of me. The bed was still warm, and the frog had started up his croaking again. The night was still young. We could linger here a while. I longed to bring the light back to Ash's hard grey eyes, remind him that there were good things in the world, too, and at least one person he could let down his guard with.

I kissed him, feeling heat bloom inside me as he returned the kiss almost with desperation. He held me like a drowning man catching hold of a rope, all the pain of the last few days in the insistence of his lips and the way his hands held me tight.

"You are a light in the darkness," he said, looking down at me with wonder in his eyes. "Too good for me."

"Rubbish." I tried to pull him back down. My heart pounded, desire twisting in my core. I wanted more from him. So much more.

But he pulled away, sitting on the edge of the bed, half turned away. His shirt stretched tight across the muscles of his back and I sat up, leaning against his warmth, and letting my hand move in long, slow strokes across them.

"I'm tainted," he said. "Death and torture are all I'm good for. You deserve so much more."

"You're not tainted," I said. "The king forced you to do a shitty thing. It doesn't mean there's anything wrong with *you*. You're a good man."

"Not good enough. I'll never fit in. I'll never be like *them*."

"Like who?"

He shrugged. "Your friends. The king, his knights." He paused. "Raven."

That reminded me. "About Raven." I sat up straighter. "I need to tell you something. I went to—"

I meant to tell him all that had happened at Lord Nox's funeral, and that I was done with Raven for good. The only man in my life who mattered now was the one staring at me right now with haunted eyes, his body suddenly still.

But I felt a sudden huge drag on the energy all around us, the life force of the plants. Now that I had access to my full Spring powers, I could feel the way the garden responded as if it were one great living thing, drawing on itself to answer the call of another Spring mage.

"What was that?" I asked.

"What was what?" He stood up, tucking his shirt back into his pants, half-turned away from me. He stood very still, head raised slightly, listening for something outside.

"A surge in Spring magic." I was wearing my favourite pair of Teenage Mutant Ninja Turtle pyjamas, but I didn't stop to change.

Though I did stop for a knife.

I ran out into the garden, towards the source of that magic upheaval, a horrible feeling of déjà vu sweeping over me. Surely we couldn't be under attack again? Ash kept pace with me, moving like a shadow under the trees, so silent it was as if I was alone. All I could hear was my own breath and the blood pounding in my ears as I ran.

A great thrashing in the trees ahead sounded like a hurricane had hit. Branches tossed wildly, followed by the sharp crack of wood breaking. The delicate white roof of Willow's pavilion reared out of the foliage and I slowed, my heart pounding in my chest. The cleared space of her garden was just ahead.

A dark shape flitted past in the corner of my vision and I froze. This really was déjà vu. How could this possibly be happening again? But, somehow, it was.

That shape had been a Viper, dressed in their customary black. And here I was in children's pyjamas and bare feet.

Ash disappeared in the direction that the Viper had gone. How many more of them were there? A horrible feeling of being watched crept over me, tightening the skin between my shoulder blades and tickling the back of my neck, but when I looked, there was no one there.

God, I hated Vipers. There could be a dozen of them lurking behind me, and I wouldn't see them. They were too good at moving unseen. I sent my awareness into the green life around me instead, trusting the plants to tell me if anyone was there.

A shout sounded from nearer the pavilion and branches thrashed again. I stepped out of the trees in time to see a Viper plucked from his feet by the branch of a massive oak. Two more had Willow boxed in by the open side of the building. She wore a long silk nightgown in deep emerald green, which was at least slightly more dignified for meeting a threat than my own attire.

Though I could move a lot better in mine. Score one for the Ninja Turtles. I dived for cover behind a clump of rhododendrons as one of the Vipers turned towards me, and opened the ground beneath his feet. Tree roots writhed out, curling round his ankles.

But, to my surprise, they subsided again. Next thing I knew, the rhododendrons turned on me, their branches wrapping around my limbs. I was jerked against the nearest trunk, and more branches tried to crush the fight out of me. I shoved at them with my magic and found them sluggish to obey my commands.

Clearly the other guy was also a Spring mage. An invisible tug of war began between us as he tried to subdue me with rhododendrons and I tried to drag him into the earth with tree roots. We were both so busy fighting off the other's attack that our own faltered.

In a corner of my mind, I registered that the oak tree had released the Viper it had picked up, and other plants were tossing and turning as if in an invisible wind between the other Vipers and Willow. Roots exploded out of the ground, snatching at Willow one minute. The next they were trying to drag the two Vipers under. The garden was a mess of churned earth.

Why were the assassins playing so nice? Where were the knives and the poison darts? I hurled my own blade at my opponent, but he dived to the ground and avoided it. The roots of the big oak got a good grip on him then, and I thought I'd won, but he soon had them under control.

It seemed that all the Vipers were Spring mages. I wondered what had happened to the one Ash had chased into the trees—he was probably Spring, too. Why had my father sent all Spring mages when he knew Willow and I were both Spring? Any other magic would have made more headway against us. This was just going to tire us all out until we'd fought ourselves to a standstill.

The rhododendron's branches snaked out for me again, and I brushed them away wearily. Not even throwing my knife had brought an answering attack from my opponent. They must have orders to keep us alive.

This wasn't an assassination attempt; it was a kidnapping.

An ice spear hurtled out of the darkness under the trees, and my opponent suddenly dropped like a stone, impaled through the neck. I opened the earth beneath him and let the roots drag him down. This time his magic didn't resist mine.

Ash emerged from the trees a moment later, snowflakes whirling around him. More spears flashed through the night, moonlight reflecting off their icy lengths, but the other two Vipers had been warned by their companion's fall. They met his spears with knives, and Ash threw up a hasty ice wall to shield himself as their blades flew towards him.

Okay, so they had no orders to keep Ash alive. Only Willow and me.

I supposed I should be glad that my father didn't want me dead. I wasn't sure I returned the feeling anymore. It hadn't even been twenty-four hours since Nuah had appeared at the funeral with her ultimatum. It certainly hadn't taken long for him to get tired of waiting for Willow to answer his summons to Spring.

Shards of Ash's ice shield peeled away from the top, directed like a deadly hail at the three Vipers still facing Willow. One of them turned to meet the threat, leaving the other two still harassing Willow, who had backed up until she was almost inside the pavilion.

Ash's opponent brought the oak into play again. Its branches lashed out, smacking the ice shards out of the air, then crashed down on the ice shield itself. I grabbed the oak with my own magic, fighting the Viper for control of it while Ash hastily repaired his shield.

In the midst of this chaos, Christian appeared, wearing only a pair of boxer shorts, and holding a gun. The gun glinted in the moonlight and I recognised it as one of mine. He must have run to my room for help when the assassins first attacked, and we'd missed each other in the dark. He was lucky the Vipers hadn't dispatched him straight away. I doubted my father even knew he existed, much less cared what happened to him.

Seeing him standing there shivering in his jocks, but determined not to abandon Willow, my opinion of him went up. But not too far, since his hands shook so badly he could end up shooting anybody.

"Get out of here," I shouted at him. Willow was too preoccupied with her battle to notice him. "Do you even know how to use that?"

"Just point and shoot," he shouted back.

The gun boomed and he jerked back. If I was being generous, I'd say from the recoil, but it was more likely fright at the sudden noise. No one went down. That was probably a good thing.

One of the Vipers facing Willow spared a moment to flick a knife at him, almost lazily. But Christian was too stunned—or too stupid—to even move, and it was right on target.

The only thing that saved him from being skewered was the sudden appearance of another ice shield, right in front of him. Shards of ice flew as the point of the blade struck it, and Christian dropped the gun in fright.

I sprinted for the gun and scooped it up. After that everything happened in a blur of speed. I fired and one of the Vipers went down. That left two against Willow, which was a fairer fight. Once I joined my magic with hers it didn't last long. The roots of the great oak tree dragged the assassins' dead bodies into the quiet earth, and I stood there, panting heavily, as Ash dissolved his ice shields.

Willow ran to Christian, who was still lying on the ground, looking surprised to find himself still alive.

"Are you hurt?" she asked, running her hands over him. It seemed a much more thorough examination than necessary. The guy hadn't been in any danger, except perhaps to his pride. The squeal when he'd dropped the gun wasn't what I'd call manly.

"I could have *died*," he said, allowing her to help him sit up.

They both looked at Ash, and Willow treated him to the friendliest smile she'd ever given him.

"Thank you. You saved Christian's life."

I looked around the once-beautiful garden and frowned at the churned-up earth and broken branches. I sent my magic out to restore order and felt immense satisfaction as plants righted themselves and grass emerged to cover the signs of our battle. Deep in the earth, I could sense the blank spots in the outpouring of green life that were the bodies of the Vipers.

"Maybe we should have kept one alive for questioning," I said. In the corner of my vision, I saw Ash wince. Damn. That was careless. I hurried on, hoping to distract him. "We need to know how they got in, at least. Otherwise we could be overrun with the bastards."

Willow stood up and scowled. "I can't understand it. The wards didn't react at all." Her face went blank for a moment, and I knew she was reaching out with her magic, checking them again.

On impulse, I did the same. Not to check the wards—they were Willow's domain, and I could sense them but not control them. Just to feel for any anomalies in the web of plant life that made up the sith.

Oh, shit. What was that?

11

"There's something by the gate," I said.

Willow stiffened, then relaxed. "No, there's not."

"Yes, there bloody is." I bolted into the trees. Not again! How were these bastards getting in?

Ash moved silently at my side and, after a momentary hesitation, I heard Willow and Christian follow. Christian sounded like a herd of elephants crashing through the trees, and I rolled my eyes. This was no way to sneak up on an enemy.

I slowed my headlong rush, ignoring the adrenaline that urged me on, and waited for them to catch up.

"Christian, what are you even doing? You're just a liability in a fight."

Guilt twinged at the hurt expression on his face, but only a little. It was true. And yeah, it made me sound like a real fae arsehole, but facts were facts. If he'd been a sharpshooter, or some kind of martial arts expert, his humanity wouldn't have been such a problem. But he wasn't even good at human fighting. And without magic he was a sitting duck—or worse, something the enemy could use against us.

"I want to help," Christian said. "I need to protect Willow."

She gave him a sappy look, but I laughed. I couldn't help it. "Mate, she is the heir of Spring. Do you really think she needs *your* protection?"

Willow glared at me.

"What?" I asked. "It's true."

"Let's keep our minds focused on the threat," Ash said. "There's no point sending him back now. Best to keep together."

"No one's sending me anywhere," Christian muttered, but everyone ignored him.

"Where is the princess?" Ash asked.

Oops. Speaking of keeping together—I hadn't even noticed she wasn't with us. The fight had taken all my attention. She could be dead somewhere—

"Gone," Willow said. "Her guards whisked her out of here the minute they realised we were under attack."

"Helpful of them," I said. "We could have used her Earthcrafting."

"To be fair, she tried to argue the point, but they insisted. King's orders, they said."

Nice to know the king considered us expendable. Neither of those guards had possessed a sword like the Hawk's, capable of opening a gate straight to the palace. By the time they got there through the Wilds, there would be no point sending reinforcements. We would either have succeeded in fighting off the attackers, or we would have died.

And after all his talk of protecting the heir of Spring from my father, too. I sighed. Maybe I should see it as a sign of his confidence in our abilities instead. I couldn't really blame him for wanting to protect his own heir, first and foremost.

"How many intruders are there?" Ash asked impatiently, bringing my attention back to the present.

I checked again, feeling for that odd flicker in the web of life that I'd sensed before. "Only one." But why were they simply standing there? Maybe they'd set up some kind of trap and were waiting to see if we were stupid enough to get caught. "They haven't moved."

"It's a trap," he said.

I nodded, a glow of pleasure warming me. Was that our Viper training showing, or did we simply think alike?

"I still can't sense anything," Willow said. "Are you sure about this?"

"Come with me," I said, setting off again, but at a much slower speed.

"Careful," Ash said.

"I'm not walking into any traps," I assured him.

When the trees thinned, I slowed even further, heart pounding in my chest. The intruder still hadn't moved, and I was beginning to doubt myself. How could I sense something that Willow couldn't, when she was tied to this sith and its wards? What kind of intruder just stood by the gate, not moving?

We reached the edge of the trees. Between us and the gate lay the open meadow, dreaming quietly in the moonlight. And there, at the meadow's end, unmistakeable even in the dark, stood a figure.

Willow drew in a sharp breath and the scent of sun-warmed rose petals filled the air as her magic swelled to meet the threat.

I thrust out a hand to stop her. "Wait."

There was something strange about the unmoving figure. Something ... familiar. Not in its silhouette, but in its presence.

What the hell? In its *presence*? My magic surged forwards—not the green power of Spring, but my other, darker magic.

I stepped out of the trees, but Ash grabbed my hand.

"What are you doing?" he whispered. "You can't just walk out there."

I let him draw me back into the cover of the trees, my mind reeling. No wonder Willow hadn't been able to sense the intruder. I thought I had sensed a life force with my Spring magic, but I'd been wrong. It was necromancy that allowed me to sense this presence.

Because that was no living person out there.

Rage boiled within me and I clenched my fists, feeling my face go hot. My father had sent a zombie into our sith. I hadn't sensed a living person but the flickering essence of a tethered soul.

My magic brushed against that soul, teased by its familiarity.

"What the *hell*."

"What's wrong?" Willow asked. "Is it a trap?"

"No." How could my father do this again? Did he have no soul of his own? Was everyone just a tool to be used to him? I drew in a deep, shaky breath, trying to control my anger. I needed to think. "But I figured out how the Vipers got in."

"How?" Ash asked.

He hadn't taken his eyes from the shadowy figure by the gate all this time. He held a knife in his hand, ready to fling it if the enemy so much as moved.

"That's a zombie out there. That bastard used Nevith *again*."

"But ..." Willow looked horrified. "But how did he find Nevith's body?"

Nevith's body had been taken home to his family, far from Lord Thistle's estate, and buried in a quiet corner of the Realm.

"He doesn't need Nevith's body." I shook with fury. I'd only just eased Nevith on his way to the Realm of Death, freeing his poor trapped spirit to its rest. And now my father had snatched him back? "He can use any body. All he needs is Nevith's spirit to access the sith. The wards identify a person by their essence, not by how they look."

Fallon had done it before, when he stuffed my mother's spirit into a random body so that I could talk to her. He'd said then that it was difficult to do, because the soul didn't have an attachment to the strange body. That was the reason, according to him, that my contact with my mother had been so brief.

I called bullshit. I would bet everything I owned that it

was no more difficult than shoving a soul back into its own body after death and that he'd lied for his own reasons. After all, he'd been trying to convince me we had to raise my mother's own body from its grave, and that it was so difficult that I had to give him Ni'ishasana for it to succeed.

Because if it was so hard to do, how could Nevith be standing here, clothed in someone else's flesh, while Fallon was back in Spring? How could he power the revenant when he wasn't even in the same world?

Unless he was.

A shiver of apprehension ran down my spine and I strode out into the meadow, ignoring Willow's protests. Ash didn't bother protesting, but strode out with me, ready for anything.

I stopped in the middle of the meadow, grasses waving against my bare legs. It was a warm night, and I was quite comfortable in my Ninja Turtle pyjamas, however ridiculous I looked. Still, at least I looked better than the zombie.

This one clearly hadn't been long dead, and my stomach seized with horror as it turned its head to face me, in case it was someone I recognised from Spring. The Lady alone knew how many people there had died in Fallon's coup.

It was a woman, wearing a long white dress, only slightly smeared with dirt, and I didn't know her. I breathed out in relief. Her face had that waxy look that corpses had, and her colour was so sickly no one could have mistaken her for a living, breathing person. But she wasn't decomposed at all, and her hair hung in fine golden strands, just as it must have when she was alive.

It was that contrast that made her so hard to look at. In a strange way, the zombies that were practically falling apart were easier on the eye. There was no doubt what they were. But with this woman, every time my gaze was drawn back to her dead face, it shocked me all over again with its wrongness.

"Nevith," I said. "Do you know me?"

I had no idea how this worked. Nevith was clearly in some kind of thrall to Fallon, who had trapped him in this body—did that mean he was a pure extension of my father's will? Or did his soul retain some awareness of its own?

The zombie nodded. "Sage."

"Is Fallon here?"

"No."

Emboldened by the zombie's calm manner, Willow joined us. "Is he still in Spring? Tell us what's happening there."

The unnatural eyes rested on Willow's face. "My purpose is only to hold the gate open for my master's Vipers."

She made a noise of frustration and glanced at me. "Can't you make it talk?"

"How would he know?" I asked, emphasising the word *he*. This was no thing. It was Nevith's soul trapped in there, whatever the woman's outward appearance. "Nevith was in the Realm of Death when Fallon grabbed him and shoved him into a random body. He hasn't been hanging around Spring keeping up with events." I contemplated the zombie. "And I suspect he wouldn't be able to tell you even if he had. There's probably some compulsion that stops him acting against Fallon's interests."

After my experience with the Viper ghost, I knew what to look for, and there it was inside the zombie—a dancing blue flame that I had to squint my eyes to see. I could also make out the bonds that bound Nevith's soul to this body, like a cage whose black bars wrapped around the flickering light of his essence. Beyond that cage, a tether stretched off through the gate and into the distance. All the way back to Spring, no doubt.

Could I sever that tether? I probed it with my magic and found it was surprisingly strong, considering the distance it had to cover.

Or did distance make no difference? Again, I ran up against the limits of my knowledge. This was so *frustrating*. I needed to know how this stuff worked if I hoped to make good on my promises to destroy the Vipers and stop my father. At the moment I was fumbling in the dark. Fallon would be killing himself laughing if he could see me now.

Which he probably could. Damn it! Was he even now looking out of the zombie's eyes, taking in this whole conversation? He'd once spoken to me in his own voice through a zombie, as if he was right there in front of me. It wasn't much of a stretch to imagine he could also see what they were seeing.

I clenched my fists in frustration and attacked the tether with everything I had.

And ... nothing happened.

"Tell me how to help you," I said.

"I don't know," Nevith whispered.

I sighed, feeling my whole body sag with disappointment. Lord Nox had known so much. I guess that was the difference between a Lord and a regular fae. Even though he hadn't yet been to the Realm of Death, Lord Nox had known a lot about a great many things, even such arcane subjects as necromancy.

I'd sent Nevith on only hours before. He'd hardly had time to get settled in the Realm of Death before Fallon yanked him back again. And he'd certainly been no Lord when he'd been alive. I couldn't expect him to know anything helpful.

Maybe I had to find an old soul, someone who'd been dead a long time, to teach me the things I needed to know.

And then what, genius? You're going to stuff it into some random dead body so you can question it?

I recoiled from the thought. I'd vowed not to create any zombies. The whole thing was too creepy for my taste. Was there another way to speak to the dead? If necromancy came from their Realm, surely they could teach me how it worked?

"How do we kill this thing?" Willow asked.

The scent of roses lay heavy on the night air. While I'd been wrestling with my thoughts, she'd twined grasses around the zombie's feet and legs, rooting it in place. That seemed pointless—the zombie hadn't shown any inclination to run. But maybe it made her feel more in control of the situation.

I wished *I* were. "We can't kill it," I said wearily. "It's already dead."

"Then free your friend's soul," Ash said, still watching the zombie warily. "Send it into death again."

I opened my mouth to tell him I couldn't, then stopped. I'd only tried assaulting the bond between the zombie and my father. I hadn't actually tried to prise open the bars of the cage that imprisoned poor Nevith's soul.

And I knew that if I could release the soul which animated it, the body would be no more than a corpse again. I took a deep breath and turned my attention to those dark bars wrapped around the flickering light of Nevith's essence.

First I tried pushing, but that made the light flicker even more, and the zombie groaned. That didn't seem like a good sign. I didn't want to extinguish that flame. So I tried pulling instead.

At first it seemed as if that would be no more successful than my previous attempt, but something shifted. Nevith's soul flared brighter, beating against the bars of its cage. I zeroed in on the weakened element and pulled harder.

"You're holding your breath," Willow said. "Are you all right?"

I breathed out. "Just trying to focus."

I only needed one bar to break. Maybe two. It was hard to be sure, but I sensed that the cage was an all-or-nothing kind of deal. Any weakness in the structure would destroy it.

There. The bars trembled and I focused all my magic on that one spot. Power surged through me and the cage exploded. Nevith's soul burst free.

The tether leading back to Fallon disappeared with the

cage. That would give my father something to chew on. I hoped it hurt.

Before he could re-establish a bond with Nevith, I blasted my friend's delicate soul through the gates to the Realm of Death, giving it an extra-hard shove before slamming the gateway closed again. Even that much exposure to the siren call of that dark Realm left me weak and shaking with the effort of resisting it.

I bent over, hands on my knees, my head spinning. I barely heard Willow's concerned voice or felt the touch of Ash's hand on my back.

Hopefully pushing Nevith deeper would make his soul harder to find, but if I wanted to stop my father from using him against us again, I needed a surer solution. At the moment, I had no idea what that might be—because I had no damn idea how this stupid necromancy worked.

It seemed there was only one way to find out, and that was to step through that dark gate and journey into the Realm of Death.

12

I wasn't stupid. Well, maybe I was—it depended on who you asked. I had no intention of risking my life if I didn't absolutely have to. I was still thinking it over the next morning, wondering where else I could get the information I needed, when Willow threw a spanner in the works.

"I've had enough," she said, looking around at us challengingly.

Ash, Christian, and I were sitting with her around the dining table in the main pavilion, finishing off a light meal before bed—assuming anyone could sleep. Zinnia had apparently interpreted *light meal* as *light meal for twenty people*. As well as providing little sweet cakes, enough sandwiches to feed a small army, and tomatoes and wild mushrooms fried in butter, she'd also given us eggs in just about every form known to man or fae—fried, scrambled with onion and peppers, boiled, poached, and served with delicious hollandaise sauce.

Despite thinking I was too stressed to eat, I'd somehow managed to consume enough eggs to turn into a chicken. I had *definitely* had enough, but I didn't think Willow was talking about how full she was.

"Of … ?" I prompted when she said no more.

"Of having these Vipers crawling all over my garden like fleas on a dog."

"They weren't trying to kill us this time," I said.

"Speak for yourself," Christian said, a surly expression on his face. We'd said no more about his uselessness as a fighter, but clearly it still rankled. "They were certainly trying to kill *me*."

I glanced at Ash. They hadn't shown any desire to keep him alive either, but he said nothing. He'd been very quiet since the attack—even more so than usual, and he wasn't exactly a chatterbox at the best of times. He'd only said three things in the last hour, and then only because he'd been directly addressed. He sat, head down, applying himself with what seemed like excessive focus to the business of eating.

Well, I could understand that. Fighting made me hungry, too. Exhibit A: the five million eggs I'd just consumed. My stomach felt as though it were full of lead. If any more Vipers showed up now, I'd have to ask them to take a rain check. There was no way I was fighting again until I digested these babies.

Willow smiled briefly at Christian, her hand resting on his on the white tablecloth. "I don't care what their intention was—I'm fed up with having them waltzing in here like they own the place. It's ridiculous. A sith is supposed to be impenetrable."

I sighed. "Tell that to the Vipers."

She glared at me, as if all this was my fault somehow. "Can't you stop your bloody father from using Nevith to get in here? This is insane."

"Can't you fix your bloody wards so Nevith no longer has access?" I returned, feeling peeved. How was I supposed to stop Fallon doing anything? I'd known about my necromantic powers for all of five minutes. Did she expect me to be an expert in their use already?

She threw her hands up in exasperation. "No, I can't. That's the real kicker. Because he's not alive anymore."

"Really?" I'd never realised that before. Not that it was the kind of thing likely to come up in casual conversation.

"Yes, really. So you'll have to fix it. Are you a necromancer or not?"

"Not," I said, anger burning its way up my throat and spreading in a hot flush across my face. I would *never* be a necromancer. I could admit that necromancy had some good uses—I'd been able to help both Lord Nox and Nevith with it. There might be *some* circumstances where I'd consider using it again—but embrace it wholeheartedly? Nope. It was never happening.

"Then we'll have to go to Spring and force your father to stop."

Right. Now I saw where she was going with this antagonism. She was trying to create a situation where she was justified in defying the king's order to stay away from Spring.

My anger died, understanding. She was worried sick about her parents and itching for an excuse to go save them. Though what hope she had of succeeding where Lord Thistle had failed was beyond me.

"King Rothbold expressly forbade you—forbade any of us—from going near your father's estate," I said. "Ash, tell her she's crazy. You know how dangerous my father is now."

Fallon had been bad enough before, when he was only a necromancer. Now he was a necromancer with the powers of Ni'ishasana behind him, with an army of zombies and a full complement of Vipers as well. Not even the king could stand alone against that much strength. Willow would be no challenge at all.

"Sage is right," Ash said. "Fallon is a dangerous man. What is your plan to defeat him?"

"My plan?" she echoed. There was a long silence. And she thought *I* was the impetuous one. Even I had more sense than to go running off to face Fallon without an ace up my sleeve. "I'll think of something on the way."

"You will die," Ash said gently. "Maybe not immediately. Clearly Fallon wants you alive for something, or those Vipers wouldn't have been so gentle. But make no mistake, once he has what he wants, you will die. He is simply too strong to resist."

Her face crumpled and she looked down in a futile attempt to hide the tears that glimmered on her lashes. Christian put his arm around her and tried to pull her into a hug, but she sat straight, refusing his comfort.

"I don't care," she declared. "Time is running out.

There are less than fourteen hours left till Fallon's deadline. Even less until the king attacks."

"The king will—"

"I know, I know, the king doesn't think Fallon will harm them. But what if he's wrong? What if the king's attack tips Fallon over the edge? I'm starting to think sending Rothbold in with guns blazing is the wrong approach. What if Fallon kills them because I don't show up? I couldn't live with myself, knowing I could have saved them, but I stayed away like a good little girl just because Rothbold told me to." Tears swam in her vivid green eyes. "I have to go. You said you thought Fallon was baiting the king—what if Rothbold attacking plays into his plans? Maybe that's exactly what Fallon wants, and he's going to take them all out at once. I can't just sit around waiting for that man to take over the entire world and do nothing."

"Do you think that's what he wants?" Christian asked, startled. "To take over the world?"

She shrugged as if she didn't care one way or another. "The fae world, at least. Why else was he after the dagger, if not for the power it gives him? He wasn't content living in hiding. He's taken Spring for now, but why would he stop there? I'll bet he sees himself on Rothbold's throne."

I took a deep breath—as deep as I could with my diaphragm constricted by the weight of all those eggs in my stomach. A moment ago, I'd been rejecting necromancy, but even I could see that it might be our only advantage at this point. "You still don't have any chance alone against Fallon. Throwing yourself away for nothing is stupid. You can't go off alone—"

"I can do what I like, and you can't stop me," she said fiercely.

"You can't go *alone*," I said. Was I really about to suggest this? The very thought scared the crap out of me, but Willow had made up her mind, and I couldn't see any other option that gave us a chance at success. "And you can't go without some kind of plan. We need an edge."

"And? You think we have one?" She was so focused on me that she didn't even notice Kel leap up onto the chair next to her and eye the tableful of food with keen interest. Usually she'd be yelling something about *that damn cat* the minute he poked his nose into the room.

"Not yet. But I'm pretty sure I know where we can get one."

"Where?" She was trying to play it cool, but she couldn't hide her eagerness.

"In the Realm of Death."

"No," Ash said instantly, his face paling. He'd barely looked at me since the attack, but he was looking now, horror in his eyes.

"You haven't even heard my plan yet." Maybe *plan* was a little generous for the bare glimmerings of my idea.

"I don't need to hear it," he said. "The Realm of Death is no place for the living."

"Necromancers go there all the time," I objected.

There was a fierceness in him as he sat forward, pinning me with his gaze. "And I could count the number of necromancers in the Realms on one hand. Do you know why?" The question seemed rhetorical, so I didn't answer. I felt sure he was about to tell me. "Because they *die*, Sage.

People trying to become necromancers *die* when they travel to the Realm of Death."

"But I already *have* necromantic powers, thanks to dear old Dad, so it shouldn't be as much of a risk."

"You're hardly a necromancer. You might have the power, but you don't know how to use it."

"So I need to go there to learn to use it."

"This is a totally circular argument."

"Look, I know it's risky—"

"Risky? It's almost certainly a death sentence."

"But not *completely* certainly. See? There's a difference."

Something flashed in my eye and I glared at Christian, who was fiddling with his ring. It was a massive rock—surely fake? Or had Willow given it to him?—and it caught the light in its facets, casting it in an array of moving spots on the wall. And, more annoyingly, in my eyes. He seemed to have checked out of the conversation altogether now that we weren't discussing any danger to Willow.

She studied me thoughtfully. "What is this edge you think you can get by going there?"

I didn't know whether to be pleased or offended that she wasn't trying to talk me out of this. A giant ball of nerves had taken up residence in my stomach, next to the eggs, at the thought of crossing into that Realm. But what else could I do? We were out of options.

The Lady knew I would never knowingly have taken this power. But since I had it, it seemed stupid not to put it to use in our hour of need. Because that mutinous look on Willow's face meant this was an hour of need for sure. I was only surprised she'd obeyed the king's edict this long.

It was written clearly in her face that she would be going to Spring soon, whatever anyone said.

Short of locking her up, there was no way to stop her. So I had to find a way to help her instead.

The cat blinked as refracted light from Christian's ring hit him in the face, and he stilled, gaze fixed on the huge stone. His interest gave me an overwhelming sense of déjà vu, but the memory escaped me. Couldn't Christian keep still? It would serve him right if Kel clawed him.

Then Kel's tail began to twitch, and he suddenly leapt from the chair, paw outstretched. We all jumped as he slammed against the wall. He was trying to catch the moving, rainbow-edged spots that Christian's damn ring was throwing up against the white surface.

Impatiently, Willow took Christian's hand and moved it so that the stone no longer caught the light just so. The rainbow spots disappeared, leaving Kel hunting fruitlessly for them.

"Well?" she prompted.

At least Kel's attack on his imagined enemy had lightened my mood. I shrugged. "I won't know until I get there, will I? But there must be something." I shot a sly glance at Ash. "People don't kill themselves trying to become necromancers for no reason, do they? It's a huge power boost."

"Which your father also possesses." Ash frowned at me. "Plus he has the dagger."

And what could any of us do against a combination like that? He didn't have to put his thought into words; it was written plain as day on his face. But I refused to share his pessimism.

"The king won't sit by and let Fallon steal Spring from under your parents' noses," I said to Willow.

"But him turning up with an army might be as good as signing their death warrant," she said. "Fallon wants *me. I* have to go. I'm not sitting here any longer."

"Just a *little* longer," I said. "We still have fourteen hours."

"Probably only twelve until the king attacks."

"Twelve, then." I looked at my watch. It was just after seven in the morning. "I'll go to the Realm of Death and see what I can find out. Promise you'll wait until I get back."

She grimaced. Reluctance was written all over her face, but eventually she nodded. "All right. But I'm not waiting long. I need to get there before the king. You have two hours, no more."

"Don't do this," Ash said. He shifted restlessly in his seat, as if he wanted to grab me and physically stop me from leaving. "You're acting as though this was just another walk through the Wilds to another Realm. You can't be sure you'll ever return."

I took his hand and his fingers tightened around mine in a desperate grip. I squeezed back, caught by the desolation in his eyes. He thought he was losing someone dear to him. Again.

"I promise you, I'll return."

"You can't promise that. You don't know what will happen."

"When do we ever know what the future holds?" The dining room seemed to fade away. Willow and Christian disappeared and all I could see was his beautiful face and those stormy grey eyes locked on mine. "All I can promise is my ... intention." I almost said love, but my tongue stumbled over the word. He'd been so strangely cool since the attack. "I'll do everything in my power to return. You will be my lifeline, anchoring me to this world."

"I wish I could go in your place."

Frankly, I kind of wished that, too. But he wasn't the one with necromantic power, so it had to be me. The idea of passing through that alluring portal scared the crap out of me. The living were never meant to enter the Realm of Death. Was I strong enough to fight my way back out again?

But, in the Vipers' garden, when I'd almost followed Atinna's ghost through that final gate, it had been his voice which had called me back to the world of the living. I had to trust that the bond between us would be strong enough.

"Give me something of yours to carry with me," I said on impulse. That would remind me of what was important.

He drew one of his many knives and I shook my head. I didn't want one of his instruments of death. But he surprised me by using it to cut one of the locks of hair that fell across his face. Willow gasped.

"Are you sure?" I breathed, searching his face. Some fae magics used locks of hair, nail clippings, even spots of blood, against a person. For that reason, fae were usually very particular about keeping such things out of others' hands. It was why swearing in blood, the way the king's knights swore to the king, was so powerful.

To offer one's hair freely was a sign of absolute trust. Even lovers usually didn't go so far. Sharing a bed was one thing, but sharing pieces of one's body was considered more intimate. And riskier. Passion could always turn sour, and the gift, once given with love, could become a weapon in the hands of an ex-lover.

His face was grim as he folded my fingers closed around the soft, silken strands. He might have been offering me a rock for all the expression there was in his eyes, though his touch lingered for a moment longer than necessary. He offered his heart and soul as if it were of no importance to him, as if he didn't care what I did with it. As if he expected me to rebuff him.

"Take it," he said. "May it bring you back safely."

13

I called the final gate into being, right there in the garden outside Willow's dining room. Ash's hair was safe in a golden locket around my neck, which Willow had supplied.

"You will be careful, won't you?" she asked. Her expression was tight, her emotions locked down. Her fear for her parents stiffened every limb.

I could tell she was busting to *do* something. Anything. No one liked feeling helpless, but it wasn't an experience that came very often to the heir of Spring, and she was only just hanging on.

I nodded. "Of course. I'll be fine."

If she could have seen the gate before me, she might have realised what a lie that was. It shimmered, sparks of blue magic zipping through the thick silver mist that roiled in the gateway and spilled out over my feet. I had no idea what I was doing, and the longing I felt, the deep yearning in my soul that wanted nothing more than to step through life's final gate—frankly, that scared the crap out of me.

If the lure of the Realm of Death was this strong when I was still outside, what would it be like once I was in there? My hand tightened reflexively around the golden locket as I glanced at Ash. His face was as emotionless as Willow's, but a muscle jumped in his jaw. He was worried, too.

Well. No point standing around being terrified. Maybe this was the last time I'd see either of them, and maybe it wasn't, but I had a job to do. We were hopelessly outclassed at the moment—going to Spring now would only play into Fallon's hands. To have any hope of helping Lord Thistle and Lady Feronique, we needed something more. Some kind of ace up our sleeve.

And it was up to me to find that ace. I drew in a deep breath, pleased that it wasn't shuddery with nerves.

"Back soon!" I said, trying for a cheery note. "Don't wait up."

Then I strode forward and passed over Death's threshold.

The pain was intense. The threshold magic attacked my living body with needles of fire. This must be what being swarmed by angry bees felt like. And yet, even as the gate itself warned me away, the Realm beyond called to me, and I strode forward eagerly to meet the pain.

The mist swirled around me, blinding me. I had the sense of other presences walking beside me, behind me. A sound like waves against the shore, or perhaps some great animal breathing, *shush-shushed* somewhere in the distance. I let out a ragged breath as the fiery pain faded.

Which way? Was there even any direction in this strange place? And how would I find the gate again? I couldn't see much past my nose with all this damned mist —it would be so easy to get turned around. My heart beat a frightened tattoo in my chest.

This was a terrible idea. No. In my long history of terrible ideas, this was without doubt the shittiest one ever. What had I been thinking? This was no place for the living. The mist billowed against my face, as if ghostly hands caressed me.

I froze to the spot, clutching the gold locket so hard it dug into the soft flesh of my palm. It was warm against my skin. I opened my hand and looked down. The locket glowed with soft, warm light, which trailed behind me, disappearing through the mist in the direction of the gate.

Okay, that made me feel better. I was still connected to Ash and the world of the living, and all I had to do when I was ready to leave was follow the trail of light. I squared my shoulders. No point cowering here by the gate. I'd come here to find us some help in the fight against my father. Time to get on with it.

I took a step, then another, gaining confidence as I moved. The mist began to clear, and I stopped again in surprise. I stood on a high promontory. Laid out below me was a great green forest dappled with moonlight, dotted with clearings bursting with flowers. A river meandered through it, looping in lazy coils through the trees. Far off in the distance, almost too far to see, I glimpsed a deeper darkness that looked like the ocean.

Well, what had I expected the fae afterlife to look like? They were a people who loved green, growing things, even the cold Winter folk like Ash. Nature was their first love—and, apparently, their last. This was the kind of reward a fae heart would dream of.

There was no sign of buildings among the trees. Perhaps fae souls didn't need such things. Did they eat or drink? There was no one around to ask, though I could have sworn that I'd been surrounded just moments before, when I'd stood in the mist.

I glanced behind me uneasily, but no one was there. A mountain towered above me—the height where I stood was only one of the foothills. There was no sign of the gate, but my bright golden thread of light still stretched back into a tumble of boulders behind me.

The top of the mountain disappeared into the clouds, so that decided me on direction. Even if I'd been equipped for mountain climbing, the forest below looked far more inviting, so I took the path that curled down around the hillside towards the trees.

Wisps of blue light flocked to greet me, some clinging to my arms like tiny flames, others dancing about my head. The path was smooth, and my steps sped up until I was striding out as I hit the level ground, almost breaking into a run. The forest pulled me forward, its leaves whispering though no wind disturbed them. Somehow I knew that everything I had ever wanted waited within its shadowed depths, and the blue flames danced, lighting my path under the branches.

In the deep shadows of the trees a larger light appeared, human-sized. It flickered at first, but became clearer as it approached, its soft glow shining on the tree trunks. At first, I could only make out that it was a woman, but a sudden certainty gave my feet wings, and I rushed down the path.

The woman pushed one last branch out of her way, her figure solidifying as she appeared before me. "Stop!"

My heart leapt. "Mama?"

"Sage," she breathed, and then I was in her arms. "You mustn't go into the woods, my darling. It's not safe for you."

Her body was as warm and solid as my own, though it glowed with soft blue light. Tears burned my eyes as I breathed in her familiar floral scent. It brought a flood of memories with it that I'd thought long forgotten, little flashes of domestic happiness. My small hand in her larger one. Her laughing down at me as we walked in her garden. Curling up against her side as she read me a story. Eating from her plate, perched on her knee at dinner while the cool night breezes of Spring ruffled her long dark hair. The call of the forest was silenced by the joy of her presence.

"What are you doing here?" I asked, hardly believing my luck. After, all, she was human. "Isn't this the fae afterlife?"

"Your father found me and brought me here. He said he didn't want to spend eternity without me." She held me away from her, letting her gaze travel up and down as if she wanted to impress every inch of me on her memory. "I never thought I would see you again," she said, her eyes glistening with unshed tears. Blue flames danced along my arms, and she brushed them away impatiently. "But you shouldn't be here. The secrets of the dead are not for the living."

"The secrets of the dead are why I'm here, Mama. I'm a necromancer now. Sort of. I didn't kill anyone," I added quickly, as she drew back, a look of horror on her face. "I stole these powers from Papa. And now I need to learn how to use them."

She still looked aghast, so I hurried on, stumbling over an explanation of all that had happened. She scowled at the first mention of my father's name, and the scowl only deepened as the story unfolded.

"That man has lost his way," she said when I'd finished. "What happened to the man I married?"

"He didn't kill me," I offered, though I didn't know why I should feel I had to defend Fallon from my mother's displeasure. He certainly hadn't earned my support.

"*He didn't kill me,*" she repeated with a curl of her lip. "That's a very low bar, darling. Most people would expect more from their own father." She sighed. "Necromancy changed him. At first, I was happy—he would summon me and it was a joy to speak to him again. Though I never agreed with his decision to leave you with Thistle and Feronique. But then he started to change. I begged him to give up necromancy, but he wouldn't listen, so I refused his call after that."

"Did being a revenant bother you?" I asked, thinking of

the decaying vehicle her soul had inhabited the time my father had summoned her to speak to me.

"It felt uncomfortable," she said. "Like wearing ill-fitting clothes. But he rarely did that. Raising bodies takes power. It's easier to simply speak. He summoned my shade to the living Realms many times before I realised how blackened his soul had become."

"Wait." I frowned in confusion. "He could speak to you *without* stuffing your soul into a body?"

"Of course. Communing with the dead is necromancy at its simplest."

"But ..." Had I just assumed? He'd put my mother's soul into a random body so I could speak to her, making me think that was the only way to do it. But he'd wanted me to think that, hadn't he? It was all part of his story of how hard it was to hold my mother's soul there, and how he needed to raise her own body so that her soul could stay.

"He lied to you?"

Of course he'd lied to me. He'd been playing on my desperate need for my mother, trying to convince me to give him the dagger—and I'd fallen for it. "Yep."

"He's more lies than truth these days. Once I realised that, I refused to have anything more to do with him."

"But you came to speak to me."

She lifted one glowing blue shoulder in a shrug. "He trapped me into that body using stronger magic. I couldn't resist it." She smiled and stroked my cheek. "But it was worth it to see you. Tell me all about your life. I've missed you so much!"

Since I was short on time—I'd promised Willow I'd be

back in two hours—I gave her the condensed version. It felt wonderful to be with her again, to be able to touch her and see her expressive face change from frowns to laughter as she followed my story. But every so often my gaze drifted over her shoulder, to the forest behind her and the path that led so invitingly into the deep shade of the trees.

I took a sideways step, trying to get past her. What could be so wrong about going just a little way into the forest? It was the most beautiful thing I'd ever seen, and the need to walk under its dark branches was like an itch that demanded scratching.

She caught my arm in a firm grip. "No, Sage. The forest is not for you." She frowned as she brushed at the tiny blue flames that danced all down my forearm, sending them spinning into the air.

"What's wrong?" I asked, watching as some shredded and dissipated, while others drifted back towards me. They were beautiful, and I couldn't see the harm in letting them hitch a ride.

"These are souls," she said. "They're attracted to your life force. They're feeding off it. They'll drain you dry if you let them."

Hastily, I brushed a few stragglers off my arm. I *was* feeling more tired now than when I'd arrived. My hand crept to the glowing golden locket at my throat. It warmed my fingers, and the connection to Ash and the world of the living reassured me.

"Why don't they look like you?" I asked. Mama was solid, as real as I was. The tiny souls looked like they should have been heating the kettle on a gas stove-top.

"There are two types of dead here," she said. "Those who want to move on to their reward"—she waved a hand in the general direction of the forest behind her and the vast ocean beyond it—"and those who want to return to the mortal Realms. Of those who long to return, most drift aimlessly here by the gate, gradually disintegrating until they're nothing but mindless longing." She indicated the blue flames.

"And the others?" I asked. "The ones who don't wait by the gate?"

"They journey deep into the lands of the dead, amassing power and knowledge, always hungry, always seeking a way back. Those are the dangerous ones."

Right. I mentally scrubbed *journey deep into the Realm of Death* off the list.

"So these ones are old?" I asked, nodding at the blue flames. "I mean, *you're* near the gate and you're not disintegrating. I guess these ones have been hanging around for a while."

She smiled. "Yes. A while."

That could mean anything from decades to millennia. I decided not to go down that particular rabbit hole. There were so many things I wanted to ask, and most of them were a lot more relevant than how long it took souls to disintegrate.

Stay focused, I reminded myself. *You don't have much time.*

Willow wouldn't wait forever. Hell, Willow might not even wait the two hours she'd promised. The word *impa-*

tient had been invented to describe her. I needed to get something useful fast and hightail it out of here.

Except ... it was my *mother*. I didn't want to leave so soon when I'd just found her again. I chewed on my lip, drinking in the sight of her. Apart from the slight blue glow, she looked just as I remembered her. Thick masses of dark hair tumbled down her back. Her eyes were dark, too, her nose a little wider than mine, her face broader. Now that I was grown, she seemed smaller than I remembered, not quite as tall as me, but her smile matched the warmth of the one in my memories perfectly.

I sighed. I'd stay forever if I could. This was so comfortable and cosy.

Wait. *No.* That wasn't right. *Focus.*

"Mama. I need to find out how necromancy works. I've got all this power and no idea how to use it. Is there someone here who could teach me?" I looked beyond her, my eyes trying to pierce the dark depths of the forest. My feet itched to carry me into that darkness, but my mind insisted that it would be a bad idea. I rubbed absently at my arm, dislodging a handful of the dancing flames. A great weariness was creeping over me.

"You already know," she said, taking my hand in her own warm, blue one. "It's just like using any other magic. The only reason you can't use it properly is because you're afraid of it. You have to stop thinking of it as evil."

Maybe my tiredness was making me stupider than usual, but that didn't make any sense. "You just told me how you tried to get Papa to give it up because it was turning him bad."

"Necromancy by itself is neither good nor evil. It merely *is*—just like any other power. If you use Spring magic to kill someone, does that make the magic bad? Of course not. Your father was putting necromancy to evil uses."

"But everyone hates necromancers. They're afraid of them." A memory tugged at me. "And to become a necromancer you have to kill someone. Nobody has to kill someone before they can use Spring magic."

She shrugged. "It *is* the magic of the Realm of Death. How living souls access it is their business. *You* didn't kill anyone, did you? Yet here you are."

I eyed her doubtfully. Something seemed wrong with that logic, but I'd come here for answers. No one had guaranteed that I'd like them.

"You've already seen how your necromancy can be used to help free ghosts who are stuck in the mortal world." She gave my hand an encouraging squeeze. "That's not a bad thing, is it? And what's so bad about talking to the dead? We live in the Realms the same as you. You might as well object to speaking to people from Ocean, or Autumn. It's just that this Realm is harder to get to."

I wasn't sure I agreed with that, either, but I was too tired to argue. "So you're saying that whether necromancy is good or evil depends on the wielder. So if I embrace it, it will answer to me just as my Spring magic does, and I can use it for good."

"Exactly." She gave me a smile I remembered well from my childhood. I'd earned that smile whenever she was satisfied with my progress. She patted my hand. "But why do you need it?"

Oh, Lady save me. What did I say? "There are ... dangers in the Realms at the moment. Papa is creating problems. I just need to be ready."

Ready for what? *Please don't let her ask me.* She wasn't Fallon's biggest fan anymore, but still. Even *I* didn't have the balls to tell my mother to her face that I was planning to ... well, that I might have to ...

I could hardly stand to admit it to myself. *I might have to kill my own father.*

I rubbed a hand over my face as a wave of tiredness washed over me.

"Are you all right? You should go, before you attract unwanted attention."

I glanced again at the dark forest. What was hiding in there, and in the ocean beyond? I should be scared, but my feet wanted to carry me into the shadows of those trees. None of my mother's warnings made any difference. I felt like the tide, pulled by a moon beyond its understanding.

Mama brushed another swarm of blue flames from my shoulder and shooed them away from my head. "You mustn't stay too long." Her hands lingered on my arms. "You are so bright, my little whirlwind. You shine like a beacon to our eyes." Her fingers tightened. "Even I feel the hunger."

I stepped back, unnerved by the need in her eyes.

"But you are my child," she said, "and so I resist."

I clutched the locket for reassurance. It didn't feel as warm as it had before, and a quick glance over my shoulder showed that my link back to Ash wasn't as bright as it had been earlier either. I really should go—but I still had so many questions.

"What about necromantic rituals?" I asked hurriedly. "How do they keep the necromancer safe?"

Suddenly I felt the need for every possible safety precaution. I flapped my hands at the encroaching blue souls, chasing them off.

"Mostly they're just for show," she said. "To frighten people, or impress them. But some necromancers use them to help connect them to the real world so they don't get lost when they leave their bodies."

"Leave their bodies?"

"You don't think they come here in physical form any more than they have to, do you? This place is dangerous for the living. Necromancers who don't realise that quickly become dead necromancers. The smart ones travel here in their dreams."

Every question she answered only led to more questions. Dream travel sounded promising. Maybe that would allow me to return more safely, so I could continue my search for answers. "How does the ritual help connect them to their bodies?"

"The dead exert a pull on the living. A necromancer needs an anchor—a drum beat to hold them in their body, or a light to guide them back should they leave it. But you have found your anchor already." She gestured at the locket. "Look at that cord."

I looked. The golden magic trailing behind me that connected me to Ash was looking less like a cord and more like a thread now. My heart lurched uncomfortably. It looked so fragile.

"If it breaks, you'll struggle to find your way back," my mother whispered.

As if in response to her words, more of the blue flames flocked to me, latching onto my arms and head, swirling around my body in an eager cloud. Their touch was no more than a brush of air against my skin, but exhaustion seeped deep into my bones, and my legs started to shake.

I brushed them off, but they only rose into the air for a moment, then settled back down. I felt an insistent tug at my core—the golden thread, trying to drag me back.

"I want to stay," I said. "It's too soon. I haven't learned enough yet!"

"The dead will feed," Mama said. "You will never return to the world of the living."

The hunger in her eyes chilled me. I took a shocked step back. The tugging sensation increased, as if sensing my change in mood. Blue flames swirled around me, blocking my mother from my sight.

I batted them away, trying to shield my face, but they surged closer, sensing victory. I staggered, weakness making my arms heavy, my steps slow and clumsy.

And then I was falling ...

14

I fell straight back through the gate and would have crashed to the floor in a humiliating heap if Ash hadn't caught me. For a moment I sagged against him, breathing in his warm ironbark scent, taking comfort from his solid physical presence.

Then I realised the terrible weakness was gone, and I pushed myself upright. Somehow my connection to him had dragged me to the gate—or perhaps it had brought the gate to me. The last moments were a bit of a blur in my mind. I shuddered, remembering that look in my mother's eyes and the dreadful sapping weakness as the blue souls fed on my life force.

"Are you all right?" Ash gripped my shoulders, holding me away as he examined me, much as my mother had done earlier. But unlike her, he was searching for damage. Evidently finding none, he let go, carefully distancing himself. His expression blanked, as if shutters had come down over his face. "You were gone too long. Did you hear me calling?"

"No."

He looked away. I hadn't heard anything, but something had sure been dragging me back. Was it his need? My hand crept to the locket that held his precious hair. If it hadn't been for the pull of the golden thread that tied me to him, I wasn't sure I'd be standing here now. I opened my mouth to tell him so when Christian stepped forward.

I hadn't even noticed he was in the room until then. That was the effect Ash had on me—other people just faded into the background when he was around.

Unless they were particularly in-your-face, like Willow. Who, I realised as I looked around the dining room, was *not* here.

"I didn't think it would take so long," Christian said.

Seriously? "It couldn't have been more than fifteen minutes."

"You were gone for nearly four *hours*, Sage." He sounded aggrieved, as if my absence had been a personal insult. "Willow wouldn't wait any longer."

"She's gone?" I shifted my attention back to Ash, who nodded.

"She left an hour ago."

I felt a small sting that she hadn't even waited to see if I would make it back alive from the Realm of Death.

"She said her parents could be *dying* while we waited around," Christian said in a bitter tone. "I hope you found something useful."

Clearly, he blamed me for Willow's departure. I

sighed, giving up my pity party. Of course she wouldn't have waited. If I'd been gone four hours, there were only ten hours until Fallon's deadline, even less before the king attacked. She would be beside herself with fear, and Willow wasn't the kind of person who could stand around in a crisis. She liked to be doing something useful.

Come to think of it, *I* was that kind of person, too. That was probably why we got on so well.

"Did she have a plan?" I asked Ash. His face was so impassive I wasn't getting anything from him.

"I don't think so."

"Figures." I took a deep breath, trying to force down the panic that clawed at my insides. Of *course* she'd gone without a plan. My father and the damn Vipers would make mincemeat out of her. "Doesn't she realise she's playing into his hands?"

"I don't think she was thinking at all. She's making decisions with her heart, not her head. Zinnia and Yarys went with her."

"*What*? They're no fighters."

"They have people they love back in Spring, too," Ash said. "They wanted to help."

"She said she could rally the survivors," Christian said. "She told me that being in her own Realm would give her an edge." He rubbed the back of his neck wearily.

"It didn't give Lord Thistle an edge," I pointed out.

"Yeah, but she thought he must have been caught by surprise for Fallon to be able to defeat him."

"Hasn't she listened to a word I've said about the

dagger? Fallon isn't just Fallon anymore." I turned to Ash in frustration. "Why didn't you stop her?"

He frowned. "For the same reason I didn't stop you going to the Realm of Death. Love is not a prison, and I am not its warder." He stared at me with such seriousness that I had the feeling he wasn't just talking about the current situation. But whatever he saw in my face must have disappointed him, because he sighed and turned away to gaze out into the garden. "People must be free to follow their own hearts, Sage. Willow did what she had to."

"So," Christian said impatiently, "did you find something? Tell me that *you* have a plan now."

He fidgeted with the ring Willow had given him, turning it round and round on his finger. Clearly it was a nervous habit. *If he cared so much, he could have gone with her*, I thought. Ash would never have let me go into that kind of danger on my own.

Admittedly, Ash was a hell of a lot more qualified to get *out* of danger than Willow's changeling boyfriend. Christian had no combat skills—didn't even know one end of a gun from another. Willow was right to leave him behind. He'd be nothing but a liability.

I stared at the ring, my attention caught by the flash of the diamond catching the light as it spun round his finger.

"Maybe I do."

Necromancy might have answers for me, but I was out of time to go hunting for them—Willow's action had taken my choices away. So I would fall back on good old human guts and cleverness. As a people, fae relied too much on their magic, and the more they had, the more they wanted.

It was inconceivable to them that anyone might want to destroy something as powerful as the dagger. It simply wasn't in their make-up.

But it was in mine.

"Let's go," I said to Ash as I strode to the door.

"To Spring?" There was a quiet resignation in his voice.

"Yes. Is that a problem?"

"I guess we'll find out."

Ash stayed quiet as the Greenway began to unspool in front of us. It was important to get your intentions firmly fixed before you began your journey in the Wilds, otherwise you could end up at the opposite end of the Realms from where you wanted to be—or even nowhere at all, doomed to wander endlessly through the trackless wilderness. The magic that lived here was capricious, as wild as its name. It took power and concentration to tame it.

The trees closed in behind us as we passed, the path disappearing as if it had never been. I'd been through here often enough not to be alarmed by the odd noises that came from either side now and then. Here a sharp, barking cough; there a frantic rustling, as if a herd of elephants passed unseen just the other side of the trees that lined the path. Oak, ash, and birch spread their branches across it, casting those who walked the path into an eternal twilight.

"So, what's the plan?" Ash asked softly, judging I'd had enough time to fix our course. "I assume you do have one."

"We'll get into Spring—"

He cut me off. "How? We won't be able to sneak in the back, the way we did last time."

Last time we'd been Vipers, exploiting my connection with Spring to fool the wards. But the Vipers weren't stupid enough to leave that route open to us. Fallon would have removed my automatic access to the estate. The wards would consider me an enemy now.

"I figured we'd just walk in the front gate."

"And?"

"And trust that my father doesn't want to kill me."

"Lady's tears, Sage." I could hear the frustration in his voice, though I didn't pause to look back. It was dangerous to take your eyes off the path. One wrong step and you could be off the narrow track, never to find it again. "That's a lot of trust. He almost killed you last time we met."

"And *almost* is the key word in that sentence. He could have, but he didn't—even though he knew I'd stolen something from him."

"That damn necromancy is probably the only reason he *won't* kill you," Ash grumbled.

"Right. Because he'll want that power back. If he kills me, it's gone. So I'll suggest a trade—I'll give him the power back if he gives me Willow."

"I doubt giving back his black magic is going to be as easy as you're making out."

"Oh, that's okay," I said cheerfully. "I'm not actually going to give it to him. That's just a trick so he'll let me in."

There was a thoughtful silence behind me. "I see," he said. "So what's the real plan?"

"The real plan is to destroy Ni'ishasana."

Without that dagger, Fallon would be only a necromancer again and not the world's most dangerous fae. Admittedly, "only" wasn't a word usually applied to necromancers. He would still be a threat, but without the support of the Vipers the threat would be more manageable. The combined might of the Spring Court would probably do it.

"Bold plan," he commented, his tone dangerously polite. "But I fail to see how we are to destroy a centuries-old dagger that contains unimaginable power."

I pushed aside a slim branch that stretched across the path, letting it spring back against him. Served him right for doubting me.

"Have you ever noticed how Kel is entranced by the light catching Christian's ring?"

"By the—what has that to do with anything?"

I grinned and let another branch thwack into him. "You remember cats can see ghosts, right?" I'd told him before about my dealings with Lord Nox and his cat. "I was thinking about it, and all of a sudden those two facts kind of connected, and I remembered how Kel was fascinated by the ruby on the hilt of Ni'ishasana."

Umarenthe had been quite annoyed by it. *What is that cat doing?* she'd demanded, as Kel swatted delicately at the ruby. Except there'd been a tone in her voice that was more than mere annoyance. In hindsight, there'd been a note of dismay, too, almost fear.

And there'd been that time she'd told me that the dagger had one weakness, though she wouldn't say what it was. Maybe it was stretching, but I'd put these little facts together and come up with one enormous answer.

"Well, his eyes tracked Umarenthe around the room, so I'm pretty sure he could see her, too. Add that to his interest in the ruby. It made me think that the ruby must be the source of the 'ghosts' of the dagger, and he sensed that. So, I'm thinking that if we smash it, the souls and their power will be destroyed."

He sucked his breath in sharply, and there was an even longer silence this time.

"You're basing your plan of attack on your *cat*?"

"Do you have any better ideas?"

"I thought you went to the Realm of Death to find some necromantic power you could use against your father?"

"Well, that didn't work out." I'd found my mother. I'd found the freaky little blue flames. But what I hadn't found was any concrete advice, only *don't be scared of the magic* and *you already know what to do*. Nice little pep talk, Mama, but not much useful detail.

Ash caught my arm, forcing me to stop. "Then you're walking in there to die. This is ridiculous."

I eyed him impatiently. "You sound as scared as Christian. You're an assassin. You spent years walking into dangerous situations every day as part of your job. How is this any different?"

His eyes bored into mine. "The difference is that I walked in with a plan. And that plan was based on days, if not weeks, of reconnaissance and tweaking and re-tweaking my approach. I didn't become the Serpent's right hand by rushing off with more enthusiasm than fore-thought. For Lady's sake, Sage, wait for the king. Lily will have told him of the attack by now. He knows that Fallon's plans for Spring have been set in motion. Reinforcements are probably on their way already. Or send for your friend Allegra. She is the Lady of Illusion, isn't she? You need an Illusionist to slip in unnoticed."

I glared right back at him. Couldn't he understand? "Willow doesn't have *time* to wait for reinforcements from the king, or for someone to tramp all the way through the Wilds to Illusion. Fallon didn't want her so he could have a nice little tea party with her and her family." She might even already be dead, but I shied away from that thought. No. I would be in time. I could still save her. "We are the only two people with a chance to get there in time to do anything for her. I can't risk her life to take time for complicated plans and reconnaissance and tweaking."

"It's *your* life I'm concerned about," he said simply. "Let me go in there and offer a trade. You don't have to risk yourself."

I looked down, unable to meet his gaze. The words were cool, matter-of-fact, but his eyes were so bleak, as if his life wasn't important to him. As if he didn't care one way or the other whether he lived or died. That look frightened me. It was too much like the old Ash, trapped in the hell of life as a Viper, who had nothing to live for.

What was wrong with him?

My heart clenched, but a deadly countdown had me in its grip, and I was conscious of every tick of the clock. It was my fault that Fallon had ended up with the dagger, so it was up to me to fix it.

It was up to me to save Willow, and I was running out of time.

She'd only left an hour before us. I clung to the hope that that meant we could arrive in time to save her. Sometimes the Greenways could surprise you, and deposit you at your destination in half the usual time. They seemed to sense the urgency of the traveller.

I twisted out of his grip and resumed my march through the Wilds. "What good will that do? I'll still have to face him eventually, in order to make this supposed trade. You talk as if there's no chance of my plan succeeding."

"Calling it a plan is a little generous," he said. "It's more of a wild speculation."

"You'll never get a job in a cheer squad. Have a little faith."

"Faith is a luxury I've never been able to afford."

There was a scuffle in the bushes to our right, followed by a desperate squeal, cut short, of some small creature's life ending. I sped up my pace. I didn't know why my father wanted Willow, but I couldn't imagine it was for any good. He'd already tried to kill her once and I was determined there would be no second attempt.

Maybe half an hour later, an archway hung with blooming wisteria appeared on the path ahead. We were here. I took a deep breath and rolled my shoulders to loosen the tension in them, then stepped through, Ash hard on my heels.

We emerged between two mighty oak trees, whose leaves rustled in a slight breeze. As the mist of the threshold cleared, I looked around, noting the sunlit ribbon of road leading off through the trees.

"Front gates are this way," I said, leading Ash to the road.

We followed it around a bend and found the high hedges that guarded the main approach to Lord Thistle's estate. Large golden gates split the greenery. Normally they stood open, but today they were closed. Without breaking stride, I marched up to the gates and confronted the lone Viper who stood on guard behind them.

"You've come down a little in the world, haven't you, Seph? Reduced to guarding the gates like an underdressed doorman."

The short, dark-haired man sneered at me. "One could say the same to you, Lady Serpent. Oh, wait, you're not the Serpent anymore. What are you doing here?"

"That's none of your business, doorman. Take me to my father."

Seph nodded to another Viper who had been concealed among the trees by the gate, and he headed off, presumably to announce our arrival.

A few minutes later he returned, accompanied by several more Vipers, led by a figure I knew well. It was Mezzi, one of the Serpent's Adepts.

"Well, well, well, I didn't expect to see you again so soon," Mezzi drawled. "Come to beg some scraps from your father's table, have you?"

"You'll be begging for your life if you don't open this gate," Ash growled.

Mezzi laughed. "You've picked the wrong side in this war, Ashovar. Lord Fallon has great plans for the Vipers."

"I've got some pretty big plans for the Vipers myself," I said, smiling sweetly. "Unfortunately, they don't include any of you staying alive much beyond sunset."

Mezzi laughed and opened the gate to show that he didn't fear my threats. I mean, they must have looked pretty empty. There was no way the two of us would be taking on the might of the Vipers on our own. But Rothbold would have something to add to the discussion, and then Mezzi might be laughing on the other side of his face. If only I could afford to wait for the king to arrive, this could be a very different conversation.

"Behold me trembling in fear," the Viper said, motioning the others forward with a jerk of his head.

They searched us, taking every weapon they could find —and since they were Vipers and very thorough about such things, they took them all. Beside me, Ash held his anger on a tight rein, but I could feel it emanating from him in waves as his former comrades extracted every hidden weapon, even the darts concealed in the heel of his boot.

It didn't bother me. A few knives weren't going to make any difference. If we were to make it out of here alive, it would be through trickery, not blades.

Once the search was done, I strode forward, impatient to see my father and make sure Willow was still in one piece.

"You seem eager to die," Mezzi said as the Vipers closed in around us. He walked beside me, as relaxed as if we were going for a country stroll, though I noticed he had his men push Ash ahead. If he felt uncomfortable with Ash's formidable presence at his back, even weaponless, he wasn't as relaxed as he was making out.

And clearly he felt I was the lesser threat. I might have to force him to re-evaluate that judgement.

"Eager to finish my business here and go," I said.

A couple of the Vipers chuckled at the idea that I might leave here alive. I ignored them.

The path was wide but shaded by trees that had flourished here for hundreds of years. Three people, arms outstretched, couldn't have joined hands around their massive trunks. Their plentiful shade shadowed the path even from the afternoon sun, sheltering us in a cool green world.

Usually someone walking this path would hear the sounds of laughter and many people chattering as they approached the large open pavilion where Lord Thistle's throne stood, and where he conducted the business of the Realm most nights. Smells of roast meats and freshly baked bread would waft on the night breeze to tempt the visitor's appetite, and the faelights bobbing in the trees would shine brightly, inviting them to surrender to the music of fae flutes and drums.

Now there was no music, no delicious smells, and only a very subdued sound of talking, as if no more than three or four people were in conversation. I strained to pick out

Willow's voice as we got closer, but I couldn't make out what anyone was saying.

The trees opened up, revealing a wide sunlit lawn studded with tiny flowers. In the centre of the lawn stood the main pavilion, open to the air on all four sides. Behind it, a series of smaller pavilions disappeared into the trees. It was a familiar sight, but I had never seen it like this.

I stopped at the edge of the trees with a gasp. Mezzi took my arm and urged me into motion again as I stared. My father sat on Lord Thistle's throne, with Lady Feronique beside him on her lower one. That confused me —had Fallon's idea all along truly been to take the rule of Spring for himself? I hadn't believed Nuah when she'd come to the funeral to announce that. It had just seemed like posturing to bait the king.

Spring's former ruler slumped at the bottom of the steps leading up to the throne, draped in so many chains that the weight alone would have been enough to hold him in place, even without the draining effect of iron. If Fallon kept him chained like that for too long, he could die of iron poisoning.

Feronique was in chains too, though hers were less showy. A simple cuff of iron around each wrist was attached by a short length of chain to her seat.

There was no sign of Willow.

Dozens of tall black candles, unlit, surrounded the perimeter of the pavilion, as if standing guard. That was *not* a good sign. Fallon had used candles like that in his ritual to raise my mother's body from her grave. Also alarming: the fact that he was awake and busy at one o'clock in the afternoon, when any self-respecting fae should have been asleep. He must be particularly eager to accomplish whatever this goal of his was.

"So nice of you to visit," Fallon called as our little group of guards marched us across the grass. "I didn't expect to see you again so soon."

Or ever, probably. "I missed you so much I just couldn't stay away."

A group of very nervous-looking servants huddled together to one side of the dais on which the throne sat, as if hoping to escape their new master's notice. Half a dozen Vipers were also present, arrayed to each side of the throne, silent and watchful. Nuah wasn't among them. I wondered where the bitch was—probably causing trouble somewhere.

A faint blue glow around the servant nearest my father caught my eye, and I looked again more closely. Damn it. I could see the trees in the background through his cowering shape.

He was a ghost.

Once I'd spotted him, I realised more of the crowd of servants were also ghosts. The blue glow was hard to see in the bright afternoon light. Only five or six were actually alive. I bit my lip and looked away. I recognised all the faces of the dead.

Where were the other inhabitants of Lord Thistle's estate? The courtiers, the councillors, the musicians? The stable boys, the weavers, the ladies' maids? A deathly silence lay over the place, as if the world held its breath.

I caught Lady Feronique's eye, then wished I hadn't.

There was no love lost between us, but the look of barely controlled fear on her face would have moved a harder heart than mine. She hadn't stopped staring at me since I'd walked in, as if silently begging me to help her, to somehow stop my father.

A woman mounted the dais from behind and came to stand beside the Lady of Spring—a woman made of shadows. I drew in a shocked breath. It was Umarenthe.

"Can you see her?" I whispered to Ash. "Beside Lady Feronique?"

"There's no one there," he responded.

Either this was some new facet of my necromancy, or Umarenthe wanted me to see her. A man joined her, materialising from the air—Celebrach, Ash's father.

Umarenthe reached out to stroke Feronique's hair and smiled at me. "I'm glad you could join us. You're just in time for the show."

Feronique didn't react, confirming my suspicion that the souls of the dagger only appeared to me—and my father, of course, as the current wielder of Ni'ishasana. They *shouldn't* have been visible to me, and the fact that they were was troubling. The smile on Umarenthe's shadowy face was the smile of a bully delighting in torturing their helpless victim.

I squared my shoulders. I was no victim, and I refused to be cowed.

The dagger itself was thrust through my father's belt, the ruby in its hilt winking in the light when he moved to nudge Lord Thistle with his foot. Its strange, twisted blade glistened with an oily sheen.

"Wake up, Thistle. We have guests."

Thistle wasn't asleep, but he barely responded—perhaps unsurprisingly, given the chains that bound him. That much iron would keep even the strongest mage helpless, barely able to remain upright, much less use any magic. He shifted slightly on the step but didn't raise his head. His expression was hidden by his long red hair, the exact shade of Willow's, which tumbled loose across his face.

Had he been tortured? There was no sign of physical damage, but magical pain left no outward marks. I had expected a little more fight from him, even if words were the only weapon he had left. The Lord of Spring had never been slow to tell the world exactly what he expected from it, and the current situation could hardly have been further from his desires.

Fallon gestured to Mezzi, who left my side and disappeared into the trees. The rest of our Viper guard melted away, leaving Ash and me standing alone before the throne. It was a show of strength. There was nothing to stop us from attacking Fallon right now—except the fact that we knew that all it would take to obliterate us would be one twitch of Fallon's little finger. Ni'ishasana's wielder was virtually unstoppable.

I remembered that power well. I eyed the dagger again. This was the tricky part. It was all very well to make a plan to break that massive ruby in an attempt to destroy the dagger's power—but how exactly did one go about it? A blow from a hammer would do it, but Fallon was hardly likely to stand idly by while I let loose on his dagger. How did I even get it off him in the first place? I was hoping to get him alone, perhaps for a meal where his guard might be down. I'd have to play it by ear.

"Where's Willow?" I asked him. "Why are you holding Lord Thistle and Lady Feronique in chains? What exactly are you hoping to accomplish by all this?"

"As to your first question," he said, "I believe that will be answered momentarily."

As if on cue, Mezzi reappeared with Willow in a fierce grip. Her hands were wound about with chains like the ones that bound her mother. She held them out in front of her, trying to keep the iron from touching the rest of her body, but she was otherwise unharmed. A wave of relief swamped me. She was still alive.

Her eyes met mine. "I hope you brought the cavalry. Your father's insane."

"Now, now," Fallon said, his eyes glittering with unholy delight. "Is that any way to talk?" He clapped once, and blue flames shot up from the black candles that encircled the space. They cast an eerie glow over the scene as the sunlight faded, leaving us in an unnatural twilight. He stood up, arms spread wide as if inviting us all to dine with him. "Shall we begin?"

15

Mezzi hustled Willow to the steps and shoved her down to sit beside her father. She moved her bound hands awkwardly over so she could take his hand and leaned against him.

Two other Vipers released Lady Feronique's chains from her throne. One on each side, they grasped her arms and forced her down the steps. She tried to touch her husband and daughter, but they shoved her roughly away.

"On your knees," Fallon said.

When Feronique refused to kneel, the Vipers pushed her down. Fallon strolled down to stand beside her, stroking her hair as Umarenthe had done. This time she was aware, and flinched away from his touch.

"Would you say Feronique has been a good wife to you?" he asked Thistle.

He had turned his back to us, as if he'd forgotten we were there, and his head was tilted to one side as he waited for Thistle's answer. Thistle glared at him through his tangled hair, his eyes burning with hatred.

"Not feeling chatty today?" Fallon asked with mock sympathy when there was no answer. "That's a shame."

He waved a hand in Willow's direction, and she cried out in agony. I started forward, but I'd taken no more than a step when my limbs locked, holding me immobile.

"Leave my daughter alone," Thistle growled.

"Then answer my question."

I strained against my invisible bonds, but couldn't move anything except my head. Ash was still beside me. He must have surged forward at the same time as me, driven into action by Willow's scream. The tendons in his neck stood out from exertion, and his fingers twitched, but that was all he could do. We were caught like two flies in amber, straining for freedom but unable to move.

Thistle shook his hair from his face and glared at Fallon, his green eyes full of a poisonous hatred. "Feronique is an admirable wife."

Admirable? That was the best he could do? I knew theirs was no love match, but still. *Admirable* was pretty cold.

"Admirable," my father repeated. "Not beloved? Adored?"

Well, would you look at that—miracles could happen. For once, my father and I agreed on something.

"Not your soulmate," he continued, "who brings joy to every moment you spend together?"

Thistle's glare only deepened. "I love my wife."

"But she's not the centre of your universe, is she? Not the sun around which your whole world revolves?" He gripped the hair at the back of her head and shook Feronique hard to emphasise each point. "You call it love, but perhaps you only love her because she gave you the heir you so desperately craved." He glanced at Willow, whose glare rivalled her father's. "Perhaps you only love how easy she makes your life. The fine hostess she is for your parties." He shook Feronique's head once more for emphasis. "You enjoy the alliances that your proper fae wife brought with her, perhaps more than you enjoy her company. It's all right. You can tell me." He glanced down at Feronique, twisting her head so she was forced to look up at him. "Wouldn't you say I'm right, my dear?"

"What's your point, Fallon?" Thistle demanded before his wife could answer.

"Or would you rather tell it to the king when he gets here?" Willow said pointedly.

Fallon ignored her; he didn't so much as glance in her direction. He was focused on Thistle. "My point, Thistle, is that you don't know what real love is—you with your fae wife, so perfectly acceptable in every way. What a cold-hearted way to spend your life. I almost feel sorry for you." His hand drifted to the hilt of Ni'ishasana and Umarenthe glided down from the dais, her shadowy form sliding right through Lord Thistle. "You never knew what real love could be, but I did. I did, Thistle, until you took it away from me."

I sucked in a sharp breath. Finally, I knew what this was about.

"I took nothing from you except the daughter you didn't want," Thistle said.

For a moment, all eyes were on me.

"She's turned out quite pretty, hasn't she?" Fallon's fingers stroked the ruby on the dagger's hilt as he contemplated me. Behind him, more of the shadowy figures were gathering, like crows to a battlefield. "She has her mother's eyes and something of her smile, but she isn't the beauty that Anita was." He laughed; a small, deprecating sound. "But of course you don't remember what Anita looked like, do you? She was nothing to you. You killed her with your pride and disdain."

"I never touched your human," Thistle protested, his eyes darting to Feronique. His Lady was beginning to tremble, coming to the same realisation that I had. Fallon meant to kill her.

"You didn't *need* to touch her," Fallon said, smiling. "In fact, I'm sure you would never have wanted to sully your hands by doing so. Even now, you call her *my human*. But she was my *wife*, and I loved her. She was my sun, my springtime, and my joy. If we had been living here with you—if I had still been in my rightful place at your side—she wouldn't have died. But you couldn't stand to have her here. You said it upset your digestion to look upon her human face. Do you remember that, Thistle? You said her footsteps tainted the land she walked on. You said I had disgraced Spring and disgraced you. Is any of this ringing a bell?" His hand tightened around the hilt of Ni'ishasana, and he drew the blade from his belt.

"I remember what I said. You said some vile things to

me, too, but perhaps you have forgotten those." Thistle's gaze had snagged on Ni'ishasana's undulating blade, which gleamed blue in the sickly light of the candles. Umarenthe had drifted to Feronique's side. She wasn't looking at the dagger; she had eyes for nothing but the trembling Lady of Spring.

"Fallon, stop," I said. "Do you think this is what Mama would have wanted?"

"Your wife's death was a tragedy." Thistle was careful now to call her a wife. "But childbirth is dangerous for humans. She might have died even with the best care my House could offer."

"She might," Fallon agreed. He tilted the dagger this way and that, as if admiring the play of light on its shining twisted blade. "But perhaps you put too little stock in the skills of your healers. Unfortunately, we will never know, because you took the choice away from us. You, who have never had anything taken from you in your long and golden life."

"Papa," I said desperately. Anything to get his attention, to divert him from this monstrous course. Beside me, Ash strained against the magic that held him fast. "If Mama were here, she would be the first person to tell you this is wrong. You can't cure your own pain by inflicting it on someone else."

Fallon sighed. "You see, that's my point. Anita is *not* here. And it is long past time that Thistle should pay for our loss. You should find this interesting, actually. It will be a fascinating use of necromancy. I doubt that any such thing has ever been done." He dragged Feronique's head back, exposing her long white throat.

Chains clinked as Thistle somehow found the strength to struggle against his bonds. Willow's eyes were wide with fear, but she was obviously bound by magic as tightly as we were. Only the almost imperceptible trembling of her body spoke of her struggle to be free, to move. To save her mother.

Umarenthe knelt, facing the terrified Lady of Spring. She was so close her shadowy form was touching Feronique's shaking body. Fallon brought the dagger to Feronique's throat, passing it right through Umarenthe's body, which merely rippled and reformed behind the blade.

"Are you ready?" he asked the shadow woman and she nodded. Only I saw the gleeful anticipation on her face as she pressed closer. It must have looked to everyone else as though Fallon addressed the empty air. "The timing is important," he said to me. "Of course, my colleagues have every incentive to get it right."

"Please," I begged him, straining uselessly against the invisible bonds that held me. "Don't do this. I'll give you back the power I took. Just stop this."

He shot a cool glance my way. "I'll deal with you later."

Feronique swallowed convulsively against the dagger's edge and a thin line of red appeared on her pale skin as it tasted her blood. Her eyes were wide and flooded with terror.

"Mama," Willow said, her voice high and frightened like a child's.

Then Fallon slashed the blade across Feronique's throat. Willow screamed. I closed my eyes against the horror. When I opened them, Feronique was sprawled on the ground, her life blood glistening darkly as it coated the grass. Willow was still screaming—a wild, inchoate sound of rage and loss. Beside me, Ash jerked as he fought his bonds.

Did Fallon mean to make a servant of the Lady of Spring? The dagger could kill a person like any other blade, so that they died and their soul moved on to the afterlife, or it could choose to destroy their soul and keep their body as a slave. That would be a twisted revenge—to force Thistle to see his wife reanimated as an empty shell, still walking around as if alive, but dead in every way that mattered. A soulless puppet of the dagger.

The ruby on the hilt of the dagger suddenly flared so brightly it was if Fallon held a molten sun in his hand. The shadow of his bones was visible through his skin. That wasn't normal. What was happening? Something settled on Lady Feronique's body as the pumping blood slowed, something dark and insubstantial ...

And yet, vaguely human-shaped. In a heartstopping moment, I realised I couldn't see Umarenthe, though she'd been right there a moment before. The darkness sank into Lady Feronique's skin and disappeared.

The blood stopped flowing, but nothing else happened. Maybe Feronique was simply dead. That would be the kindest thing, at this point. I held my breath, hoping.

Willow's screams choked off into sobs that wrenched

her whole body. I only realised I was crying too when I tasted the salt of the tears tracking down my face.

"Willow was only a child when his wife died." Ash's voice shook with fury. "Why did she have to see this? What does he have against *her*?"

Lord Thistle glanced sideways at his daughter, and there was real fear in his gaze. A chill swept through me. Yes, she was next. That was why Fallon had wanted Willow here so badly. Not to force her to watch, but to take her, too. Thistle would care far more about the death of his heir than of his wife. Lady Feronique was only the first taste of what was to come.

But wait—something was happening to Feronique's body. A faint blue light streamed off it, the same colour as the blue flames of the souls that had attacked me in the Realm of Death.

At the same time, a red tide rolled in to take its place, a ruby glow seeping into the places that the blue light had departed, filling her with the same light that glowed around Fallon's hand. Dread settled heavily in the pit of my stomach. Where was Umarenthe? This was something to do with her, wasn't it? When the whole body glowed red, the light flared brightly, then went out.

Fallon lowered his hand. He paid no attention to Lord Thistle or Willow. My nerves tightened. In the moment of his revenge, shouldn't he be revelling in his enemy's pain? Instead, he watched Feronique eagerly, waiting for something. This was *not* good.

Even so, when she sat up, I gasped. The front of her dress was drenched with blood. Her hair clung in sticky strands to her bloody shoulders. But the wound was closing as I stared, and she held her hands out in front of her, turning them this way and that, as if seeing them for the first time.

She saw me watching her and smiled—a gloating smile of triumph. Lady save me, I knew that smile. I'd seen it on Umarenthe's shadowy face too many times. Fallon offered his hand and Umarenthe took it, clambering to her feet a little awkwardly, as if unused to the feeling of a body after so many years of being an insubstantial soul.

"Mama?" Willow whispered, a desperate hope in her tearstained face.

Thistle's expression was grim. "You mean to torture me by raising a revenant?"

"Not at all," Fallon said. He gazed at Umarenthe with a fond smile. "She is far more than a revenant. It's all in the timing, you see."

The timing? I stared at Umarenthe. It was uncanny—even though she wore Lady Feronique's body, it was clear that Feronique's soul was no longer the animating force. Something in the way she stood and moved, in the expressions she wore, made it clear that this was a very different person. Not a necromancer's revenant—and not the mindless husk of a servant of the dagger, either.

It's all in the timing. If Fallon could somehow use his necromantic powers to create a conduit from the dagger to a dying body ... and if a soul crossed from the dagger at exactly the right moment ... could that work?

It must. The evidence was right in front of me.

Adding Fallon's power to the dagger's changed everything. Suddenly, everything that had happened since I joined the Vipers as an unwilling apprentice made sense. A new, horrible sense.

I'd always wondered why the dagger, the most powerful magical artefact in the fae Realms, had chosen me. I'd realised recently it had only been interested in me as a way of getting to my father. And now I could see why it had been so interested in *him*.

Fallon had used his necromancy to give the trapped souls of Ni'ishasana the one piece they'd been missing—a way to cross from the dagger into a body at the moment of death.

A way to live again.

"She's not a revenant," I said. "She's really alive. He's stealing bodies for the souls of the dagger."

16

Umarenthe clapped—slow, mocking claps. "She's finally figured it out. Maybe she's not as stupid as I thought."

Fallon slanted a glance at me. "Stupid enough to come here. What do you think you're going to do against me and the might of Ni'ishasana, Sage? No one can stand against us."

"Ni'ishasana won't be anything but an ugly knife if you free all the souls inside it."

That had to be the end game. The other souls wouldn't stand for remaining trapped if Umarenthe had been freed. And if Fallon thought he'd be able to control them once they were free, he was even more stupid than he was accusing me of being.

He shrugged. "It's only a means to an end. Once I've achieved that end, I'll disappear again."

His gaze fell on Willow, and he smiled.

"Leave her alone," Lord Thistle said at once, unable to

197

hide his fear and desperation. "What do you want, Fallon? I can give you riches. Reinstate you at my right hand. Anything you want."

Fallon nodded to Mezzi, who dragged Willow to her feet. Thistle strained against his chains, panic in his eyes. That same panic surged within me, making my heart pound and my breath come in short gasps. This was my worst nightmare come true, the very fate I'd come to save Willow from. But now I was trapped, helpless to do anything to stop this horror. My only hope was to shatter the ruby in the dagger's hilt—but how was I to do that when Fallon's magic rooted me to the spot? The dagger was only a few steps away, still clenched in his fist, but it might as well have been on the moon. Those steps were an impossible barrier, and Willow's time was running out.

She could see that as well as I could, and struggled in Mezzi's grip, her face pale, green eyes wide with fear. But Fallon's magic held her, too. She could walk, but she couldn't unbind her hands or access her magic.

"I only want one thing from you, Thistle," Fallon said. "And I'm about to take it."

Mezzi forced Willow to her knees in front of his Serpent. Desperate, I looked around for another option. Something. Anything. If only there were some way to distract Fallon. Then we might have a chance to break free of his control. The ghosts, maybe? I called to them, reaching out with the deep strength inside me.

Surprisingly, they moved, flocking to my side. So Fallon's bonds didn't stop me from using necromancy. Perhaps necromancy was what powered them.

I directed the ghosts to attack him, remembering how Atinna's ghost had been able to inflict real damage with her magic. If he'd killed these with the dagger, that might have forged enough of a connection for them to use theirs. But they seemed afraid of Fallon and milled uncertainly in the space between us.

He glanced at me, raising a mocking eyebrow. "You won't scare me with ghosts, Sage. You're wasting your time."

If only I had more experience with necromancy. I didn't know what to do. He was right; there was nothing I could do with this stolen power that might catch such an experienced necromancer off guard.

Umarenthe smiled mockingly at me before turning her attention to Willow. There was something truly chilling about seeing the former Lady Feronique's eyes gazing at her own child with that hungry glint. Willow avoided that gaze, staring defiantly up at Fallon through unruly red curls.

Though her face was tearstained, she still fought her bonds. She wasn't the type to give up. But she couldn't look at her mother. *Former* mother.

I knew the pain of losing your mother. How much worse must this be, to have a monster take your mother's form?

That unsettling look on my own mother's face, last time I'd seen her, had been bad enough. But that was different. Mama was a dead soul, attracted to my living vitality. It wasn't her fault that she craved my life force. It hadn't made her gloat as someone tried to kill me.

A sudden, desperate thought occurred to me as Pardiz, another of the dagger's souls, came to kneel opposite Willow. Mama had said Fallon used to call her, to speak with her, without dropping her into the body of a revenant. I had no real idea how it was done, but need made me desperate.

I opened a gate to the Realm of Death and cried out to my mother with all the terror and desperation of my soul.

Mama stepped through the gate, and I slammed it shut behind her, cutting off its siren call. Fallon's head whipped around. Her form shimmered, surrounded by that strange bluish glow of the afterlife, as she drifted across the grass towards him.

"Anita!"

I strained against my bonds, feeling them burst like bubbles on my skin, and then I was free. So was Ash.

More importantly, so was Willow, who surged to her feet as Fallon turned away from her, his attention wholly captured by the spirit form of my mother.

"Enough, Fallon," Mama said in a firm tone that I remembered from my childhood. "No more death. No more vengeance."

Fallon took a step towards her. Willow lashed out with her bound hands, striking a startled Mezzi across the face with the dangling ends of her chains. He fell back as Ash leapt forward, blasting him with icy Winter magic.

A moment later, Mezzi was caught in a block of ice. Umarenthe was trapped from the knees down in a smaller one. Ash snatched a knife from Mezzi's belt and flicked it at Fallon's back, but it stopped short and fell harmlessly to the grass, repelled by some protective magic that surrounded him.

Umarenthe raised her hands, but her magic was slow to respond. Being encased in flesh again after so long probably took a little getting used to. Willow wielded her chains against her, too, catching her across the face and sending her crashing to the grass, feet still encased in ice.

More knives zipped through the air as the gathered Vipers responded to the threat to their Serpent. I willed the ghosts of Spring on, sending a bit of my life force to them. Abruptly, they became apparent to everyone and swarmed the Vipers. Though they had no weapons, their chilly hands were distraction enough to buy us precious time.

Fallon shouted, but Mama surged forward and caught his face between her spectral hands, and he turned back to her, helpless as a moth before the pull of the moon.

"Open a gate!" I yelled at Willow. The wards protecting the estate wouldn't allow anyone but a member of the ruling family to open a gate within their boundaries.

She held up her bound hands in mute response. Shit. No one could work magic encased in that much iron.

Ash, seeing the problem, directed such a focused beam of Winter magic against her chains that they snapped, and Willow hurriedly freed herself.

A gate materialised to one side of the pavilion, between two saplings that bent towards each other like dancers making a graceful bow. The mist of the threshold magic billowed forth, making the strange scene even more unearthly. Willow turned as if to run to her father, but Ash grabbed her and bundled her through the gate.

"Sage, come on!" Ash called.

I hesitated, my eyes drawn to the dagger in Fallon's hand. All I had to do was break that ruby. I launched myself toward it, but Umarenthe screamed a warning.

With a casual flick of his hand, Fallon sent a great wave of power at me. I crashed to the ground, all the breath knocked out of me. Ash darted forward and hoisted me into his arms. He leapt through the gate, and it slammed shut behind us.

Two Vipers made it through on our heels. One, a short, compact man, lashed us with a bolt of searing heat and Ash only just got an ice shield up in time. Winded and still dazed from my father's attack, I groped wildly for my magic as Ash dumped me on my feet.

Before I could pull myself together, Ash returned fire with spears of icy Winter magic. I felt a huge surge in Spring magic, then the sun was momentarily blotted out as a tree bent over the narrow path and plucked the other Viper from her feet before she could attack. Her scream was abruptly cut off. Once off the path, a person was lost forever.

Willow stood there, arms outflung and a vicious look on her face. Ash diverted another blast of Summer heat from the remaining Viper, and I flinched.

Willow joined him and the forest around us came alive at her urging. My own Spring power flared in response, but sluggishly. It felt as though the power of the Wild resisted my call. Here, there was a darkness at the heart of the forest's green life, and a surly resistance to any form of magic other than Earth. I probably would have had an easier time overcoming it if I hadn't just been pounded into the ground by my father's magic.

At least he'd stopped short of actually killing me, but my head was still spinning and every muscle was begging for mercy. I stood there, swaying like a drunk, as Willow brute-forced the trees into submission, and branches lashed the remaining Viper from the path. His despairing cry was swallowed up as the forest closed in. I shuddered.

Willow stood for a moment, breathing hard from effort. Then she pinned Ash with a ferocious glare. "Why didn't you bring my father? He was *right there*. We could have saved him!"

"There was no time." Ash returned her glare with a cool look. "Do you think Fallon would have stood by while we hauled your father up and dragged him with us? We barely got out ourselves."

"Then I'm going back for him," she said.

"Don't be stupid," I said. "You can't go back. The three of us alone are no match for Fallon."

That had just been demonstrated to us in the most compelling way. But she stared at me, her chest heaving, her eyes bright with unshed tears. "I can't just *leave* him there."

"Of course you can," I snapped. "He'll be fine."

"But he's in *chains*," she protested.

"So?" Usually she was way smarter than this, but her fear was blinding her to the truth. "Don't you get it? Fallon was about to kill you—to hurt your father. That's his big goal, to take away every single thing that Thistle loves—his wife, his daughter, his people, his Realm—*and make Thistle watch him do it*. That's what it's going to take to satisfy his thirst for revenge. As long as Fallon doesn't have *you*, your father is perfectly safe. He won't kill him before he gets to make him suffer watching *you* die. So the best thing you can do for your father right now is *stay away from Spring*."

"But the deadline—"

"The deadline was always false," Ash said. "It was only a means to get you to come to him."

"And it worked, didn't it?" I said. "You went there, without a plan, without any backup, because you were so afraid of what would happen if you left it to the king. If we hadn't got there when we did, you'd be dead now, and so would your father and everyone else he cared about."

And thank the Lady and her blessed silver tree that we'd been in time. If we'd waited for the king or wasted time trying to get help from Allegra it would have been a very different story, one that made me feel ill even to think about.

I let her digest that for a long moment. After myself, she was the stubbornest person I knew. I had to be certain she understood.

"We should get moving," Ash said.

The little bit of path we stood on barely extended a foot on either side of us. Willow had opened the gate, but she hadn't yet formed an intention for where the path should lead us.

I nodded. It was dangerous to stand idle on a Greenway. The Wilds might decide to pick a direction for you.

"Fine." Willow sighed, seeming to deflate. "Let's go to Whitehaven and join up with the king."

Ash didn't object or even move, but his very stillness told me he didn't want to return to Whitehaven. I had no particular desire to go there either, after what the king had put him through.

"We'll catch up with you. I need a couple of hours' sleep before I fall down."

"Sleep at Whitehaven." she said. "It could be hours yet before the king is ready to move."

I glanced at Ash's stony face. "I think we'll be more comfortable at the sith."

Clearly, as things stood, human trickery alone couldn't get me close enough to the dagger to destroy it. I'd tried that and failed. My father was just too powerful. Fae magic could probably do it, in great enough force—but how many of the king's people would have to die to stop Fallon?

There had to be another way. A way that combined human trickery and fae magic without costing dozens, or even hundreds, of lives. Using my mother to distract Fallon wouldn't work again. I needed something else.

But I had to figure it out without telling Willow what I was up to, or she'd find a way to get involved. Right now, all of us—including Thistle and the survivors in Spring— were safer if she stayed safely under the king's protection at Whitehaven.

"The sith isn't safe," Ash reminded me. "Your father can breech its wards."

Damn. I'd done what I could to hide Nevith's soul from Fallon, but there was no denying that my father was a much better necromancer than I was, and I couldn't be sure I'd been successful. But I'd feel more comfortable risking my neck again in familiar surroundings.

"Then we'll go to The Drunken Irishman," I said. "Randall has rooms upstairs there."

There wasn't really any other place I'd feel safe enough to do what needed to be done.

17

———

If Randall was surprised to see us at three o'clock in the afternoon, he didn't show it. He took one look at my drooping state and the hard look in Ash's eyes and held his hands up. "If you're in trouble, I don't want to know. This is neutral ground."

"I just need a place to sleep for a couple of hours," I said, trying to look reassuring.

"And there's something wrong with that palatial home of yours?"

"The sith's off limits for the moment. Long story," I added when his eyebrows rose.

"Fine, fine," he grumbled, heading into the office behind the bar. He came back with a key, which looked tiny in his enormous hand. Randall was part troll, and he towered over most people. "Room 204. Don't make a mess or you'll be scrubbing it clean with a toothbrush."

"Thanks." I hugged him, ignoring the threat, which I knew was empty. Despite his alarming appearance,

Randall was a marshmallow. It was a little like hugging a boulder.

His massive arms came around me and he patted me awkwardly on the shoulder. "Everything all right?"

"You don't want to know," I reminded him.

He sighed and gave me a gentle nudge towards the stairs. "Go on, before I change my mind."

Room 204 wasn't anything fancy, though it did have its own tiny en suite, unlike most of the rooms here. I threw myself face down on the bed, my eyelids falling shut of their own accord. The cheap cotton quilt felt like purest swansdown beneath my cheek.

"I'll stand guard while you sleep," Ash said from the doorway.

I wriggled round so I could see him, standing tall and powerful in the opening. He was a long, cool drink of water, and I was a woman dying of thirst. I could think of nothing I'd rather do right now than lose myself in the depths of those clear grey eyes. Feel his hands moving on my body.

I sighed and patted the bed beside me. I didn't have time to indulge my daydreams, but he'd been awake for hours. A cuddle and some sleep couldn't hurt. "Why don't you join me?"

Something flickered in his eyes, but he shook his head firmly. "I think not."

Then he shut the door on me, leaving me alone and confused. Okay, then. A little niggle of hurt twinged. Maybe I wasn't looking my best, having just survived a fight with my father. I sniffed cautiously at my underarm. Didn't smell the best, either.

Sure, this wasn't the most romantic setting, but I'd seen more expression on the faces of dummies in store windows. It was as if he was holding himself apart. In fact, he'd seemed a bit off for a while. Had he changed his mind about us?

It was surprising how much that thought hurt.

I rolled over with a groan and buried my face in the quilt. I was too tired to think about it now. Maybe I was imagining things. Ash had always had a good poker face. He was probably just concerned about the situation with my father. I was imagining rejection where there was none.

Yeah, and my father would hand over the dagger without a struggle.

My eyes were closed, but I could feel the room spinning around me. I couldn't remember the last time I'd been this tired. It was probably just as well that Ash was being all alert and distant in the hallway. Fallon could march his whole zombie army in here and I doubted I could muster up the energy to do anything about it.

The size of that army, combined with the power of Ni'ishasana and the might of the Vipers, would pose a serious threat to the king's forces. Rothbold wouldn't risk moving against such a threat before he was ready, even with Willow lighting a fire under his arse, but he'd have to move soon. There was too much at stake.

The king only ruled the Realms by agreement of its Lords. They swore fealty to him in return for his protection, among other things. He'd already failed spectacularly to protect Illusion when Summer had invaded it. That hadn't been his fault, since he'd already been incapacitated beforehand, but still, with a strike like that against him, he couldn't afford to let down another Lord. His fate was tied to Spring's fortunes now. If he let Fallon keep it, his days on the throne of the Realms were numbered.

It would be a tight contest—the king's powers against Fallon's. But every soul that Fallon released from the dagger was a point in Rothbold's favour. As individual mages in bodies that could be killed, the dagger's souls were less of a threat than as part of Ni'ishasana, where they lent their power directly to Fallon, making him virtually invincible.

It made me doubt that Fallon intended to release them all, or even most of them, whatever deal he'd made. Having stirred the hornet's nest, he couldn't afford to weaken himself. Perhaps the deal had only been to free the most dominant souls, like Umarenthe, Pardiz, and Celebrach.

Whatever. It would be a tough battle, with major casualties, if it went ahead. But maybe I could remove the need for battle altogether. I owed it to all those people who would otherwise die to at least *try*.

My last visit to the Realm of Death hadn't gone too well, but I had to try again. I needed to find someone in that shadowy Realm who could teach me more about necromancy than my mother. I didn't want to risk my body again, but Mama had mentioned another option, had even hinted it was easier.

I hadn't told Ash what I intended, because I had no

strength left for another argument. I pulled the locket containing his hair out of my shirt. It was warm from resting against my chest, and clasping it made me feel more secure, buoyed by a little of his strength. I sank back into the soft mattress and closed my eyes.

My thoughts began to drift, giving way to strange imaginings. Dream images whirled through my tired brain: my father morphing into a bird which flew away at the approach of the king's army, which was now inexplicably made up of dolphins carrying streamers of red and gold in their mouths. The dolphins swam through the air as if it were water, strong tails driving them forward. They brushed past me, flowing around me as if I were a rock in a stream, and their skin was surprisingly smooth.

I began to float, drifting up into a grey sky. My body remained below, but it was also above, and the two parts of me were connected by a thin golden string. The winds caught my floating body like a kite, and I moved faster through the sky.

Below me, the land whipped past as I picked up speed. Fields and forests rolled by, faster and faster. The king's army had been left far behind. Then the forests were gone, too, replaced in the blink of an eye by a rocky landscape.

The colour leached from the world. Only grey rocks remained, though little blue sparks flitted in front of my face like inquisitive fireflies. I passed over a mountain range whose jagged peaks speared into the sky, but I didn't stop, rushing on ever faster, a great hunger growing in me. Somewhere up ahead was the answer to all my problems. I just knew it.

Strangely enough, considering the speed I was going, no wind battered me. My flight was silent and smooth, as if I merely hung in place in the sky while the whole world turned beneath me. An ocean appeared on the horizon, growing rapidly larger as I approached. The hunger only increased at the sight of it. *Yes.* This was where I needed to be, where I wanted to stay forever. If I could cross that ocean, all my cares would disappear.

The blue fireflies crowded closer, and I shooed them away impatiently. I started to slow, and realised I was looking down at a gently wooded landscape, softly lit as if it were twilight, though the light had no source. *No.* I couldn't stop here. I struggled, flapping my arms, straining towards that watery horizon.

There were people down there, gazing up at me. I was going slowly enough now that I could make out their faces —even the expressions on their faces. Lady Feronique gazed up at me wistfully. Maybe she wished she could fly, too. A Viper I recognised was beside her.

The wind caught me, and I soared on, leaving them behind. More Vipers appeared as the ocean loomed larger and larger ahead, but I paid them little attention. My heart was fixed on the ocean and the bliss I knew awaited me there.

A handful of people I knew from Lord Thistle's estate waved up at me, distracting me from my goal. When I recognised my old friend the stable master among them, my heart gave a little jolt, and it was as if I woke up, though nothing changed in the landscape.

Except now I knew I'd done it. I'd dreamwalked my

way to the Realm of Death. I was looking down at the dead, soaring through their Realm, unhindered by a body. That ocean was the place my mother had warned me against, and the blue fireflies were souls that had withered. But even knowing that, my yearning to cross the ocean didn't fade.

I held my hands out in front of me. They, too, shone softly blue, and I drew in a ragged breath. Had I messed it up somehow? Was I actually dead? Somersaulting in the air, I looked back the way I'd come. Behind me a thin golden thread stretched as far as the eye could see, until its bright light was lost in the grey sky.

No, I wasn't dead—only asleep. *Don't panic.* I'd fallen asleep on the soft bed in room 204. Ash was standing guard outside. Back there, my body still lay on that bed, but my spirit self, connected to it by that *alarmingly* thin thread, had travelled beyond the borders of the living world.

When my mother had said this was something necromancers could do, I'd assumed it would be a lot harder to manage than this. I'd meant to meditate and try to get in touch with my necromantic power before I made the attempt, but I'd been so tired I'd simply fallen asleep before I could.

There'd been none of the agony of physically crossing Death's threshold, either. But the terrifying longing to stay forever was just as strong. Maybe the hard part was getting back. If I'd had a spine, a cold shiver would have gone down it for sure at that thought.

I tried to stop flying. There had to be someone closer to

the gate, back where it was safer, that I could ask. But it was as if I were caught in an invisible current. Like a rip that dragged the unwary swimmer out to sea, it refused to release its grip on my soul. When I tried to grab hold of the golden thread and haul myself back to my body, hand over hand, my fingers passed right through it. Though it looked solid enough, it had no physical presence here.

Awesome. I was on a one-way ride through the Realm of Death.

Before I could descend into full-blown panic, everything abruptly changed, and I found myself in a small sailing boat in the middle of the ocean. There was no sign of the rocky landscape, the forests, or even the mountains. Nothing but white-capped waves as far as the eye could see. The thin golden thread back to my body stretched off into the distance.

I tried to lift into the sky again, but I remained earthbound—or waterbound, I guess. I glanced nervously up at the sail above me. It wasn't a very big boat. It had a tiny cabin that looked barely big enough to lie down inside. At the rear of that—or should I say *aft* on a boat?—was a small open space with two short bench seats facing each other. I sat at the stern, my hand inexplicably on the tiller that steered the little boat as it skimmed across the grey sea.

Hurriedly, I removed my hand. I had no business being in charge of a boat—I had no idea how to sail, and only knew the handle thing was called a tiller because of some movie I'd watched. And this boat was nowhere *near* big enough to be this far from land.

A more experienced necromancer probably would have been able to stop the dreamscape changing so randomly—yet another sign that I needed a little guidance on this whole necromancer gig. I was uneasily aware that I was now sitting on the very ocean Mama had warned me against. She'd said that was where the old souls lived, and they were hungry for life. And now that I was here, the mindless hunger for the ocean had completely disappeared, as if the Realm of Death had me exactly where it wanted me. Not a happy thought.

The little boat continued to sail itself, arrowing straight through the waves, their salt smell fresh in my nose. Where the hell was it taking me? And should I be hoping to arrive—or fearing it?

Before I could decide, something large surfaced, then rolled back under the water. Way too large, and way too close. My fear spiked and I eyed the water with growing unease. It was impossible to see what was under there, but my imagination was only too happy to provide some horrifying possibilities.

It could have been a whale. All I'd got was a brief glimpse of barnacled skin. It had only appeared for a moment, and not enough of it had broken the surface to be able to tell. Not that I was big on marine biology—particularly the kind likely to be found in the fae afterlife. Chances were good that it would involve teeth or tentacles.

"Let's just go with *whale*," I muttered, checking my golden connecting thread. It still stretched off behind me. Was there a limit to how far I could go? What happened if I passed that limit?

Something bumped the boat and I yelped. A little blue soul drifted closer, landing on the roof of the small cabin. Only then did it occur to me that I hadn't seen one for a while. Perhaps the powerful old souls chased these lesser ones away. Out here, there was only me and the ocean—and whatever had just nudged the boat. I scanned the water around me, fear building inside me.

"Now would be a good time for another change of scenery," I suggested hopefully, but whatever magic controlled this strange dream travel ignored me.

The boat picked up speed, the wind filling the sail above my head. Water slapped at the hull and sprayed in my face. Or was that something else slapping the hull? I eyed the grey depths with deep suspicion.

The boat jerked again, and I took a death grip on the seat. Why did it have to be water? I had nothing against it generally, but I liked my water to come properly contained. Streams were nice. Ponds, too. I could even go for a smallish lake.

But I'd never realised before how isolating such a large body of water felt. My Spring senses reached in vain for the green, growing energy of plants. Until this moment I hadn't noticed how the hum of that natural magic formed a soundtrack to my whole life. Even in the urbanised human world, there were still trees and gardens and other patches of greenery all around. Never before had I been so disconnected from nature's energy.

Never had I been so cut off from the source of my magic.

The sound of water bubbling brought my head around

so fast I nearly gave myself whiplash. A vast creature reared up from the water, its massive body dwarfing the boat. Somewhere way above the sail was a mouth full of jagged teeth. A suckered tentacle curled out of the water and looped lazily around the boat. The mast creaked warningly as the sail collapsed, then it shattered into kindling. I threw up an arm to shield my face from splinters of wood the length of short spears. Salt water drenched me as they splashed into the water.

The finned head dipped lower, mouth opening.

"Where are you going, little fish?" Its voice was the deep rumble of thunder, of waves crashing on the shore.

One enormous eye examined me. It was faceted like a black jewel, with a tiny red glow in its inky depths. It was also twice my size. I backed up until the tiller pressed into my back and there was nowhere else to go, dwarfed by the enormity of the creature.

"What's it to you?" I asked, my voice a little squeakier than normal. The creature's dripping skin was covered in barnacles, and even a few fish, attached to it like suckers. It glowed almost as bright a blue as the firefly souls, and lit up the dark water in a wide circle around us. When Mama had said *old soul*, I'd pictured something a little more human-like, but the power emanating from this creature was so strong I could taste it, like metal on my tongue. Like blood. This nightmare vision had to be as old as they came—I couldn't bear to imagine anything *more* powerful.

I clung on for dear life as it hoisted the bow of the boat out of the water, the tip of its great tentacle curling and uncurling. The wood beneath my fingers was wet and slippery, my hands numb with cold.

"I can smell the life within you," the monster boomed, its voice vibrating through the wood. "You are caught in my net. I will taste you."

I shrank back. "Find another snack!" I yelled.

Then I blinked, and I was hanging in an actual net from the branch of an enormous tree. The ocean was gone. The creature was gone—*thank the Lady*. A vast grey forest surrounded me. Apart from the fact that I was suspended in a net far above the ground, my life didn't appear to be in imminent danger. Things were looking up.

The ropes of the net cut into my spirit self, compressing me into an awkward ball. I wriggled around and was groping for a knife inside my shirt when I felt a sharp sting in my calf. I jerked and twisted, setting the net to spinning, and found a glowing blue bird hovering like a hummingbird. Not much bigger than a hummingbird, either. Its beak was long and thin, ending in a wicked point. And it turned out there were no weapons inside my shirt or anywhere else.

For a moment, the bird and I stared at each other while its wings beat faster than thought, holding it in place, then its head darted forward and it stabbed me with that vicious beak again.

"Get lost!" I tried to kick it. Not very successfully, considering the net and the spinning. The sky rotated dizzyingly, and when I next spun back around to face the bird, it had a friend. Great.

Both of them stabbed at my legs. The pain was sharp

and somehow hot and cold at the same time, like the burn of ice on the skin. But there was no blood. Instead, a warm golden glow leaked from the wounds.

I wriggled an arm through the holes in the net and tried to knock the little bastards from the sky. But they managed to avoid my clumsy swings, darting around my cramped hanging body, stabbing at me with their nasty little beaks.

New wounds opened up every moment and soon the golden light was leaking from everywhere. More birds joined the first two, until a whole flock of the stabby little horrors surrounded me. I flailed and cursed. Unsurprisingly, they took no notice.

I reached for the tree's life, to use its branches as weapons against the birds. But there was no answering surge, no green life to do my bidding. In the shock of the birds' attack, I hadn't noticed, but the woods in which I hung were as empty of the growing energy my Spring magic called on as the empty reaches of the ocean had been.

What had I expected? This was the Realm of Death.

But tears still leaked from my eyes as the birds stepped up their attack. Everything felt hopeless. I should just give up. My feeble efforts at fighting back were getting nowhere, and I was tired. So tired. The golden light leaked away from me, and I watched it go, almost numb, as if the pain was happening to someone else.

Even the golden light was giving up, its bright glow dimming. In one of the net's revolutions, I caught sight of the thin golden thread that connected me to my sleeping body back in the mortal world. It, too, was dimming, its glow fading into the grey sky.

Somewhere under the exhaustion, I was aware that going to sleep would be a bad idea, that I mustn't give in to the lethargy. I tried to stand up inside the swinging net, struggling to reach the branch where it was tied. My foot slipped through a hole, jerking me facedown against the rough rope of the net. Willow's golden locket swung free of my shirt.

I squinted at its bright glow. That was right, it held a lock of Ash's hair—a priceless gift of love and trust. Its light bathed my face as the memory of his strength filled me with a new strength of my own. I wanted to go back. I wanted to feel his arms around me again.

The net tore apart, and the birds scattered in surprise. I lifted into the air, light as a feather, and surged up past the branches of the tree into the open sky. The golden thread leading to my body beckoned me on, and I followed its pale light, the locket clutched tight in my hand.

Faster and faster I rushed through the sky, leaving the birds reeling away from the wind of my passage. The light of the golden thread grew brighter, pulsing in time with my heartbeat.

Far behind me, the deep voice of the old soul wailed in anguish.

18

"**S**age. Wake up."

Ash's hand on my shoulder shook me back to wakefulness. The lights in the room were low and it took me a minute to remember where I was.

Dingy grey paint. Faint scent of old beer. Bed as blissfully soft as a cloud. Good old Room 204.

The bed took up most of the space, and I was sprawled across it diagonally. Ash perched on the very edge, so that the only part of his body touching mine was his hand.

I blinked. Once. Twice. Everything felt odd—the light was different, the softness of the bed beneath me felt for a moment as if it should have been the strands of a net cutting into my flesh. My clothes were completely dry, though my body remembered freezing salt water.

I held my hand in front of my face, inspecting it, but nothing glowed anymore. I was really back.

I sat up and threw my arms around Ash's neck. "You saved me!"

Again. The memory of his love had woken me from my lethargy and given me the strength to force my way out of the trap I'd been caught in. Its symbolic representation in the Realm of Death, the glowing locket around my neck, had brought me back to him.

Shuddering at the memory of the monster's great faceted eye, the red glow like hellfire in its depths, I pressed a grateful kiss against Ash's skin where the pulse beat in his neck. I was lucky to be here. That thing had been nothing but hunger. If it had consumed my soul, my body would never have woken.

"From what? You were asleep," Ash said. Of course—he had no way to know the danger I'd been in. "Were you dreaming?"

"I dreamed myself right into the Realm of Death."

He frowned and pushed me away, holding me at arm's length. "Was that wise?"

"It was necessary."

"I can't believe you risked yourself again. Without even telling me." He stood up and turned away abruptly.

I wanted to nestle back against him, but he definitely wasn't in a nestling mood. Seemed like he'd been stand-offish for a while now. I swung my feet to the floor, frowning at his muscled back. I'd thought we were beyond keeping this distance between us, now that Ni'ishasana no longer stood in the way. When he'd given me that lock of his hair, he might as well have been announcing his love for the world to hear, but now here we were, with him apparently unable to stand my touch.

What was going on behind those cool grey eyes? Was

he regretting throwing his lot in with mine? He'd made enemies of the entire Night Viper organisation for me—plus he'd gained himself a whole bunch of new enemies, too. It was clear Rothbold didn't trust him and only suffered his presence for my sake. Nor were any of the Lords likely to welcome a former assassin into their Realms. Everywhere he turned, he was faced with rejection.

And it wasn't as if his life had improved all that much now that he was with me. He'd swapped killing people on the Serpent's command to torturing them on the king's. Not much of a step up, really. Our lives had been nothing but drama and trouble since we'd escaped the Vipers.

"Ash," I said. My heart quailed at the thought that he might be regretting his choices—regretting *us*. But I had to know.

"It doesn't matter now. You're back, and we need to move." He opened the door a crack and listened a moment. His attention was firmly fixed on something outside the room. "Something's wrong downstairs."

"What do you mean, *something's wrong*?" I joined him at the door, laying a tentative hand on his muscled arm.

His eyes flicked down to my hand, then away. "There was a scream a moment ago. I couldn't go to investigate and leave you, asleep and defenceless."

"Maybe someone dropped a glass."

"It wasn't that kind of scream." He stepped out into the corridor. "Stay here. I'll go see."

He shut the door in my face, but I wasn't having that. If he was right—and he probably was; let's face it, he'd heard his share of screams in his day—and there was trouble downstairs, I wasn't letting him face it alone.

I slipped out of the room as quietly as I could. He was already gone, silent as a shadow. I padded down the carpeted hall to the top of the stairs and found him on the landing. He glared at me as I joined him.

"I told you to stay in the room." His voice was so low I barely heard him. His breath tickled my ear in such a delicious way I almost forgot what we were doing there.

Then I heard a voice I recognised downstairs, and my stomach clenched.

"It's Umarenthe."

I knew Lady Feronique's voice well, though I couldn't make out exactly what she was saying. What was she doing here? Had she followed us from Spring? That shouldn't have been possible.

Unless this was one more use of necromancy that I was unaware of.

He nodded, his face set in grim lines. "Go back to the room."

Okay, this protective thing was getting out of hand.

"I'm not made of glass," I hissed into his ear. "She's just an Air mage now. Between the two of us, we should be able to take her down, no problems."

"Just an Air mage," he repeated. "And you're a Spring. Do you see any plants in here?"

I rolled my eyes, but he wasn't looking at me anyway. "We can do more than just work with plants."

He was at the bottom of the stairs already. Fine. *Ignore me, why don't you?* I followed him down.

A scene of carnage greeted me. Blood splashed across the top of the bar and dripped down its side. A body lay on the floor. From this angle, I couldn't see who it was, just a pair of legs encased in black pants sticking out beyond the end of the bar.

Probably staff, then. Black pants were part of the uniform. I had no idea who'd been on—we'd only seen Randall when we arrived, and the legs were way too slim to be his.

It was four in the afternoon, too late for the lunchtime crowd, and too early for those stopping in for a drink after work. Beyond the legs, two patrons sat frozen at a table, their faces pale, eyes fixed on whatever was happening just around the corner from us. Otherwise, the place seemed deserted.

Once we left the staircase, we would be able to see Umarenthe, and she would be able to see us. I pulled a knife from my boot. At least here my weapons hadn't disappeared.

"Unless you want another death on your conscience," Umarenthe was saying in a bored voice, "you'd better call her."

"I don't have her number," Randall protested. He was still alive, then. "And even if I did, she's probably in the Realms. Phones don't work there."

Call her? Was Randall protecting *me*?

"You have ten seconds to miraculously find this number you claim not to have before someone else dies. Who will it be this time? Your chef? Or one of these fine customers?"

The two guys at the table hadn't noticed us. Their horrified attention was riveted on the scene in front of them.

Ash caught my eye and held up three fingers. He appeared to have accepted the fact that I wasn't returning meekly to the room. Good call. He put one finger down. *Two*. Then another. *One*.

When the last one folded down, we leapt out into the room. In a split second, I had my bearings. Umarenthe was at the bar, seated on one of the bar stools as if she'd dropped in for a pint. Randall, his face like stone, stood behind the bar opposite her, though he wasn't serving drinks. I let my knife fly, but Ash was ahead of me. A hail of ice spears was already in flight.

Umarenthe raised a casual hand and flicked them aside with a well-timed blast of Air. They sped straight for the two men at the table, who hurled themselves to the floor, chairs toppling with a crash, to avoid being pierced. The knife clattered against the table and thudded to the carpet.

Ash charged forward, and Umarenthe surged up from the stool. Not to meet him, but to grab Randall by his shirt and drag him across the bar.

"Stay right where you are, or this man dies."

Ash froze. Randall did, too, sprawled awkwardly across the bar, conscious of the knife at his throat. His face was turned towards us, his expression unreadable. Umarenthe must have used Air magic to lift him. There was no way a woman of her size could have budged a giant like Randall without it.

I joined Ash, hands held up to show I was unarmed. Umarenthe smiled pleasantly at me, as if her knife wasn't poised to slit Randall's throat, as if she hadn't already killed someone in a particularly bloody fashion. The body on the floor was a guy about my own age, his blond hair pulled back in a short ponytail, the end of which was soaked in his own blood.

"Just the person I need," she said.

"You can let him go," I said. "I'm here now."

"Oh, it's not you I want, but I'm sure you'll prove useful." The hand holding the knife twitched and blood flowed in a thin line down Randall's thick neck. The big man didn't react at all, lying completely still. "Assuming you care what happens to our troll friend here."

"What do you want?"

I couldn't see any options here, not with that knife at Randall's throat. We couldn't attack faster than she could use it.

As if to prove the point, she wiggled the knife again, opening a wider slice in Randall's skin. Blood flowed more freely, soaking through the collar of his shirt, and smearing the polished gleam of the bar.

"Unless you get Willow here, alone, within the next five minutes, the troll dies."

mpossible. No one could get here that fast, even with magic.

"Do you think I've got her stashed out the back in the carpark? Or have you been so long without a body that you've forgotten how long things take in the real world?"

She pressed the knife a little harder against Randall's skin, and I did my best not to flinch at the fresh trickle of blood.

"If I were you, I wouldn't be throwing insults around. I suggest a little less lip and a lot more action. Unless, of course, you don't actually care what happens to him."

I pulled out my phone, avoiding Randall's stony gaze. "I can try ringing her, but I think she's in the Realms."

I knew perfectly well she was. By now, she should be at Whitehaven. Probably throwing her weight around and demanding the king mount an immediate rescue of her father. But I made a show of finding her number in my contacts and listening to the ringing.

"Put it on speaker," Umarenthe demanded, and I did.

All the while, my mind raced, considering possibilities and discarding them almost as quickly. If I could just get that damn knife out of the picture, things would be very different. Ash and I between us could defeat a single Air mage—and that's all she was now, without the full might of the dagger at her disposal. Had she considered that in her quest for a body? After so many centuries of limitless power, she might find the limitations of a body less appealing than she'd expected.

The call eventually went to Willow's message service.

"Shall I send her a text?"

"I find your flippancy disturbing. Perhaps you need a demonstration of the seriousness of the situation."

"And perhaps you need to give me a chance to actually get hold of Willow, if you really want her," I said hastily, before she could get too invested in the idea of demonstrating anything. I knew how that would go for Randall. "What do you want her for, anyway? You don't have to do my father's bidding now. You're a free woman."

"For the moment, our goals align."

"And what would those goals be?" I doubted she'd tell me, but I wanted to keep the conversation going. I thought I knew how to beat her, but I wanted her more relaxed. My plan would have a better chance of working if she believed I'd given up on the idea of fighting her.

"Fallon wants to take Willow's body for Pardiz." She shrugged. "You know how obsessed he is with revenging himself on Thistle."

Umarenthe might be wearing Lady Feronique's body,

but no one would have believed they were the same woman, at least not for more than a minute. Umarenthe moved differently, without the stick-up-the-arse rigidity that Lady Feronique had. Her speech was different, too, delivered with more animation. Even the expressions on her face were livelier. Perhaps it was Umarenthe's excitement at finding herself in a body after all those centuries trapped inside the dagger.

Even so, it was strange to hear someone who looked like Willow's mother speaking so calmly about killing her.

"Does he mean to empty the dagger completely?" Ash asked.

I wasn't sure how many souls it contained, but I knew it was a lot. "Is he going to kill *everyone* in Spring? How will he rule if there are no more subjects?"

"Subjects?" Umarenthe laughed. "Fallon doesn't care about ruling Spring. Only about hurting Thistle's family."

"So you and one other soul are the only ones to leave the dagger," Ash said.

She looked at him, and I wondered if he'd realised my strategy, and was doing his bit to distract her.

"I didn't say that, did I? I suppose he'll just kill most of them. After all, who wants the body of a stable hand or a kitchen maid? Not when there are so many available at the peak of physical perfection with the deadliest of skills."

It took me a minute, but then it clicked. She was talking about the Vipers. Fallon was going to put the dagger's souls into Viper bodies, not what he considered the lesser specimens of Spring. That explained the number of dead Vipers I'd seen in the Realm of Death. He must have started already. I'd thought it was odd that so many of them could die in the takeover of Spring.

Ash shrugged. "He might find he has a revolt on his hands."

I tuned out of the conversation. I was almost ready.

Once, I'd seen Willow make a hole in glass with Spring magic. She'd said the glass *wanted* to be sand again. Spring was a power of growth and change, but change could be reversed.

My magic had seeped into the wood of the bar. It was a long time since it had been a tree, and by any human means of measurement, the wood was dead.

Magic, of course, didn't play by human rules.

I *pulled* with Spring magic and a branch burst forth from the wood of the bar, shoving Umarenthe's hand aside in an instant, forming a barrier between the blade of the knife and Randall's vulnerable neck. At the same time, I used my necromantic power to open a gate to the Realm of Death behind her, and gave her soul a violent shove. I could see it if I looked just right—a blue flame hovering inside her stolen body.

Best case scenario, it wasn't properly tethered and went flying over the threshold into the Realm it had avoided for centuries, leaving Lady Feronique's body behind for a proper burial. Worst case scenario, it was held in place just like anyone else's soul—but even then, the force I'd applied to the soul ought to be enough to take the body with it. So no last rites for Lady Feronique, but Umarenthe still ended up dead. That seemed a fair trade, in the circumstances.

Several things happened at once.

Umarenthe flew backwards with a yelp of surprise. Randall sprang away from her, producing a baseball bat from underneath the bar. A roar like thunder crashed into the room. Beyond the gate, the old soul that had almost caught me raged, trying to force its way into the world of the living.

Unfortunately, one thing *didn't* happen. Umarenthe bounced back from the gate as if she'd collided with a rubber wall. *Why* hadn't she fallen through? A tiny thread of blue light that I hadn't noticed before drifted behind her, disappearing into the distance, just like the one that had connected that Viper ghost in Willow's garden to the dagger. Damn. That bloody dagger ruined everything.

I slammed the gate shut in the old soul's terrifying face. I didn't need any more enemies in this fight.

Randall vaulted the bar with more agility than I ever would have believed he possessed, the baseball bat swinging with all the power of his massive muscles. She swept him aside with a blast of Air. He crashed into Ash, who had also leapt forward in a storm of ice spears, all sharp edges and glittering deadliness. She turned most of them aside, and for the moment the scene was obscured by flurries of snow as a freezing wind swirled through the room, sending ice spears in every direction. I focused on the bar, dragging a few spears of my own from its wood and hurling them at her. With so many attacks coming at her at once, surely she couldn't fend them all off?

One of my spears *did* manage to catch her a glancing blow, and she staggered towards the bar. Quick as thought, more extensions shot out from the wood, this time to capture and hold her.

I thought I had her as one of them closed around her wrist like a handcuff. But she was stronger than she looked. Before the circle of the cuff could close completely, she had wrenched her arm free and leapt away, evading another wild swing from Randall, and scooped a body up from the floor.

A body?

The bottom fell out of my world. It was Ash, his head lolling, eyes shut, and she held his limp form in front of her like a shield. One of his own ice spears protruded from his chest, as thick around as my wrist. All his quiet strength, gone.

No.

Time stopped as I stared at his pale face. Was he dead? *No.* How could there be a world without him? He was the one constant in the madness my life had become. I *needed* him, the same way I needed air to breathe.

The whole front of his shirt was soaked in blood. A chill that had nothing to do with the ice and snow in the room seized my heart. How could he lose that much blood and still live?

Randall's bat fell to his side, and he looked at me uncertainly. What did we do now?

"Ironic, isn't it?" Umarenthe said. She was breathing heavily but otherwise seemed unaffected by the fight. "Poor Ashovar, fighting at your side, brought down by his own weapon." She backed away towards the door, dragging Ash with her.

"Let him go."

"I think not. I'm sure we can find a use for him before he dies. Celebrach might like this body."

My whole body clenched as I held in a silent scream of protest. Celebrach, alive again in Ash's body? It would be the ultimate agony. Ash would rather die a thousand times over than let his body be taken by the father he hated.

I must have made some noise of protest despite my effort to hide my feelings, because Umarenthe's smile widened. She tipped her head to one side, pretending to consider. "I suppose we *could* let him live, if you decided to be helpful. His life for Willow's, perhaps. You could bring her to us. She'd trust you."

"I would never betray Willow," I said hotly.

"No? I must have been mistaken." She was almost at the door. "I was under the impression that you were rather fond of this man. That maybe you even loved him."

"I do." It didn't matter that he'd been so strangely cool to me lately. I had a long memory, and I cherished the memory of every single thing he'd ever done for me, every time he'd saved my life without hesitation or consideration of what it would cost him. Every time he'd comforted me. Every brush of his lips, every touch of his hand. "I do love him."

"You have a difficult choice to make, then. This spear is probably the only thing keeping him alive at the moment. It's stopping him losing even more blood. But once the ice melts ..."

She left the rest to my imagination, which was well and

truly up to the job. As the ice melted, the blood would be able to flow freely, faster and faster, until Ash was dead.

With a swirl of Air magic, she opened the doors behind them and stepped through. "Under the circumstances, I'd advise a quick decision."

20

Willow or Ash?

Who lived and who died? That wasn't a decision I could make, even if I'd been the kind of person who gave up my loved ones to my enemies—which I most emphatically was *not*.

Willow was my oldest friend, and Ash was ... well, Ash was my life. There was no other way to put it, no other way to do justice to the enormity of my feelings for him. He was the rock supporting my whole world.

Wow. Such good timing I had. *Now* I realised that, when he was dragged off by that bitch with a goddamn spear stuck in his chest? *Now*, when he might be about to ...

No. I would find a way to save him, without involving Willow—or anyone else, for that matter. Ash was dying, and he didn't have time. But I'd save him. I *would*. I couldn't bear to contemplate any other outcome.

I just had to come up with a way to do it.

Randall looked around at the devastation of our fight. Chairs and tables were overturned or smashed into kindling, and melting ice and snow lay everywhere.

"Who the hell was that bitch?"

"Umarenthe, lately a soul inhabiting Ni'ishasana, now riding Lady Feronique's body around."

His eyes widened. "That was Lady Feronique? Willow's mother?"

"No. Well, kind of. Her body, anyway."

"What happened to the lady herself?"

"Dead," I said briefly. My mind whirled, desperately coming up with ideas and discarding them almost as quickly. I couldn't spare the time to fill Randall in on every detail. Safer for him not to be involved, anyway.

"Ah. Poor Willow." His eyes dropped to the body of the guy on the floor, and he shook his head. "And poor Ileyn. How am I going to tell his parents? He was so young."

He knelt down by Ileyn's side and rested his big hand on the dead guy's shoulder. The carpet made the most awful squelching sound when his knees hit the floor. I shuddered. At least Ileyn had been fae. It would have been even harder to explain to a human couple exactly how their son had died.

I scrubbed my hand tiredly across my face, watching as the two patrons who'd survived the attack muttered hurried farewells to Randall before scuttling out. They were fae, too, which was just as well. Humans would have been calling for the police long before now, which would only have complicated matters.

My head pounded in time with my heartbeat. My sleep

had been short and unrefreshing, but that wasn't the main reason I felt so sick and fuddled. I kept seeing Ash's face, drained of blood, and Umarenthe's cruel smile as she dragged him away.

I had to come up with a plan, but I couldn't *think*. The pressure was freezing me in place. "What a nightmare."

Randall gave me a sympathetic look. "Where will she take that fella of yours?"

"Back to Spring."

"He could heal from that, if it didn't pierce his heart."

"Maybe if someone gave him some urgent care to stop him bleeding out while he was healing." Which Fallon might do, if he wanted Celebrach to have Ash's body. Or he could just as easily decide to short-circuit the whole healing process and kill Ash straight away with the dagger, so Celebrach could take over. Both scenarios led to the same horrific outcome for Ash.

Randall stood up, wiping his hands on his already-bloodied shirt. "Seems to me he's no good to her as a hostage if she lets him die."

I sighed. I knew he meant to comfort me, but he didn't have all the facts. Ash's time was fast running out, and I was the only person in a position to help him. I needed a plan *right now*, preferably one that dealt with the threat of the dagger as well as saving Ash. I hadn't forgotten all the other lives that were also hanging in the balance if it came to a battle between the king's forces and Fallon's.

Think, dammit. There has to be something.

Something that I'd missed, some little edge that would mean the difference between life and death for Ash. I shut my eyes, but all I could see was Umarenthe's grinning face as she emerged from the swirling snow with Ash's body. That moment would be forever seared in my memory. Her shit-eating grin, the vicious cold, and the furious noise of competing magics in such an enclosed space.

But even that noise had been nothing compared to the roar of the trapped soul raging at the gate to the Realm of Death. A jet engine would have been quieter than its howl.

No wonder I had such a headache. "My ears are still ringing from the noise of that damned soul."

Randall gave me an odd look. "I didn't hear anything but the wind and the sound of my furniture being destroyed." He looked ruefully around the room and scratched the back of his head, as if in disbelief. "This is going to cost a fortune to clean up."

"Won't your insurance cover it?"

"Believe it or not, my insurance doesn't have a clause that covers attack by a psycho Air mage."

"You could say it was a bar fight."

"Would *you* believe a bar fight could cause all this?" He waved a hand at the blood, the water damage, the smashed furniture. "And my poor bar." He patted one of the new protuberances. "It looks like one of those weird pieces of modern art. Not that I'm not grateful, of course." He rubbed the cut on his neck. "That woman was far too eager to taste my blood. Thanks for saving me."

"You're welcome," I said automatically, my thoughts more than half elsewhere—wherever Ash was.

I needed a way to save *him*.

The glimmerings of a plan suddenly formed in my

mind, coalescing out of my desperately spinning thoughts. That soul had been so eager to cross the barrier between the worlds, raging to get out of the Realm of Death and live again. My mother had said the old ones were dangerous. They could suck a necromancer dry like a grape, leaving nothing but a shrivelled raisin behind. Or drain one with a thousand small stabs, as those birds had almost done to me when I dreamwalked. The birds had probably been another manifestation of the same old soul, which seemed to have latched on to my presence in the Realm.

"Have you got a hammer?" I asked Randall.

Could this work? The weight of fear and helplessness began to lift. Maybe it could. Maybe I had a real chance.

He frowned. "A warhammer, you mean?"

"No, just a regular old hammer."

His frown deepened. "I think there's one in the storeroom. I'll go and have a hunt around and see what I can find."

"Never mind." I'd seen Randall's storeroom. He could be hours looking for something down there, and I couldn't spare the time. *Ash* couldn't spare the time. "I'll improvise."

I headed for the door, but Randall's voice stopped me. "What about Willow?"

"What about her?"

"That woman wanted you to fetch her." He watched me with a wariness that surprised me.

And hurt me, once I realised its source. He was afraid I was going after her, to deliver her to Umarenthe. He thought I might sacrifice my best friend to save Ash.

Ouch. He should have known me better than that.

"She's at Whitehaven, or maybe even already on her way to Spring with the king's forces." She'd had enough time to kick Rothbold's preparations into high gear. By now, taking on a mighty necromancer might even look like a better option to him than having Willow in his ear every five minutes. She was relentless. "There's no point looking for her now."

His wary stance relaxed. "So where are you going?"

"Where else? I'm going to save Ash."

21

———

I was outside the gates of Lord Thistle's estate less than an hour later. The Wilds must have sensed my urgency, because the Greenways had never taken me there so swiftly from the human world before.

Once again, Seph challenged me as I stepped up to the gate. Thank the Lady, I was here before the king and his forces. I still had a chance to prevent a bloodbath.

Besides, if the battle had already begun, the life of one insignificant ex-Viper would *not* be top of Rothbold's mind. Rothbold's goal was holding his kingdom together. He would be focused on saving Lord Thistle and regaining the Realm for him.

In fact, there was a chance he might even take the opportunity to remove—or at least allow someone else to remove—what he might consider an annoying loose end. I liked Rothbold as a person but, as a king, he was a tad more ruthless than I was comfortable with, and he'd already shown that he barely tolerated Ash. I needed to secure Ash before an "accident of battle" conveniently removed him from the scene.

Right now, of course, Fallon's intentions were a more immediate threat. Not to mention Umarenthe's. She seemed to have a personal grudge against me, which hardly seemed fair, since I'd been the means to her getting everything she wanted.

"Why are you sniffing around here again?" Seph sneered. Clearly he hadn't forgiven the doorman insult.

"Don't waste the time of your betters, Seph. My father wants to see me."

Perhaps Umarenthe resented me because I'd been the only Serpent in all the Vipers' long history to escape eternal imprisonment inside Ni'ishasana. Or maybe she was just a psycho bitch. Whatever. Her motives didn't interest me, only her actions.

Seph glared at me for long moments. I pretended to examine my nails—I wasn't joining his pissing contest. Eventually, he signalled to one of the Vipers half-hidden among the trees.

I yawned, making a show of boredom as time passed. The plan was as solid as I could make it, given the amount of time and the resources I had at my disposal. Anxiety was gnawing a hole in the bottom of my stomach, but there wasn't anything else I could do except pray. Given everything that had happened lately, I wasn't sure the Lady was even listening.

The Viper returned with Mezzi, as before, then returned to his post. I breathed a sigh of relief. Getting Mezzi alone made Step 1 of the plan easier.

"Back so soon?" Mezzi jeered, as Seph swung the gate open. "I had a feeling you'd come crawling back when I saw Lady Umarenthe drag Ash in."

"Is he still alive?" I asked, then kicked myself for showing weakness in front of the Viper.

His smile widened. "Maybe. I didn't bother checking. It'd be funny if you'd come all this way for a corpse, wouldn't it?"

"Hilarious. Take me to my father."

"Ask me nicely." His eyes glittered with amusement.

Let him enjoy flexing his power over me. It would be the last enjoyment he ever had.

"Please take me to my father, dearest Mezzi."

He bowed with an extravagant flourish of his arm. "Of course, dear ex-Serpent. Come this way."

He checked me over for weapons first, of course. I'd tucked a dagger into my boot just so he'd have something to find. Satisfied, he led off down the path through the trees, a swagger in his step. *Tut tut, Mezzi. Never turn your back on a Viper.* Isn't that what they said? Even an ex-Viper. But he was so confident that he held the upper hand here, convinced I was desperate to see my father.

He never dreamed that he was in any danger.

The path wound its way through the trees, and the gate was soon out of sight. I examined the gardens to either side, but I saw no sign of any more hidden Vipers. Fallon probably thought that having them at the gate was enough of a precaution. Like Mezzi, he hadn't foreseen that anyone he admitted would become a problem once they were in. There might be guards all over the boundaries of the estate, but there were none here in its heart.

"You've come to grovel, I assume?" Mezzi said over his shoulder, his eyes still gleaming with enjoyment of the situation.

"Something like that," I said.

This seemed as good a place as any. The white roof of the main pavilion loomed above the trees ahead, still five minutes' walk away, but getting closer. Flowering bushes grew close to the path, forming a sweet-smelling green tunnel. A Spring mage in a garden always had weapons to hand, but Mezzi knew I'd been a weak half-fae before I became Serpent. I'd barely been able to float a couple of faelights.

That had all changed when my father returned the Spring power he'd stolen from me, and I came into my full strength. I was counting on the fact that Mezzi didn't know about that.

"I have to warn you, I don't think your father is in a receptive mood. After all, you have nothing he wants anymore." He sounded positively gleeful at the prospect of my failure. "Weren't you supposed to bring the Spring heir with you?"

"She'll be here soon," I said.

"Probably not soon enough to save poor dear Ashovar," he sighed.

Anger heated my blood. I held my hand out to the side, and a perfectly formed wooden spear touched my palm, born from an overhanging gum tree. The overpowering perfume of the flowering bushes hid the scent of my magic from him. I lunged forward and slammed the spear into his back, angling it up between his ribs to pierce his heart.

Just the way the Vipers had taught me.

He made an odd gurgling sound. Tried to turn. Found his legs would no longer support him. He sagged to the ground, staring up at me with fury in his eyes.

"Not even soon enough to save *you*," I said as those eyes glazed over.

I stood over him for a moment, taking deep breaths to quell the sudden rush of emotions as my anger abruptly cooled. Taking a life was never easy. Even if that life belonged to a scumbag like Mezzi. I had to fight the urge to vomit.

My hands shook as I grabbed Mezzi's body under the arms. The bushes at the side of the path parted for me, responding to my Spring magic, then rustled closed again to hide us.

I rolled Mezzi onto his back, then wiped my hands furiously on my pants, though there was no blood on them. Some necromancer I'd be. Dead bodies gave me chills—especially if I'd been the one to make them that way. Guilt gnawed at me as I gazed down at him. I needed him dead. I'd come here, knowing my plan depended on killing a Viper. But I still struggled not to lose the contents of my stomach.

Swallowing convulsively, I closed my eyes. Maybe it would be better if I didn't look at him. I rubbed my hands on my jeans again. He'd still felt *warm*.

Get your shit together, I told myself firmly. *You're in*

enemy territory. You can't afford to stand around with your eyes shut.

Right. Okay, next steps.

I took a deep breath to settle my shattered nerves. And then another. The problem was, the next steps were pretty bloody vague.

I'd hated zombies—excuse me, *revenants*—since the first time I'd met one. And that one had been a prince, compared to the rotting messes I'd come across since then. The whole concept of stuffing a soul that should be resting peacefully in the afterlife into a rotting body, so it could shuffle around doing a necromancer's bidding, made me want to heave. It was so *wrong*. Against nature. And Spring people were all about nature.

Yet here I was contemplating doing that very thing. Ever since I'd discovered my necromantic powers, I'd been determined *never* to raise a revenant. It was the ultimate misuse of power—maybe even worse than killing someone.

I glanced down at the body at my feet. He deserved it. He'd killed untold numbers of people, without a care, simply for gain and personal glory. Like the other Vipers—except Ash, of course—Mezzi was a shit stain on the underwear of the universe. I shouldn't be hesitating on this.

Ash didn't have time for me to hesitate.

That thought straightened my spine. There was no other way out now. I'd killed Mezzi, and leaving his body here to be found did Ash no good. The only way to save

Ash was to follow through with the plan, flimsy as it was. Time to get on with it.

Except I didn't actually know *how* to get on with it. If only my mother had been a little more forthcoming with the actual details of necromancy. This *you'll figure it out, it's just like any other power* stuff wasn't cutting it. How did I even begin to call another soul to inhabit the body that Mezzi's soul had abandoned? How had my father done it?

Forget him, said a little voice inside my head. *How will you* do it?

In an ugly, makeshift way that would probably make any real necromancer shudder. Despite the gravity of the situation, my mouth quirked into a half-smile at the thought. Master necromancer I most definitely was not.

Sage Domani, Quick and Dirty Deeds Done Here. I should get cards made up.

I called a gate into being between two silver birch trees. That part, at least, was familiar. Forming a gate was no different, whether it led to the Wilds or the Realm of Death. Mist billowed out of it, snaking around my legs, and hiding the body at my feet.

Before I could lose my nerve, I stepped through.

A great roaring greeted me. The old soul was now a spinning tornado, not a sea monster, but I recognised it all the same. There was no mistaking that great yearning hunger. It towered above the grey landscape, a black whirl of malevolent force. It bent towards me, eager to snatch me up.

My hair streamed behind me as I squinted against the

rush of wind. "Come on, then! If you want me, come and get me."

The tail of the twister whipped across the ground, faster than any real tornado could move. It wrenched grey trees from the dead earth, tossing them into the air like matchsticks. The roar was overwhelming as it surged towards me, blue lights flashing within its dark heart.

I fought to stay upright against the howling pressure of the wind, bracing one leg behind me. I spread my arms wide and urged it on, but my voice was lost in the fury of the storm.

The tornado dipped down toward me, and I held up my hand to it, grasping at the wind. Little lines of gold darted out from my fingers and disappeared into the black heart of the storm, seeking the soul at its core. Eagerly, it surged towards me, and my hand closed around a wild blue flame.

Quick as thought, I stepped back through the gate, dragging it with me.

This side of the gate, the soul lost the appearance of a tornado and all its howling energy. That was a relief— might have been a bit hard to hide that racket from dear old Dad, even if no one else could hear the dead. Now it was a flickering blue shape, but I could still feel its power as it lunged at me.

With all my strength, I rammed it down, shoving it toward the body at my feet. My gold threads were still tangled about it, and they whipped themselves around the raging soul, forcing it into Mezzi's still form. Quickly, I built a cage around it, its black bars like the one that had trapped Nevith's soul. My father had made a mistake in sending that zombie to our sith, because it had shown me how to anchor a soul inside a dead body to make a revenant.

And I was a quick learner.

The creature that had been Mezzi sat up, a snarl contorting his dead face. The next minute, he was on his feet and lunging for my throat like an animal.

"Stop!"

He jerked to a halt, still growling. Deep in his eyes, blue flames danced.

"Behave yourself," I said, and the growling stopped. "I haven't brought you here to act like a starving dog. You will do as I tell you."

"Huuuuuuungry," he moaned.

"I promise you, you will feast. Now be silent and come with me."

22

———————

I stepped back out onto the path, the creature following. It made no sound, walking with all the catlike quiet that Mezzi himself had possessed. I guessed that was the advantage of having such a newly dead body. What would happen in a few hours? Would rigor mortis set in? A sudden vision of the creature caught mid-stride, unable to move, almost made me giggle.

Get a grip, I told myself firmly. This was no time for laughter. That was just my nerves talking. The hairs on the back of my neck prickled at having it behind me. Was it my imagination, or could I actually feel its hunger swelling back there? Now I could feel its breath hot on my skin.

I spun around and grabbed it by the throat. The creature jerked and spasmed, but it didn't seem to have full control of the body yet. My action had caught it by surprise.

Deep inside it, the blue glimmer of the trapped soul blazed between the bars of its prison. Hmmm. That wouldn't do. Might as well march in with a big sign saying, *hey, Fallon! Treachery afoot!*

I reached for the cage with my magic, wrapping strands of power around and around it, until the black bars had become an impenetrable wall. That was better. Fallon would have to look very closely to see that Mezzi was now a revenant. And why would he? He had no reason to be suspicious. I tightened the cage a little more, and the body shuddered and moaned.

"That's right," I said, giving the soul another squeeze. "I'm the boss here, and I can rip you out of this body as fast as I put you into it. Don't test me."

The creature nodded and I released it. Despite my bold words, I was far from feeling confident. The soul was old and wily; I was afraid it would slip free. Its hunger still beat at me. If I let it, it would swallow the whole world in its search for satiety. Inside the prison of the body, I could still feel it testing the bounds of its cell, pacing like a caged tiger.

It wanted to truly live, not ape living. It didn't want to be trapped for a time, then sent back, as revenants usually were. This body would soon decay. It wanted the real deal —to live again—and its hunger would only be sated when it fed on a living soul.

I motioned it to walk ahead of me. "We're going to the main pavilion."

It nodded, as if it knew where that was, and began walking again. Had it once walked this path as a living person? Maybe it had lived in Spring. Maybe it had been a Lord or Lady of some other Realm, who had visited here in state. I got the sense of immense power from it, as well as great age.

As long as it could play the part of Mezzi convincingly for a few moments, that was all I needed to know about it.

That was the million-dollar question, of course. Would it convince Fallon? There might be some other way for him to tell that "Mezzi" was now a revenant, despite my efforts to hide the evidence.

My eyes fell on the creature's back. Lady save me, but I was stupid. Fallon wouldn't have to rely on any esoteric senses if "Mezzi" turned around. He'd see the hole where the spear had entered his body.

Fortunately, the Vipers always wore black, so the blood soaked into the fabric wasn't easy to see. But that hole was a dead giveaway.

I couldn't do anything about the hole in Mezzi's back, but I could at least fix the hole in his shirt, and that would hide the wound. With Spring magic, I coaxed the threads of cotton to stretch out towards each other, reforming over the hole. When I was satisfied, I pulled one of Mezzi's knives out of his belt and pressed it to the creature's throat, my other hand holding him tight. Then I marched him down the path and into the meadow surrounding the main pavilion.

Lord Thistle was still seated in chains on the bottom step of the dais. Laid on the ground in front of him was the still form of Ash. My heart skipped a beat at the sight of him. He lay on his side, but his hair covered his face. I couldn't tell if he was alive, though I watched his chest, desperate to see it rise and fall, as we approached.

Fallon sat on the fallen Lord's throne, with Umarenthe beside him on Lady Feronique's throne. They were watching two Vipers spar in the cleared space at the centre of the pavilion. My father looked up as we emerged from the trees, shuffling awkwardly so that my knife never left the throat of my "prisoner". He frowned, then waved the two fighting Vipers to stillness. They bowed and withdrew to the edges of the pavilion.

Ghosts still crowded there, I noted, but I was having trouble focusing on anything but Ash.

"Have you come alone?" Umarenthe asked. There was smugness in her voice, as if she'd expected me to fail and was eagerly anticipating Fallon's reaction.

I ignored her and met my father's eyes as the creature and I came to a stop before the dais. He didn't look pleased to see me.

"You have some nerve, turning up here again. How dare you use Anita against me?"

"I learned from the best. You did the same to me not so long ago."

"That's true," he said, succumbing, as I knew he would, to the compliment. He'd always loved flattery. "I assume you have some reason for taking my Viper hostage?"

I forced "Mezzi's" head up with a movement of my blade. "I've come to offer you a trade. Ash's life for this one."

It was a desperate gamble. My whole plan hinged on Fallon agreeing, but I wasn't exactly his favourite person right now. The fact that he hadn't struck me down as soon as I turned up was encouraging—it suggested he still had some vague fatherly feeling left for me.

"What makes you think I care what happens to the Viper?" Fallon asked.

"I'm sure you don't. But perhaps you care for me. Give me Ash and I'll leave." At least Fallon had no grudge against Ash.

Fallon's eyes narrowed. "You cost me Willow. I find myself disinclined to do anything for you."

Umarenthe's eyes glowed with spite. "You're not in any position to be asking favours."

"Willow will be here soon enough," I said. "You can take her back then."

Lord Thistle raised his head long enough to shoot a poisonous glare at me. No doubt I'd just fulfilled every miserable expectation he had of me.

Fine. He thought I'd betray Willow? What did I care about his opinion? He was as wrong now as he'd always been.

"She's on her way here with the king's forces." I glanced at Ash. What I could see of his face was so pale he might already be dead. A worm of panic coiled through my gut. I had to persuade Fallon to let him go *now*. His time was running out. "What difference can Ash make to you? You're winning. You hold all the cards."

Umarenthe shifted restlessly on her throne. "Lord Celebrach might feel that Ashovar makes a great deal of difference."

I resolutely ignored her, though bile rose in my throat

at the thought of that hateful man taking his son's body for himself.

"If you don't care about the Vipers, why should you care who gets sacrificed to provide a body for Celebrach? This one will do just as well." I gave the creature a little shake. "Take him and give me Ash. Please, Papa."

His mouth tightened and a strange expression flitted across his face at the childhood name, as if it took him back to a happier time. It was gone in a flash, but I sensed I was close and pushed on. After all, if he didn't care for me at least a little, he wouldn't have let me go after I'd inadvertently stolen some of his necromantic power.

"I love him the way you loved Mama. I would do anything for him. Anything at all. I would pass through the gates of Death itself."

A change shivered over my father's face. There was an almost human look, a memory of suffering, in his eyes as he met mine. The silence stretched interminably between us.

"Very well," he said at last. Umarenthe made a noise of protest, but he ignored her as he rose from his throne. "Celebrach will have to be happy with this one. You may take the other—but not until I have Willow back. And I'll have your assurance that that will be the end of your meddling."

"Of course, Papa." He was making the same mistake Mezzi had—the same mistake all fae made. Underestimating me. "You'll never see me again after this." It wasn't only the fae who knew how to twist the meaning of words to suit themselves. A pang of regret pierced me as I contemplated what I had to do.

"Good. Then you'd better pray that you were right about Willow arriving soon. Otherwise, you may be taking him only to bury him."

That meant he was still alive *now*. I drew in a shuddering breath of relief as I forced the revenant to his knees.

Fallon descended the steps of the dais and drew Ni'ishasana from his belt.

23

$\mathcal{A}$ distant sound of fighting reached us. Fallon paused on the bottom step and nodded to the attendant Vipers. They all melted away into the trees, moving towards the front gate of the estate.

"That will be the king," I said.

Fallon shrugged, closing the distance between us. "Let him come. I am more than a match for him."

"Willow," Lord Thistle croaked. His red hair, so like his daughter's, was matted with blood. He looked as though he'd been to hell and back, bruised and battered, but his eyes were still fierce with disgust as he glared at me.

"That's right," I said. "She'll be here any moment. Just let me get Ash to safety first, Papa, and you can have your revenge."

"Not so fast, child. Not until I have Willow in my hands again. That was our bargain." He waved the tip of Ni'ishasana dismissively. "But you may tend to him if he means so much to you. Come, Celebrach. Let's get you into this fine new body."

I dropped to my knees at Ash's side, confident that Fallon's magic would hold the revenant in place. Tenderly, I swept the hair back from Ash's face. Was it my imagination, or did he stir? His skin was clammy and cold. He didn't look good, though someone must have taken the trouble to stabilise him at some point, because there was no sign now of the ice spear and he was still breathing.

My heart clamoured to get him out of there, *right now*. He needed safety and time to heal. Deep inside, I could sense his soul, and it was only tethered to his body by the thinnest of threads. But I wasn't finished here. More than Ash's life was at stake.

A figure made of shadows joined my father, glancing across at me as it did so. Celebrach. It was too much to hope that look on his shadowy face was concern for his son. More likely regret, that he couldn't torture Ash one last time. He knelt down, facing the revenant.

Fallon placed one hand on the revenant's head. The dagger hung loosely from the other. The creature glanced up at him, and my heart nearly stopped at the hunger in that dark gaze. I clamped down more firmly on its soul, holding it to my bidding, and it looked down instead.

The next moments were vital. Timing was everything. I leaned over Ash, pretending to be engrossed with his wound, trying to make myself so small that everyone would forget I was here, so close at hand. Close enough to touch.

Or to kill.

Umarenthe leaned forward in her seat, eyes fixed intently on the scene before her. A small smile of anticipation played about her mouth and her hands gripped the arms of the throne tightly, as if she held herself ready to launch from the dais the minute the transfer was complete.

"Ready?" Fallon asked Celebrach.

The shadowy figure nodded. My father's arm drew back, almost in slow motion—or so it seemed, but that was probably my nerves. My heart was pounding about a thousand beats a minute. Then the dagger came flashing down and lodged itself in the revenant's heart.

Go! I urged the old soul, releasing it from the bonds that chained it to Mezzi's body. A vast wave of darkness surged up, rushing straight through the dagger into Fallon, following the path that connected him to the dagger's power.

Fallon's body froze in place. Nobody else realised anything was wrong. Umarenthe still leaned forward, that same anticipatory gleam in her eye. Celebrach's shadowy form began dissolving into Mezzi's body. And Fallon stood there, a wild look in his eyes, but unable even to let go of Ni'ishasana.

Inside my father's body, a battle was being fought. I saw it as a great black beast, tentacles lashing, giant teeth devouring Fallon from within as he struggled in vain against it.

A faint voice floated on the still air. "*Hungry.*"

No one heard it but me.

Fallon jerked, and Umarenthe sat up straight, a frown

forming on her smooth forehead. The shadow beast feasted, devouring my father's soul. His hand fell away from Ni'ishasana's hilt at last, and he staggered back.

Umarenthe stood up. "Lord Fallon? What's wrong?"

But he couldn't answer her. His face was caving in, his body crumbling under the ferocious onslaught of the ravening soul. He abruptly lost his grip on the magic that held the revenant in place, and its body toppled over, landing in the grass with a thud. It was nothing but a dead body now. Celebrach had disappeared. I had no idea where he'd gone—clearly not into the revenant. Since the body was already dead, he couldn't switch places with a departing soul.

My father sagged to his knees, aging a thousand years in an instant. His skin sagged and wrinkled, his hair greyed then fell out, leaving only a few sad strands. His body shrank, hunched over itself as he gasped for breath. Then he collapsed onto his side, nothing more than a skeleton with aging, wrinkled skin stretched over it. He looked tiny inside his clothes.

Umarenthe hurried down the steps, panic in her face. "Lord Fallon?"

Fallon's dimming eyes found mine. "Sage?"

Inside me, a little girl's heart broke for her beloved Papa. *I'm sorry, Papa. I had to.*

At least he would be with Mama now.

The light went out of his eyes, and the old soul roared in triumph. It burst out of his body, hovering above us like a cloud that dimmed the light. It was still hungry, and it was looking for another soul to feed on. Shadow tentacles writhed within the darkness, flicking out as if to test the air.

But part of it was still in the dagger. I tugged hard on that connection, trying to force it back. It strained against me as Umarenthe dropped to her knees in the grass by Fallon's side, a look of horror on her face.

I *pulled* with all the power I had within me, with all the love and fear I possessed. I knew Ash and I would be its first victims if I couldn't tame it. The need to protect him gave me strength that I hadn't known I was capable of.

It roared again, struggling against me. It was strong, but it had made a mistake in leaving Fallon's body. A body would have sustained and sheltered it, but it had been too greedy. It had fed on Fallon's life force and destroyed him —just as I'd hoped it would—instead of taking his form for itself.

Gasping with effort, I forced it back into the dagger. Umarenthe glanced at me, her eyes narrowing with suspicion as she took in my sweaty, straining face.

"What have you *done*?" she whispered, her voice filled with menace.

Then her eyes widened in horror and her gaze jerked to the dagger, standing up from Mezzi's dead chest like a flagpole. Even *I* could hear the screaming of the souls inside as the monster devoured them. Her body jerked, and she lunged for the dagger, scrabbling desperately across the grass.

But I was there before her. I ripped it from Mezzi's chest and whirled around, nearly tripping over Ash in my haste. I had no hammer, but the steps of the dais were made of stone. That would have to do.

With all my magic-fuelled strength, I slammed the hilt of the dagger down on the step. The ruby cracked, and the shockwave as the magic within it burst free nearly hurled me from my feet.

From the corner of my eye, I saw Umarenthe crumple to the ground like a discarded doll, but my focus was still on the dagger. The old soul still lingered inside it, feasting on the last of its souls. In a moment, it would turn its attention elsewhere, and it would only be strengthened by the souls it had devoured.

So I opened a gate to the Realm of Death and hurled the dagger through it.

24

———

"*W*hat just happened?"

I'd forgotten Lord Thistle was there. I turned, reeling like a drunk after what I'd just been through, and found his green eyes glaring at me through the lank strands of his hair.

"I killed my father and destroyed Ni'ishasana."

Wow. I'd killed my father. My whole body trembled as that sank in. I'd killed my *father*. Maybe he'd been right to abandon me all those years ago. What kind of daughter killed her own father?

But I had to. What other choice had there been? He was bound to the dagger until death. There was no other way of separating him from its power—and Fallon, the necromancer bent on revenge, was an unstoppable force with the dagger in his possession. I wouldn't have been able to destroy it if I hadn't killed him first.

And Ni'ishasana was a power so dark and dangerous that it never should have been created in the first place.

"That blade has been nothing but trouble since Amuethis forged it." Thistle echoed my own thoughts.

Well, would you look at that? I'd never expected to agree with the prickly Lord of Spring on anything.

Before I could fall down, I sank to my knees by Ash's side. He looked no worse, but I was horribly conscious that every minute that passed without getting him proper medical treatment was a minute more that his life hung in the balance.

"So you never meant to sacrifice my daughter?" Thistle asked, a grudging respect in his voice.

"Don't be ridiculous." That wasn't the way Lords were usually addressed, but I had passed way beyond caring. "You, sure. I wouldn't shed any tears over *your* death. But Willow is my best friend."

He grunted at that. "Unchain me."

It was on the tip of my tongue to tell him to say *please*, but Ash didn't have time for me to be scoring points off the Lord of Spring.

"Where are your healers?" I asked instead, ignoring his request. Ash also didn't have time for me to muck around helping Thistle when, judging by the growing sounds of battle, the cavalry would be here shortly. Thistle could wait a few minutes longer.

"Dead," he said succinctly.

Damn. I chewed my lip, wondering what to do. I couldn't lift Ash myself—not without hurting him further. I needed bandages and I'd probably find them in the vast kitchens of Spring, but most of all, I needed a healer who knew what they were doing. *Hang on just a little bit longer*, I urged him silently.

A shout rent the air, then two people burst from the trees, running hard across the grass towards us. Willow's green eyes, so like her father's, were flashing with temper, and Raven had a sword in his hand and a deep gash down one cheek. Raven stopped short, but Willow hurried to her father's side and began attacking the chains that bound him.

Lord Thistle gazed into her face as she worked, and spoke softly. "Are you well, daughter?"

"I'm fine," she said shortly. "You?"

Neither of them would meet the other's gaze. Lady Feronique's death lay between them. I knew Willow too well. She didn't want to cry in front of her father, certain that he would see it as a sign of weakness.

"What has happened here?" Raven demanded, taking in the bodies of Umarenthe and Mezzi, and the strange, shrivelled corpse of my father. Then his gaze landed on Ash and his face filled with concern. "Is he dead?"

"No." I pressed two fingers to his neck. The pulse there was weak and thready, and fear seized me in a crushing grip. I couldn't move; I couldn't think. *I'm losing him, I'm losing him* repeated over and over in my mind. "Help me carry him."

He crouched next to me. "Where to?" Struck dumb by panic, I didn't reply. Where should we take him? Raven turned to Lord Thistle. "Where are your healers, my lord?"

"Dead," he said again, just as surly as he'd been with me.

"And our other people?" Willow asked anxiously as she removed the last chain. "What happened to them?"

Thistle shook his head. "Some managed to flee. Many were killed by the Vipers. Some are being held captive. I know Zinnia and Yarys still live." He met his daughter's eyes briefly, then looked away. "Any whose deaths would cause me particular pain have been left till last."

Willow leaned in to hug her father. For once, the aloof Lord of Spring didn't reject her comfort.

The clash of swords had grown louder as we spoke. I heard the thrum of an arrow being released very near. Raven leapt up, sword at the ready, as more people arrived, but he relaxed when he realised they were the king's forces.

The Hawk was first among them. His dark hair was bound back in a leather thong, and he wore silver armour that was almost too bright to look at in the afternoon sun. On his breastplate were the leaping dolphins of the Brenfell crest.

"Sir Hawk, your aid is required," Raven said formally.

The knight strode over to us, his sword Ecfirrith clasped firmly in one mailed fist. I'd never seen him in full armour before. He certainly cut an imposing figure, towering over Raven and managing to exude an air of menace, despite the fact that he was on our side. The dark blood glistening on Ecfirrith's blade only added to the effect.

I wouldn't want to meet him in battle. Possibly Ash could give him a run for his money, but I certainly couldn't.

I wasn't a short woman, but he was a good head taller than me—and swords had never been my weapon of choice.

"What do you need?" he asked, glancing down at me and Ash on the ground.

"Healers," I said immediately.

He nodded. "I will speak to the king about taking him back to the palace."

I opened my mouth to say I didn't give a crap about the king, I needed a gate to Whitehaven *right now*, but I was saved the necessity by the appearance of the man himself.

As Rothbold emerged from the trees, Lord Thistle struggled to his feet and offered his sovereign a shaky bow. Willow and Raven bowed, too, but I didn't bother moving. There was a time for bows, and there was a time for action.

"Sire," I said, before anyone else could speak, "Ash may be dying. We need to get him back to the healers at Whitehaven."

"Lord Thistle, you are well?" Rothbold asked, ignoring me for the moment.

"As well as can be expected in the circumstances," Thistle replied, glancing down at his wife's dead body.

Rothbold looked down, too, and sighed. Now that Umarenthe's soul had fled, Lady Feronique's expression had lost Umarenthe's habitual malevolence. She looked to be peacefully asleep.

"This is a heavy loss, my friend. The kingdom grieves with you."

Lord Thistle nodded, perhaps not trusting himself to speak.

"What happened here?" the king asked.

I butted in before Thistle could answer. "Short version? I killed Fallon and destroyed the dagger." Somehow it was easier to say if I called him *Fallon* and not *my father*.

The king's eyebrows almost disappeared into his dark hair. "Impressive. And the long version?"

"The long version can wait."

Lord Thistle sucked in a shocked breath at such insolence.

Raven jumped in to fill the silence. "This man needs care urgently, sire." He met my eyes. "He's very important to Sage."

Rothbold looked down at Ash as if just noticing he was there, and frowned. For a heartstopping moment, I thought he was going to deny Ash access to the palace healers. He studied my face in silence, then nodded.

"Lord Thistle," he said. "If you would be so kind as to clear the Hawk through your wards."

The Hawk's sword, Ecfirrith, could open a direct gate to anywhere in the Realms, without having to brave the twisting Greenways of the Wilds. But we were inside a Lord's estate, and they were usually heavily warded. No one wanted uninvited visitors popping in at random. A member of the ruling family had to create an exception, even for someone as highly placed as the king's favourite knight.

Lord Thistle scowled, probably because the request involved doing something nice for me, but he inclined his head to the king. A moment later, he nodded at the Hawk, who lifted his blade and made three broad slashes in the air: two vertical and one across the top, joining them into a rough doorway. The lines glowed in the air like the after-image of a sparkler, pulsing until the space between them went dark and mist billowed forth. A courtyard paved in white marble appeared briefly between wisps of mist.

More of the king's forces had joined us by now, and the king ordered two burly soldiers to lift Ash. One took his shoulders and the other his feet, moving him with surprising gentleness. They carried him through the gate, and I stepped through practically on their heels. No way was I leaving Ash after this.

The Hawk followed me through, no doubt to smooth the way with the healers, but before he closed the gate behind us, I heard Lord Thistle say to Raven, "Thank you for protecting my daughter."

Lady save us. Did the man have *no* understanding of his daughter's personality? If he was looking for a quick way to make Willow dislike Raven, he'd just found it. I wasn't looking forward to the sparks that would fly when he told her she had to marry the Night lordling.

Willow snorted. "He didn't protect me." Then she surprised me by adding, "Sage did. She saved us all."

25

When Ash opened his eyes on the third day, they were clear and focused.

Unlike mine, which felt raw and gritty from all the sleep I'd missed keeping a vigil at his bedside. The healers had tried to shoo me away, telling me I needed a proper night's sleep, but I was sure they were more motivated by the desire to get rid of the bossy woman who kept demanding their attention for Ash.

"We've done all that is necessary," the lead healer, a man whose eyes looked even more tired than my own, said impatiently after the first twenty-four hours of me summoning them for every twitch or moan. "All he needs now is rest to let his body heal. Taking his temperature every five minutes isn't going to change anything. You should rest yourself."

"I'll rest when I know he's all right."

"I promise you, he'll make a full recovery. But it won't

happen any faster because you sit there staring at him," he added with a certain irritation in his voice.

In the end, I almost missed the moment I'd been waiting for. I was sprawled in a chair by Ash's bedside, fighting the heaviness of my eyelids, when he moved his arm.

I jerked upright, half-expecting another delirious attempt to remove his bandages. He'd had a fever the first night, and he'd thrashed around, muttering unintelligibly to himself. Until the fever broke, the healers had tied his hands to the sides of his bed, to stop him picking at the bandages that swathed his chest.

But this time, he rubbed his face, then turned his head on the pillow to look at me.

"You're here." He sounded surprised.

My exhaustion fell away in a rush of happiness at having him awake and lucid. "Of course I'm here. Where else would I be?" Meaningfully, I tapped my boot, with its hidden blade. "Who else was going to protect you if any Vipers had shown up looking for revenge? These healers might be good with a scalpel, but that's about the extent of their skill with a blade."

I was only half joking. Most of the Vipers had been killed in the clash at Spring, but a handful had escaped, and no one knew what had become of them. Nuah was among the missing, which made me nervous.

His gaze wandered around the room, and he frowned. "Where are we?"

"At Whitehaven."

A gleam of amusement appeared in those grey eyes.

"And you're worried that all the king's guards and magical defences couldn't stop a few Vipers?"

I shrugged. "I wasn't taking any chances. I went to a lot of trouble to keep you alive, you know. I couldn't have anyone undoing all my good work."

It was easy to joke about it now, but I'd been worried sick. At least the long hours alone had given me time to think. Funny how almost losing someone clarified a girl's thinking, making it very clear what was important and what wasn't.

His face had always been hard to read, but as the amusement faded, it was replaced with a solemnity that seemed out of place. Most people in his position would have been thrilled to wake up at all. Something seemed wrong, but I didn't know what.

His hand picked restlessly at the crisp white sheet, his gaze sliding away from mine. "Perhaps you shouldn't have tried quite so hard."

I took his hand firmly between my own. His palm was rough with the callouses of a warrior, and I stroked my thumb over it gently.

"What kind of defeatist shit is that?" Was he worried that he would never fully recover from his wounds? "I know you took a spear through the chest, but it missed your heart, and the healers have repaired the damage to your lung. In a week you'll feel like your old self."

He muttered something that sounded like *my heart was definitely damaged*, but when I leaned closer and asked him to repeat it, he shook his head. His eyes drifted closed, and I thought he'd gone to sleep again until he spoke.

"What happened? The last thing I remember is fighting Umarenthe at The Drunken Irishman. Does Fallon still have the dagger?"

"Nope. I destroyed it."

His eyes flew open again. "*Destroyed* it? How?"

So I filled him in on what he'd missed, from following him to Spring and killing Mezzi, to summoning the old soul, the confrontation with my father, and the destruction of the dagger and all its souls. He listened attentively, reminding me of the times I'd reported to him as apprentice to Adept.

When I'd finished, he frowned. "Why did Umarenthe die? She had escaped the dagger."

"There was still a connection there." I explained the thread of magic I'd seen, connecting her soul to the dagger, during our fight at The Drunken Irishman. "It must have been enough to drag her back into the dagger at the end, when the old soul was munching on all the others like popcorn."

"I can't believe you did all that on your own," he said when I was finished. Pride gleamed in his eyes. "The Vipers are finished without Ni'ishasana. Never underestimate the power of a woman on a rampage."

"Never underestimate the power of a woman in love," I corrected him.

His expression went blank, and he lowered his eyes, those impossibly long eyelashes brushing his cheeks. "You should probably leave. I've taken up enough of your time."

"*What?*" I stared at him, astonished and more than a

little wounded. "I tell you that I love you, and you want me to leave?"

His eyes flew to my face, shock and the flaring of a desperate hope in their grey depths. "You love *me*?"

"Of course I do, you idiot." Okay, maybe I needed to work on my loverlike language. Calling someone an idiot in the same moment that you declared your love for them wasn't normally how it worked out in the romcoms I'd seen. But I was pretty new at this love thing. I'd never felt this depth and passion for anyone else before. The feeling was almost ferocious in its intensity, and it took my breath away. "Do you think I'd kill my own father for just *anyone*?"

The hope in his eyes died, and he turned his head. "Yes, you would. You have a moral compass that drives you to do the right thing always, no matter what it costs you. You needn't pretend."

"*Pretend?*" I couldn't believe what I was hearing. I'd dreamed of this moment—it had kept me going through all the killing and the drama, and the long nights sitting watch at his bedside. The moment when we would finally be able to come right out and say what was in our hearts.

Shortly to be followed by the moment when we fell into bed and I finally found out if he was as good as my fantasies had made out.

But none of my dreams had included a conversation as perplexing as this.

"I'm not pretending." Honestly, if he hadn't been injured, I would have shaken him. What was going on behind those shields of his? "What are you talking about?"

He drew a deep breath, as if to fortify himself, and said, "I know you love Raven."

"Raven? *Raven?*" I hadn't given Raven a moment's thought since we'd left him behind in Spring. "I most certainly do *not*. Why would you think that?"

I mean, sure, I'd had a bit of a thing for Raven earlier, but I'd thought I'd been pretty clear about my feelings *now*. Apparently not.

"You said ... you said you went to Lord Nox's funeral, and Raven was there. You said you had something to tell me—that night at Willow's sith, remember? Right before we were attacked."

"That's right," I said slowly, thinking back. We were kissing, and I was just about to tell him that my infatuation with Raven was over. My heart had chosen *him*. But then the Vipers attacked, and we hadn't had a moment to ourselves ever since.

The temptation to call him an idiot again was very strong, but I guess I could see how he might have misinterpreted. "That thing I was going to tell you—it was that I love you."

"But Raven ..." He was staring at me with a yearning I'd never seen in his face before.

"*Forget* Raven! He has nothing to do with anything. I was only going to say that I'd seen him and realised how much better a man *you* are."

"Sage," he said with great seriousness. "I am *not* a good man."

"Bullshit," I said, studying his beautiful face. "There's a well of goodness in you that even your father couldn't destroy." How had I ever thought him a soulless killer? Even now, he was trying to protect me—at his own expense. It occurred to me that this wasn't the first time, either. "So that time you said love wasn't a prison, and people had to be free to follow their own hearts ... you weren't only talking about Willow, were you?" I'd *thought* something was off. He'd been so serious and bleak.

"I was telling you that you didn't owe me anything. That you were free to go."

I shook my head, marvelling at how the misunderstandings had mounted. "You know, for an assassin, you're pretty damn noble." He opened his mouth to object, and I grinned. "Stupid, too, but never mind. Doesn't matter anyway. You're the only man for me."

He shook his head in wonder. "Am I still fevered? Can this really be happening?"

I pinched him hard, smiling at his wince. "You're definitely awake, buddy. I'm afraid you're stuck with me."

A careful happiness spread across his face, as if, even now, he was afraid to let down his guard in case it was all snatched away from him again.

"I was so sure you had chosen Raven. I was determined to step back and let you have your happiness with him."

Well, that explained a lot about the distant way he'd been acting lately. But that meant that he'd given me that lock of hair to keep me safe even though he thought I loved someone else. That was pretty humbling. He really *was* a good man—and *way* more selfless than I would have been in the same circumstances.

I snorted. "You must have a funny definition of *step back*. You stuck to me like glue."

"That wasn't my fault. You kept needing me to keep you alive."

"Did not! Well, except for the first time I went into the Realm of Death." Only my connection with him had allowed me to return safely to the world of the living. "And I guess the second time, too." The old soul almost had me that time.

Okay, so maybe he had a point.

I got onto the bed, careful not to bump him too much, and lay down beside him, snuggling into his good side. "I'll always need you."

He sighed, and it sounded as though he were letting go the cares of the whole world. Then his arms snaked around me, and he pulled me on top of him.

"Your chest!" I protested.

He grinned up at me, and it was the most carefree look I'd ever seen on his usually grim face. My eyes misted over. I was *such* a sucker for a happy ending, and it looked like we were about to get ours, despite the odds that had been against us.

"It's fine," he said, one hand releasing me long enough to cup my cheek, an expression of wonder in his eyes as he gazed up at me, his soul naked before me. "Everything's fine."

"I don't want to reopen the wound." The healers would *murder* me after the fuss I'd made. "You shouldn't be doing anything strenuous."

His mouth quirked as he pulled me down for a kiss. "I'm only injured. I'm not *dead*."

And then his lips found mine and he showed me how very much alive he was.

THE END

Keep up to date with new releases, plus get free stories, special deals and other book news, by signing up for my newsletter at www.marinafinlayson.com.

Reviews and word of mouth are vital for any author's success. If you enjoyed *Assassin's Bane*, please take a moment to leave a short review at Amazon.com. Just a few words sharing your thoughts on the book would be extremely helpful in spreading the word to other readers (and this author would be immensely grateful!).

THE PROVING SERIES

Everyone wants Kate dead. Shame she can't remember why.

There's a big difference between wanting to move on from a tragic past and having someone rip the memories right out of your head. When Kate returns from an unusual courier job with no memory of where she's just been, alarm bells start ringing.

Whatever happened must have been pretty wild, because now there's a werewolf in her kitchen trying to kill her—and he's just the first in line.

Kate's caught up in a war between the daughters of the dragon queen. To survive, she must remember the explosive secret she's forgotten—but first she has to live through the night.

Get The Proving series at your favourite online bookshop!

ACKNOWLEDGMENTS

Heartfelt thanks to Jen Rasmussen for some absolutely A-grade beta reading. Her comments and suggestions made this a much better book.

A big thank-you to my son Connor, who is always happy to talk about plot or worldbuilding problems. He helped me write my way out of some tricky corners.

And, as always, thanks to my husband Mal for his love and support, including always being ready to drop everything at the eleventh hour to beta read for me. Best husband. Whole world.

ABOUT THE AUTHOR

Marina Finlayson is a reformed wedding organist who now writes fantasy. She is married and shares her Sydney home with three kids, a large collection of dragon statues and one very stupid dog with a death wish.

Her idea of heaven is lying in the bath with a cup of tea and a good book until she goes wrinkly.